BURN DOWN THE NIGHT

CRAIG KEE STRETE

WARNER BOOKS

A Warner Communications Company

Copyright © 1982 by Craig Kee Strete

All rights reserved.

Warner Books, Inc., 75 Rockefeller Plaza, New York, N.Y. 10019.

 A Warner Communications Company

Printed in the United States of America

First printing: June 1982
10 9 8 7 6 5 4 3 2 1

Book design by Judy Allan (The Designing Woman)
Cover design by Gene Light

Library of Congress Cataloging in Publication Data

Strete, Craig.
  Burn down the night.

  1. Morrison, Jim, 1943-1971—Fiction.
I. Title.
PS3569.T6935B8   813'.54   81-14753
ISBN 0-446-37071-1 (U.S.A.)   AACR2
ISBN 0-446-37343-5 (Canada)

ATTENTION: SCHOOLS AND CORPORATIONS

WARNER books are available at quantity discounts with bulk purchase for educational, business, or sales promotional use. For information, please write to: SPECIAL SALES DEPARTMENT, WARNER BOOKS, 75 ROCKEFELLER PLAZA, NEW YORK, N.Y. 10019.

ARE THERE WARNER BOOKS
YOU WANT BUT CANNOT FIND IN YOUR LOCAL STORES?

You can get any WARNER BOOKS title in print. Simply send title and retail price, plus 50¢ per order and 50¢ per copy to cover mailing and handling costs for each book desired. New York State and California residents add applicable sales tax. Enclose check or money order only, no cash please, to: WARNER BOOKS, P.O. BOX 690, NEW YORK, N.Y. 10019. OR SEND FOR OUR COMPLETE CATALOGUE OF WARNER BOOKS.

BURN DOWN
THE NIGHT

CHAPTER 1

It was the kind of party where the host cuts the hearts out of small children and inserts a Coke bottle in the red-rimmed hole to amuse his guests.

Snort. Pop. Inject. Two rock bands from out of town and the local meat. Bikers. The surfer girls. The mad and the maddening.

"Don't think. Forget. Live on only what you can dream." His voice was soft. Jim Morrison was leaning against the wall making exaggerated theatrical gestures. He popped a pill. His third pill in an hour.

Later I learned it's his first lie, although possibly not

one of his own. Not drugs he ate like candy. Tabs of
Vitamin C.

Jim Morrison is handsome. I heard some girl say he
was so good-looking even his face slept around. He has
a look of practiced agony about him.

Morrison's speaking to a girl. The same one I've been
promoting. Both of us are hustling the same spaced-out
chick.

"My name's Jackie." Bored and wary, she watches us
both. She suspects we are both drug-crazed. A reason-
able suspicion. It fits almost everybody at the party.
That kind of party.

She was tall, all legs and muscles. Tight white T-
shirt with nothing to tell but a lot to show. Big made-
up eyes with the blues. Patched blue jeans with a patch
on the right front pocket that reads "Suck-em-soft."

Nervous teeth, restless hands. Tongue provocatively
edging the corners of her mouth. She was the multiple-
orgasm girl with the quick-starting engine. All living,
all breathing, but distant. She thinks we're tripping.

It still comes in sugar cubes. Those days. I am heading for a hot peak that someone sold me as an Owsley,
which I doubt, but what the hell. *Sainted, I wouldn't
burn you, Owsley Acid!*

My frying brains say I have been sold true.

I flip around, stare at Morrison, the stranger. The
cold cat cutting into my act.

Somebody at the party had already pointed him out
to me. Said he was crazy a little. A maniac.

To me he was just in the way. I saw this blond beach
bitch first.

Morrison leans forward, says, "I don't want to know
your name. I just want to remember your body and the
taste and touch of you."

She's sympathetic but confused. I already told her
practically the same thing, only more direct. Something like "I wanna jump you."

Morrison just leans against the wall, well posed.
Ragged jacket, tight bead choker around his neck.

Same interested eyes for the girl that I got.

I'm dressed in cast-off clothes from the band I traveled into L.A. with. Black velvet and ruffles. Slightly Edwardian and completely out of place.

Morrison looks like the ragged end of a trail drive, shirttail hanging out and battered jacket. Still he's real competition. And I steam about it. Shit, I saw her first, talked her up first. I resent the stranger come to jump in my game.

The chick laughs. About nothing. Small teeth and big gums. Laugh that sounds like a horse in heat.

All around us the party is jumping up and down like hot dice. People weaving in and out. Chaotic noise. Stereo blasting above the level of auditory comprehension. Heavy bass rumble from big speakers, so overloaded with vibration that we hear through our rears, not our ears.

Music that pounds against the face, screaming at the inner ear.

Tripping talk. Let's-get-laid numbers. I'm *wasted*, man! *WASTED!* Wasted is everybody. That kind of party.

Let's open a vein and see if blood is real.

"Are you like into what? I mean, are you a musician?" The girl says it to me but looks at Morrison.

I try answering but the best I can do is nod yes, which is a lie. My head is beginning to throw me. My eyes swim in and out of focus.

While I'm looking at her she becomes giant breasts with mouth wings. Harmonica ears. Wavering image and green outlined face.

Heightened sense of having lost her to a brain-damaged animator escaped from Disneyland, lost her before anything at all has had a chance to happen.

I regain audio, good enough to tell some lies. Spin out my hanging-out-with-the-rock-and-roll-bands routine. Then lay on my mysterious Indian routine. My threat trip. Ever slept with an Indian?

Absurd searching for the heat of Saturday night.

Nonsense ritual of hey-I-could-be-almost-anybody-but-let's-pretend-I'm somebody-you-want-to-sleep-with.

She just listens with the landscape of the Sahara passing for an expression on her face. Lay it all on her and she blinks and gives Morrison a hot look.

Morrison's still on the wall, still got this mysterious smile, like a transvestite Mona Lisa. My line of strutting stuff makes no dents in her or him. Morrison's into some heavy nonverbal projection. Courtship without words. This cat is knocking me off without saying anything.

Morrison gets passed a bottle of wine and drinks some. Somebody reaches to take it from him and he shakes his head. Guy who wants the wine doesn't resist. He's been outpower-tripped without any real display of power. Morrison's got the wine for the rest of the night, practically a full bottle.

Building a solid wall of resentment, I make a gesture that says leave. Fuck off. Rhetorical threat to see who's more powerful. Indian or stranger?

Jim stares at me. Just a little bit hostile. Watchful.

I get a rush. Heavy. So intense from Momma LSD that I stumble, feeling the floor sinking out from under my legs. Long screaming dive to the bottom of a well. Vertigo. Everything melting and pulled down by gravity.

Morrison's hand hits my chest, steadies me, then pushes me to the wall so I don't dive forward on my face.

"Peaking on acid?"

I'm grateful for the hand and the wall. "Mount McKinley," I admit, too suddenly disoriented. Shudders up and down my body. Mild state of convulsion. Body jerking with involuntary twitches.

Morrison's oblique nod. Meant for me or the chick, I don't know

The chick is eyes agog, staring at us. Suddenly we

see her pulling back from us, disengaging. Morrison
and I exchange a knowing look. As with the same
mind, we at once understand that she is not who we
thought she was. We suddenly know this one is not a
doper, a fellow traveler in the pharmaceutical alchemy
line. Not a head chick, more like a juice maiden. Bud-
weiser on the brain.

A dark shadow. A biker, three months in the same
shirt without once taking it off, is suddenly in our personal space. New gladiator in the arena.

Has his tattooed arms around the chick, squeezing
breasts, beer belly pushing her back against us. He and
the chick are climbing all over each other's bones like
two dogs smelling their sex places. He himself smells
like a dog pissed him into the world.

They pull apart and then the biker is using his eyes
to give us the against-the-wall-motherfucker treat-
ment. Pushes her away and gets into an ass-kicking
stance. He's got a scar across his forehead from eye to
eye and half of one ear gone. Broken teeth that smell.
Chains and leather. Sharpened bicycle chain for a belt.
The flails of the godless.

"You bastards been hustling my old lady." Not a
question, an accusation spoiling for a fight. His face
looks like a skin-colored carpet with cigarette burns.

He fixes on me, ignoring Morrison.

I fold up inside. Panic time from the skin side inside
and out. Start a paranoid dead man's float, eyes wishing not to see. Pushing off the wall, please just let me
float away?

Too alchemical, too wired to handle any threat.

The biker moves toward me, whirling me around by
the arm. Universe goes nova inside my spinning brain.
I almost lose it altogether and go down.

Jesus H! I am gonna get my head pulped in Technicolor.

I get pulled in close, watching this incredible slow-
motion movie where the biker's arm comes up, goes

back, tightening to strike out at me. Know I'm going to get stomped.

My body already writhing, gone paranoid on a cellular level in convulsive anticipation.

Morrison moves in, a smooth glide. "Hey, man, there was this drunk son of a bitch. Really on his ass from downers and booze, man. Fucker was bothering your old lady so we stood next to her so he would leave her alone. No shit, man!"

Morrison pulls me away from him, gets up in his face.

"She told us straight off she was connected up. We were just holding the fort till you could get back." Morrison's cool smile. You had to believe it when you saw it.

"Yeah?" The fist unclenches, the arm comes down. Guy has to think about it. Has a tattoo on his right arm that says "Born to Raise Hell."

Biker gives the room a once-over. No thanks for imaginary services rendered, just suspicious as hell. "Where's this guy at now?"

Morrison's vague gesture. "He got pissed off and went outside. Maybe he's waiting for her to come out. You should have heard the stuff he was saying about your old lady!"

"Son of a bitch!" says the biker, and he pushes past us, almost knocking us over. Western gunslinger rage, arms knotting up like pythons, he storms out of the room. A real meat mind, a territorial stomper.

"You lied," says the chick. Not too bright, this chick.

Morrison shrugs. "Didn't you see the guy? Didn't you hear what he said about you?"

The chick frowns, brain stretched to the limit, already confused. "What guy?"

Even rushed a million miles up, I am picking up his game. Funny trip. Strange guy.

Morrison, self-assured, as if he believes it himself: "Man, this guy was practically slobbering in your pant-

ies. We kept shoving him away. He was really wasted,
you know. Like out of it completely. Just fucking insane."

"But I didn't see nobody. I didn't hear nobody say
nothing." The chick looks a little worried. Definitely
feels cheated, like something interesting happened and
she was smelling her armpit and missed it.

She believes him. Amazing.

I nod. " *'Strue!''* The words are hard to get out at
first. This tripped out, this wrecked, you have to keep
talking or you lose your tongue. "It's . . . true. Said he
was gonna suck your armpits til they bled. Should
have heard him . . . him. Was gonna . . . was gonna rip
your tits off with a can opener."

Where I'm at, in my drug dream a million miles out
and fading fast, it even begins to seem real to me.

Chick looks at us both. We're both pretending to be
angels.

Then, incredibly, she reaches out to each of us to
shake hands.

Very formal, like a cocktail waitress in church.
"Thank you so much I am sure. I hope he catches the
bastard." Idiotic smile.

The three of us shake hands awkwardly, like three
unfrocked businessmen meeting for lunch in a toilet in
a Mexican cathouse.

"Unholy communion," mutters Morrison, catching
the absurdity of it all, bowing from the waist.

"Gotta go see if my old man is all right. Was very
nice talking to you, I am sure." She retracts her claws,
rearranges the molecules in her legs and splits.

We watch her go, suddenly co-conspirators in a Roman plot to squeeze the juice from the daughters of
Caesar, whatever that means.

I nod gratitude and add the clever line, "You saved
me from the mad biker who goes bump in the night."

"It was a newly coined chance to go mad and swallow my brain."

"What?"

"The pleasure was all mine," says Morrison.

I say, "Oh! Uh, well, we both saved each other from a social disease. We're lucky."

"We're even," says Morrison, "except you're peaking to glory and I'm pilled and not even a little bit off. Think I got burned."

Curious, I ask, "What you supposed to be doing?"

"Supposed to be mescaline. Brown mesc. That's what the asshole said. Got nothing. Probably drugstore vitamins."

I smile. Small-time dealing can make you feel so big-pocketed at times. I never go anywhere without something to bring something.

I wave a pillbox at him. "I have a cure for your disease."

Inside the box a sugar cube screams quietly with a whole lot more than sweetness going for it.

"It's yours if you can swallow." I open the pillbox, show him the goodie inside.

"Let's go out in the air. I want to catch the cure." He thrusts his hands in his jacket pockets and I nod. You need running room to get up to speed before you leave the nest.

We start walking out, a slow journey in super-slow motion through the debris of human party wreckage.

We pass a dark-haired chick giving head, so out of it she would have given head to a Volkswagen. Bodies on bodies like stacks of tongue depressors. Intense rap sessions of bodies beyond words.

Venice beachhouse party. This summer you can get wet. Wet between your legs. If you understand the thrill, you don't have to seek it.

There is no comprehension here.

"I'm having an energy rush." Morrison speeds ahead, colliding with unresisting bodies in his flight. I stumble after him, staggering in a vain attempt to keep up.

Morrison stops, waits for me to catch up. He snatches a beer bottle from a chick with zits and a loud, raunchy chest that aims up at the sky like two ack-ack guns. He up-ends the bottle sloppily, spilling some down the sides of his face.

Morrison massages her shoulder a little, watching her breasts jump. Then he thrusts the beer bottle against her chest, dead center between her bulging breasts.

Says something to her about the great black bear of the woods and his beer bottle dildo.

Just catching up, I don't quite hear it completely but she's laughing as I tumble past.

Morrison is energized, in full maniacal flight. Coasting on the party energy, the mad-orgy-mental-menstrual-cramp sensation.

A few people already getting naked in an aimless animal way. Fleshly waves crashing on each other's shores. Mindless animal couplings.

Someone screams, drugs or pain, no one knows or asks.

A girl by the door, hysterical expression and glazed eyes.

"Dachau missed a few," says Morrison, going cryptic.

This girl at the door has her T-shirt, a tie-dyed scream, half torn off and has blood on one side of her face and clotted in the pale strands of her blond hair. She looks us both over as we get to the door and suddenly starts crying.

"Don't step on her," I say. "She's probably somebody's mother."

"Daughters of ministers! Religious snakes!" says Morrison, standing over her, passing some kind of benediction. Half priest, half wired sumo wrestler.

We have to step around her to get out. As we do, she goes into a fetal position, sitting up, arms wrapped tight around her knees. My foot accidentally bumps her head and she overbalances, goes over on one side and begins to throw up violently on the edge of the door frame.

"Party party party!" Arms out like a human plane, Morrison jets out the doorway, exaltation on his face. Wild shout, arms hugging the sky. "Party!"

I tumble out the doorway, jumping high to avoid the human fountain spraying vomit. I wobble, weaving behind him with my load, melting eyes, screaming body. Face aching with the acid smile.

Just outside the door Morrison turns and looks at me strangely. Theatrical whisper. "We'll go see the phallic cannons of city hall! Erected by the city. *Erected!*"

Just my acid smile for a reply. Don't know what the fuck he's talking about and don't care. Got the feeling he's peaking two times higher than I am and I am already knocking on the gates of heaven.

We march down the driveway, out to the cars.

Our meat-mind biker friend is out there, strutting his stuff for his little blond beach bitch. He's banging some poor son of a bitch's head against the side of a blue bus.

"That's him. That's the one said those things about me," says his chick.

The meat slap of head against metal is sickening. Blood comes in a stream from nose and mouth, the guy's already knocked cold. He looks seriously damaged.

Morrison stops abruptly, going up on his toes. I almost collide with his back.

"Hey, man, stop!" Morrison shouts.

Startled, the biker lets his victim fall back against the fender of the bus, head lolling sideways like a broken-necked doll.

"That's the wrong one," says Morrison. "That's his brother. The other guy you wanted was taller and he was wearing a blue condom with a hole in the tip. You can't miss him."

The biker gets up off the body, stepping on the guy's chest.

His chick stands next to him, arms going around him, hero worship. He's successfully defended her honor again, probably the fourth or fifth time tonight.

Morrison and I just stand there, staring at them. We are watching a movie about L.A. and its opened veins.

The biker and his bitch roar off into the night on a

chrome-plated dragon with two wheels.

Killer on the highway, legs wrapped around a hot engine made out of angry metal.

"I almost didn't kill anybody back there," I say, sweating.

I don't know exactly what I mean. Morrison seems stunned. He gets excited, feverish. There is a strange light in his eyes. He says, "The dead delight in the participation of decay."

I get it. "But we still live and the living delight in the escape of souls through hands of light, through faces in the dark."

"You're a fucking poet." He makes a wild gesture with his arms, embracing the world.

I shrug. "I only bleed from my mouth menstrually is all. Every twenty-eight days my teeth get a little irritable."

Morrison nods. "Bleed me a song and we'll find a dead dog to sing it."

We keep walking. I stare into the warm night, watching the air dissemble around our heads. "Where do you want it?" I ask, meaning the acid, as if where was as important as when.

"Someplace where it would be good to die, not here. Too many asshole imitators already halfway there." Morrison spins and looks at me, eyes burning. "Let's go for a ride up L.A.'s anus! We'll find a driver to deliver graveyards! Epic journey!"

"Journey?" I spread my fingers open, sweeping them across the horizon, pointing every which way. "Night journeys are my favorite kind. I am a vacilandor!"

Morrison looks at me, puzzled. "What's that?"

"A vacilandor is someone who sets out on a quest to find something he knows is not there."

"I want to find a girl who gives birth to her heart," says Morrison. "Let's go, menstruation mouth. Let's take a trip."

Together, we had begun a journey to the end of the night.

CHAPTER 2

We walk down to the beach, down to the conquistador shore. The night is a fever breathing around our heads. Wind comes off the beach like a salty kiss that burns against the base of the spine.

Morrison keeps his head turned a little, whatever else he does, so that the sounds of the sea are always clear in his ears, as though he expects some other sound than the splashing of the waves, night crashing.

My summer night breathes in and out, me traveling where the sky gets heavy and reality doesn't.

"This isn't real," says Morrison, and his eyes sweep

the darkened sea before us. "There is no other night like this anyplace on earth."

I am on my own planet but I feel I can easily surrender to his. I try it.

I hear the faint thunder of breakers and my drug eyes see strange ghostly shapes, tattered galleons chasing phantoms, death ships wheeling darkly through strange eerie islands. It's Morrison's world, some unseen place across the dark sea.

"Something is happening out there." Morrison turns and looks at me. His voice sounds like a funeral. "I am an island creature. I . . . am . . . drowning. Drowning in an ocean that touches strange shores. Tonight . . . I will be ready. . . . Tonight something strange is going to happen."

"You're freaking me out," I say, eyes darting around, feeling paranoid rushes. Strange scuttling shapes form just outside the lines of my vision.

I got too many demons of my own making without sharing his.

Morrison moves an arm, whipping it quickly across the sky as if he held a rapier. *Ancestral Memories!* Witch kiss. The sea calls us!"

Standing beside him, I shiver. The dark is very dark.

"I'll never be buried at sea." Morrison stares out there somewhere, brooding. "My father died at sea. They scattered his ashes in all the oceans he sailed. But I'll never end up like that."

Morrison looks up at the sky. "Someday I'm going to explode into space."

"How did he die?" An inane question.

Morrison shrugs. "His heart failed. All death is heart failure."

Morrison moves away, goes down to the water's edge.

"Something is moving out there. Do you hear it?"

My mind flashes outward, frightened, imagining, beholding dark transgressors. It seems that we stand on the edge of an island surrounded by swirling waters.

The fog comes down smothering and silent. The moon is still high, for a silvery radiance filters magically through the mist, and beneath us washes the sea, dark and filigreed with white foam.

I hear a moving in the wind. The sound of wind in the rigging of a ghost ship, speaking to us in a voice none but a shaman could understand.

The waves break at Morrison's feet. "The sea conspires against us."

I move back, threatened. Frightened.

"The admiral sleeps with the sea. You can hear him crying on the conquistador shore." Morrison's cold laugh. Sad and empty. "None of his children ever sail anymore."

"*Look!*" Morrison points into the dark above the sea. "The bone ship!"

My mind follows his voice into the fantasy, into a strange terrifying world of his own making. I hear the timbers creak, hear the voices of men who sail her, who sail some great and terrible galleon.

Slowly, so slowly, like a dream you cannot wake from, a great shape, shadowy in that unearthly light, sweeps toward us.

Out of the fog the ghost ship looms, driving toward the island, its burning decks awash with blood. The mast towers above us. I sense the presence of death.

Realization, volition come back to me. In my terror I scream and turn away from the dream, from the shape stalking the night, and stare at Morrison, the conjurer.

He's turned to face me, eyes terrible in the moonlight.

"Before we sink in too deep." Morrison uses his hands to feel the outlines of his face, to touch the skin. He shakes his head as if to clear it of vision.

A scream still vibrates inside my head, echoing.

I am lost, drug gone. Paranoid, shaking. I reach for his shoulder, meaning by a touch to choke off the drug music, the painful sound of his words that do not seem to belong to his body.

I want to join his words and his body into something

less terrifying. I hear someone talking.

His shoulder passes through my fingers like the breeze. My eyes clear and I realize that he is several yards away, picking up something from the ghost-white beach.

Morrison puts the object in his pocket and comes back. "You've been talking to yourself," he says. "You must really be destroyed."

It strikes me as funny and I settle down a little. My big monster rush subsides. My face thinks it's smiling. Control comes back. The world rights itself, night creatures melting into the mist from where they have come.

"Yeah, guess I am destroyed. You wanna join my wrecking crew?"

Morrison laughs. "Only if I get to blow up the buildings. Let's go. I want to walk a ways."

Morrison leads. I follow, passing him the pillbox that seems to hum with the energy of its cargo.

I think I see sparks fly from Morrison's hands as he touches the pillbox.

We walk up a short walkway that dead-ends on a path running along the ocean. The buildings are full of lights and moving bodies.

As we pass the beachfront houses I feel them lean inward on me, like a silent row of parasites feeling the body of its host.

Strange figures like our own walk up and down the path, swimming into our visions, churning the sand in aimless patterns.

A girl runs off the beach screaming. Chased by no one we can see. Over and over again she screams, *"No! No! No! No! No! Nooooooo!"*

"This is a strange dance," says Morrison. He swallows the sugar cube whole, to let it dissolve inside, a rectangle of perception.

I catch up to Morrison, staggering a little as if leaning into a suddenly strong wind. "The dance is not strange. It is us who are strange."

Morrison hands back the empty pillbox. I toss it over

my shoulder. My eyes see a trail of sparks as it goes
across my shoulder.

Morrison's eyes are feverish, burning. "We are
strange! We are strange because we are lizards, summer lizards in the flowing heat of young rivers."

His words dance in the air like chants.

"Our bodies are ready at any moment to betray us.
To give birth to blind lizard children."

"Blind lizard children," I say, picking up the chant.

"Blind lizard children that swim rivers of dust . . .
blind lizard children with bridal tongues, caressing
scorched rocks."

Lightning and thunder crash in the places where
words come from, electric rampage in the synapse
chains. I nearly scream. "We have immense blind liz-
and children and . . . and dust rivers . . . pouring out of
TV screens."

Morrison throws back his head, like a stallion tossing his mane. He raises his arms heavenward. "*Amen
Orange Julius!*"

Then mood changing, or breaking, he turns to me
and says, "We got to find a car, find a driver. It's an L.A.
highway night! The beach is no place to sit at the fire!"

"What fire?"

Morrison shakes his head, ignoring the question. "I
promise you a journey."

"What fire?"

Impatient shrug. "We seek it or flee from it. Fire
lights the cave. Shadows wait for us, no matter what."

I give in, lost in his language. Don't know what he's
saying. "I got a car. Belongs to the girl I've been staying
with."

Morrison is suddenly energetic, whirling around like
a dust devil. Walking rapidly, talking back over his
shoulder at me. "Let's get it and go, man."

I stumble along behind, trying to catch up.

Morrison says, "All of life is a journey by car. By
their wheels you shall know them."

I just nod, flowing with him, with my acid fever. I've

already begun a journey, inside, somewhere deep, on a river that never ends. I drift out, carried by the current to make the drowning man's swim.

One edge of reality, one pain, and I panic. "I got the car but you better drive. Jesus! I'm too wasted!"

Morrison stops abruptly, turns and faces me. His eyes glitter. "Think you can drive?"

I shake my head, scared at the idea of even trying it.

"I doubt it. I mean I'm really fucked up!"

Morrison nods. "Good! Then you drive. If you're really fucked up, the fear of death will keep us both awake."

New ending for a dance of wheels
Interconnected freeways
Tunnel vision swimmers in the driver's box
The engine of the heart
Predestination between
White lines of the highway
Neither to the left
Nor the right
Straight
The highway

The dead swimmers float listlessly
Through the lines of traffic
Who among them has driven
Into uncharted desolation?
No surprises!
No changes of lanes
No thoughts in the intersections
Of erogenous zones

The driver's swim deprives senses
Eliminates pain
Beyond the tunnel
There is only

The euphoria of wreckage
The withering of dream

Jim Morrison and Craig Strete

CHAPTER 3

We get back to the party and I go in to get my coat and my car keys while Morrison waits outside.

The party is still riding high. Looks like a Hieronymus Bosch painting based on ideas by the Marquis de Sade. Party's got louder, more violent, ugly.

Lots of motorcycles outside. Looks like the bikers have landed.

The bloody-haired girl who had been throwing up on the door as we went out is being dragged into one of the bedrooms by four tough-looking guys in biker gear as I walk in. Her shirt's already ripped off. Skinny little ribs and little-girl breasts. Maybe she's thirteen years old or fourteen. She's screaming hysterically but nobody pays much attention to her.

Some party she's having, if she survives it.

My coat is in one of the bedrooms. I go round the beginning of a fight. Have to push away some drunken chick with infected pimples who wants to sit on my face while I'm still standing up. Get to the bedroom, look for my coat and discover a bunch of naked people are lying on it.

Lots of enthusiastic groping but not much accuracy. Bed is just too crowded.

A pretty little surfer girl wearing nothing but a tan puts her arms out to me, inviting me in, as she feels me tug on the coat that's under her ass.

I move back to avoid her arms and she slips off the bed, hits the floor head first and vomits all over herself.

My coat comes free and I back out of the room.

Try to get across the crowded living room. Somehow, somebody's managed to turn the music up louder and it's pounding my skull into tiny crazed pieces. Got to get out of there before I turn into a shock cube of paranoia.

I stumble over partied-out bodies. Avoid one spot on the floor that is all bloody. Jesus! Somebody must have taken a human sacrifice. Lots of blood.

A naked teenybopper, completely spaced out on drugs, mechanically fingers herself on the floor. Looks pleasureless, her face a pale, skinny mask without expression. Her biker companion is passed out drunk across her legs.

There's a crash as somebody throws a chair through a window. I walk around a guy who is standing in the center of the room, convulsively squeezing his crotch through his clothes with both hands and moaning. Probably a rising young record executive doing some of his best work.

Seems like the trip across the room takes a million

years. Feel like I am in a corpse factory and the ma-
chines are trying to snatch me up and run me through
the assembly line. By the time I get to the door I'm
scared shitless. There's a graveyard inside this party.

As I pass through the door, a biker rams some girl's
head against the wall beside the door. Blood explodes
from her smashed nose and the white corner of a tooth
spits out of her mouth. A drop of blood falls on my
arm.

She screams and I lose it. Freaked out, insane with
fear. I run with demons at my back. Blindly, hysterically.

At the end of the sidewalk Morrison grabs me,
knocks me down. Contact with hard pavement jolts
me back out of it. Good thing he caught me. Would
have run until my heart gave out. Party violence really
fried me, really wrecked me.

Morrison helps me up.

"The car?" he asks.

"What?" Disoriented.

"Where's the car?"

"What car?"

Morrison sighs. "You said you had a car."

"I said that?" I shrug. "Did I say that?"

"Far out," says Morrison.

"Far out what?" Universe is spinning, can't get a grip
on this conversation. What is he talking about?

"You wouldn't understand," says Morrison. "It's the
kind of thing which to be properly understood, you
gotta hear it through a mirror."

I nod. I've encountered lots of things like that before,
but never in other people.

Morrison puts his hands in his coat pockets, scuffs
his foot against the sidewalk. "Looks like we're gonna
have to walk."

"Why don't we take my car?" I say. "It's better than
walking."

"You got a car?" asks Morrison, suspicious.

My face feels that the smile on it is only pretending to be innocent. "Why? Did somebody say I didn't have one?"

It was a '61 or '62 Chevy. Or it was a black '62 Ford with moon hubcaps? If it was a Chevy, it was either blue or green. People you remember, your favorite rapes you remember, dirty words you remember, but cars you forget unless something special happens like her father catches both of you in the back seat wearing only each other's suntans.

There were a couple of bottles of wine in the car, two six-packs of beer, party supplies that never made it to the party.

Also some Schoenling Little Kings Cream Ale, boot-legged from the Midwest by some friends of mine in a rock and roll band. My favorite drink but hard to get anywhere but in the Midwest.

Morrison and I get into the Ford or Chevy. I open a Little Kings Ale for myself right away. Knock the cap off on the ashtray, which is all bent out of shape and makes a perfect bottle opener.

I need something to calm my nerves. Gonna be lucky to get the car started, let alone drive. Morrison declines a beer.

He opens the glove compartment, exploring. Inside he finds a nasty-looking bag of dark brown weed. Michomocaan. A friend laid some on me in exchange for a band groupie I had lent him, a funny little sleep-around girl who gave such good head she left scorch marks.

He doesn't seem to be in any hurry to get going. Me either. My hands are shaking so bad I spill cream ale on myself trying to drink. I settle back against the seat, willing to wait forever.

If I sit here long enough, I tell myself, maybe my vision will clear enough for me to be able to find the place on the steering column where the key is supposed to go. Hate to bet on it, though.

Morrison's got the bag in his hands, a weight ounce of Mexican mind boggle.

"Is that some of that there Mary Weyno, boy?" He's doing an imitation of a dumb Southern cop, the kind with raised eyebrow ridges and hairy knuckles.

I reply in kind. "Catnip, boss. Just a little catnip hyar, boss."

He opens the bag and takes out a couple of already rolled joints. I'd already rolled a half dozen or more.

"Gonna have to confiscate these here funny cigarettes."

I shrug. "Help yourself. With six you get eggroll."

While Morrison is helping himself to my dope, I am watching the windshield flow in and out. Sometimes it looks like it's coming in, sometimes it looks like it's going out. There is a tide in the affairs of men.

Morrison puts the joint under his nose, sniffing it like a rich man sniffs an expensive Havana.

The interior of the car comes into focus momentarily. I frown as the windshield stabilizes. I take advantage of this little burst of sustained reality and insert the key in the car ignition.

Getting even bolder, the lucid period stretching out, I even manage to get the car started too. Miracles will never cease.

The car is loud. I lost part of the muffler on a high curb on the way to the party. Zigging when I should have been zagging. Now the engine noise is scary. I am half afraid the car will eat me.

Morrison looks up, notices the car engine is turning over, says, "Let's hit the road." He puts a joint in the corner of his mouth.

I sigh. I almost wish I am Catholic. I don't have any comfortable little gestures to ward off death like the sign of the cross. Not that I believe in any of that crap. My religious beliefs stop at wall-to-wall carpeting.

Still, be nice to have some protective razzmatazz, no matter how fake it is.

"I don't think this is a good idea," I say. With a clash of gears I mis-shift us and we pull away from the curb. We flee somewhat erratically into L.A. night.

Car keeps weaving, jumping wildly as I mis-shift in every gear. Car's got a full tank of gas and I just aim it at the million miles of bitch goddess L.A. and let it run where it wants to go.

Up there in that part of my head that is trying to drive nothing is working except reflexes. I'm so wrecked. Too wrecked. I finish the first bottle of cream ale as we cruise down a small side street. Roll down a window one handed and toss the bottle out. Hit a parked car, cracking the windshield.

Morrison's still rummaging in the glove compartment, not paying attention.

"This is a terrible idea," I say, sweating. Road keeps melting in front of me, becoming a black thick liquid as I pass over it. Car seems to be swooping and diving, sinking down into the soft black tar of the road.

I make an illegal U turn at an intersection for no special reason and then a right turn up what I think is somebody's driveway. Shit! Now I'm going to have to back out.

Driveway seems endless so I speed up, making a curve, wanting to get to the end of the driveway so I can turn this pile of Detroit iron around if I can. Be easier than backing out.

A boat passes me, a blue-and-white cabin cruiser with twin outboard engines.

I shake my head to clear it. Don't know how I did it, but the car seems to be on the San Diego freeway, heading into the black heart of L.A. That doesn't explain the boat.

Morrison is unconcerned, searching the car for matches, unlit joint still dangling from his mouth.

"A boat just passed me," I say, trying to be calm. Sweat on the palms of my hands, a cold, heavy weight in the pit of my stomach. Feels like I am trying to give birth to an anvil. Driving in my destroyed state is making me nervous as hell. My guts tighten up like coiled ropes. I want very much to pull over or scream or both. Morrison just ignores me.

"I said a boat just passed me!" Near hysterical. I look at Morrison, pleading for some kind of help. I know I am weaving all over the road but Morrison isn't the least bit interested in how badly I am driving.

"Speed up," he says, dragging stuff out of the glove compartment. "That'll keep the boats from passing you."

"Terrific," I say and just miss sideswiping a black pimp in a white Cadillac.

I am getting worse. Car going all over the road. Windshield starting that damn flowing-in-and-out routine again. I grip the wheel tight, try to get my mind on flowing with the car. Every time I try to turn the wheel the car makes a sickening sideways plummet. If Morrison doesn't care about bailing me out, if he isn't worrying about getting multiply mangled, why should I? I say the hell with it, lean back against the seat, watch the windshield flow in and out and relax.

Best idea. The car stops weaving. Shit! Let the frigging car drive. This far gone, it's the only way. I go off dreaming.

Next time I look up from some kind of vehicular dream state, miles have passed by as quick as blips on radar. Must have made an exit off the freeway somewhere but don't remember making it. Car is back on surface streets again, lost in the horse latitudes of L.A.'s back streets.

I slow down, get with the other traffic on the street and flow with it, windshields streaming.

Sometimes I turn right, sometimes left. Sometimes I go straight for miles. No pattern to my driving or to us. We're just drifting through a highway night.

I don't have any idea where we are or where we're going. To be on the way to somewhere is all that counts.

Morrison asks, "Hey, man, you got a match?"

"Your face and my ass," I say automatically.

"That's an old one. I think Cleopatra said that to Marc Antony. You got a match, asshole?"

"Use the cigarette lighter."

"There isn't any cigarette lighter."

"Then don't use it."

"Good idea. You got a match?"

"There must be an echo in here. Everything you say sounds like 'You got a match?' "

"Your face and my ass," says Morrison.

"That's an old one. I think . . . uh . . ." I start to say but stop because I can't remember who he said said it to who. I think about the original question. "Uhm, no. I don't think I got a match."

I try digging in my pockets. Car weaves across the center line and we almost smash head on into a semi-truck.

"Shit!" says Morrison, grabbing the wheel and swinging us back into our lane. The truck roars by, horn blaring. "Take it easy." Morrison crawls across the seat, lets go of the wheel. "I'll look, you just drive, for crissakes!"

I nod dumbly and slow up for a light. Morrison digs into my tight pockets but I don't have any matches.

"What a bitch!" he says, touching the unlit joint hanging from his mouth. "I got to get this mother lit."

"I could stop at a store and get some matches," I suggest. I reach down on the floor between my legs and snatch at another bottle of Little Kings Cream Ale. The car careens off to the right and takes a long strip of chrome off a parked car.

"Pretty neat," says Morrison, looking back at the damage I've done.

"Open this for me." He opens the bottle and hands it back. "Thanks. I get a few more bottles of Little Kings Ale in me and I'll be fine. This stuff always mellows me out, if I don't pass out first."

"Too simple. It lacks class," says Morrison.

"What?"

"Store-bought matches. They are without soul."

"Oh."

Morrison sticks his head out the window and waves

at a foxy girl coming out of a bar. "Give my rhino head!" he shouts. At least that's what it sounds like.

"Like I said, stores are too simple. Stores and the products therein. Civilized fire is the worst kind. Like in the invention of porcelain. That's really corruption."

I look at Morrison. "Is that supposed to make sense?"

"No," he admits.

"Good. I'm glad to hear it. For a second there, I thought I might be wrecked on some dangerous chemical."

The girl he yelled at gives him an up-yours gesture, turns her back on him and walks away. If she yells back, I don't hear it. She's strutting off doing that phony L.A. model/waitress swivel. Like she's got a tuning fork up her ass and she doesn't want the insides of her legs to touch for fear she'll strike the wrong note.

"What was that all about?"

"Cecil B. De Mille," he says. "Without tights."

That makes perfect sense to me. His mind is fried.

"I'm sorry you didn't get off," I tell him. I try stopping for a stoplight. Perfect smooth stop. Unfortunately I'm still fifty yards from the stoplight. I'm in no shape to pass any driver's license tests.

"Didn't get off? Are you out of your frigging mind? As Black Lazarus said, I am getting off like a motherfucker! What was that shit really? I'm getting rushes that feel like they're gonna break my bones!"

The light changes as I inch up on it, gears grinding as I miss a couple of shifts and finally stall the car out. I look over at Morrison. His eyes are chasing each other. He looks like a truck is parked on his mind. "That stuff is baby laxative," I tell him. "Absolutely pure and guaranteed to be undiluted. You'll know when you get ripped 'cause you'll pass out with a diaper on your nose."

"Far out."

I restart the car, noticing a street sign. We are cruising Van Nuys Boulevard. That means we are lost in the swamp of North Hollywood. How we got there, I have no way of knowing. Me, I thought we were in Santa Monica or Pennsylvania, or someplace like that.

"How we gonna smoke without matches? I got to figure this out," says Morrison, the joint still dangling from one corner of his mouth.

I am up to the intersection by now and it turns red. I stop for it. Right in the middle of the intersection. Jesus! I don't seem to be doing so hot.

A couple of cars honk at us, perhaps in recognition of my superior driving skills.

Morrison looks out the window at the cars whipping toward us on both sides. He just shrugs, grabs up a bottle of wine, pops the cork and takes a big hit off of it. He seems bored by the whole business.

And me? Me, I am not bored. I am about to piss myself with fright. Scared shitless is what I am.

I race the restarted motor, let the clutch out, peel rubber and stall the car again, still in the frigging intersection. A red Mustang puts on its brakes and skids toward us.

At the speed of light and some left over, I get the car going again, forgetting it is still in gear, and the car lurches forward, just enough to be missed by the red Mustang as it skids sideways past us.

"Pretty neat! Pretty neat!" says Morrison, drinking some more wine. "I'm glad this is all a dream or I'd be shooting shit all over my back pew." He held up the joint. "What we need to do is discover the secret of fire."

He's beginning to sound like a scratched record.

I'm busy. Stalling the car again. I don't know how I do it but I do it. At least, we are almost out of the intersection. That counts for something.

I restart the frigging car, shift, tell myself not to panic.

Morrison is reading the wine bottle. Totally unconcerned. Love to wrap his head around the goddamn steering wheel column.

I slam the car into gear, but carefully, ease up on the clutch and depress the accelerator smoothly. We move rapidly without jerking. Ah, success!

Unfortunately the car is in reverse and we shoot back through the intersection. Amazing! Ah, failure! We pass through the intersection and go beyond it. With the speed of an ice age, I realize my mistake and go for the brake. I just ran a red light going backwards.

Morrison is drinking wine when I slam on the brakes, me practically standing up on the brakes I hit them so hard.

Wine splashes all over Morrison's face and down his shirt.

"Shit!" Morrison's wiping off his face and shirt. "What the hell are you doing! I got this bear piss all over me!"

"Pixies and camel drivers always drive backwards," I say by way of explanation.

"You're no pixie," says Morrison, wiping wine off of his neck. "You're a frigging caddy at a miniature golf course!"

I look in the rearview mirror and see a car behind us come to a tire-burning stop, turned completely sideways. Looks like somebody slammed on their brakes trying not to hit us and went into a nasty skid. Makes you wish other people could be more careful on the highway, doesn't it?

"You're really full of shit, you know that?" says Morrison.

I notice that the car is stalled again. Forgot to clutch it when I stood up on the brakes.

"You know something, you're probably right," I agree, beginning the weary routine of starting the car again. One thing I can say for this car: no trouble getting it cranked up.

I pull up to the light. The light turns green and I shift, really concentrating. Please let me get it right, I tell myself, but I got my hand on the turn signal indicator instead of the gear shift lever and it snaps off in my hand. Frigging cars anyway!

The car stalls again, bigger than shit, edged over a little bit into the intersection.

Somebody behind me honks as the light glows a maddening green. Getting through this intersection is becoming like sex for the first time.

"Enjoying the view?" I ask.

"All right," says Morrison, tapping his fingers against the wine bottle to some music only he hears. Morrison looks out the back window, then turns and looks out the front window. Has a puzzled look on his face.

"Hey, man, isn't this the same frigging intersection? What the fuck you doing? Making an epic?"

That pisses me off. The guy behind me with the horn that won't quit has already got me pissed. Now I'm really pissed. "Why don't you fucking drive then? I'm doing the best I can."

"Show me your worst and I'll sell tickets. You drive like a virgin on roller skates."

"Just for that, I'm gonna start driving with my eyes open from now on. I'm better at head-on collisions when I can see what I'm aiming at."

I get back to concentrating on my car routine. Getting it started again, getting it in gear, waiting for the light. This time, goddamn it, I'll get it right!

"Turn around! Turn around!" Morrison has his head out the car window, waving the wine bottle like Custer's personal bugle at the battle of Little Big Horn.

I turn around in my seat, figuring the back of the car is on fire or maybe fifty thousand angry drivers are coming up on us on foot with mayhem in mind. I don't see a fire and, looking out the back window, I don't see a lynch mob or room service or what have you. Whatever is behind us stays a mystery to me. I can't see doodly squat.

"Turn this monster around! Pull a U turn. Now!" urges Morrison, in a fever.

"What for?" I want to know. "Christ! I can't make no goddamn U turns! I can't even get through this frigging intersection, for chrissakes! Now you want me to make a U turn?" I threw my hands in the air. "Jesus, you got a lot of balls, asking me to—"

"C'mon, turn it around. Get this iron mother turned, man! There's some matches, I know it, and the girl with the graveyard heart. Poon from the moon!" Morrison is suffering from mental sunspots. Or maybe just suffering.

I shake my head. "No way, man. We're gonna get arrested bigger than shit." I put my hands back on the wheel, stare straight ahead, waiting for the light. Then I think about it. "Did you say poon from the moon?"

He nods, crazed.

I don't know what poon from the moon is. I sigh, watching the red light. "Is it okay if I wait for the light to change before I hang this illegal U turn?"

Morrison has this wicked laugh. "Didn't stop you before, why should it now?"

He's got a point there. It makes sense—how it does escapes me. At that point everything escapes me. Thinking about it for a few hours or seconds, I don't know which, I stab the gas pedal and cramp the wheel. Swoop into a maniac U turn against the light.

Universe threatens to turn over on its side. Citizens in the cars going the other way wetting themselves as I scream through their ranks. My U turn is about two weeks too wide. Sloppy driving. Going to lose my Ben Hur license.

Lots of freaked-out drivers slamming brakes. Tire shrieks like whips at the Roman arena.

Wham! Suitable sound effect as car lifts up and scoots over the curb, goes smashing down the sidewalk for about thirty feet. Did I say a sloppy turn? If it got any worse, I'd be driving through somebody's house.

We slam off the sidewalk, lightly kissing the tail end of a parked car, crash with a grinding clatter as muffler meets curb. Panic time. I whip the wheel in one direction, not sure which way, just keeping busy.

Car makes an unexpected surfboard twist and we suddenly find ourselves back on Van Nuys Boulevard, heading in the opposite direction. Heading for what I don't know but going after it in something resembling a straight line.

Morrison's hanging out the window. Yelling about something. What the hell is he doing? Maybe tossing his cookies. Got his head bent down toward the street. Yeah. I bet he's tossing his cookies, either that or he grew up poor and couldn't afford to have his tonsils taken out so he paid to just have them loosened.

The car sounds loud. Very loud and getting louder. I hear a scraping noise, metal against pavement. Something snaps, car now sounds like a jet engine with bad compression. I look back in the rearview mirror in time to wave goodbye to the rest of the muffler.

"Hey, what did we turn around for?"

"Over there," says Morrison, resurfacing inside the car.

I look where he's pointing. I see two chicks thumbing it in front of some kind of army/navy store, something appropriate like that.

"They got the secret of fire," says Morrison with a grin.

"And crabs and clap and—"

"*Pssssssssst!*" Sounds like steam hissing out of a steamboat snake. Smartest thing he's said all night.

I stop for another light. This time I do it perfect. Correct lane, smooth stop, proper distance. Only thing spoiling it is that the light is green not red.

"What are you going *pssssssssssst* for?"

" 'Cause I am *pssssssssssst!*" Morrison tilts the wine bottle, drinks an armadillo full of wine. Least it looks like that to me. One man's apple is somebody else's orange.

"Yes sir, I am definitely *pssssssst!*"

As I ease through the intersection on yellow (the light turns red before I get halfway through) I turn and look at him. "It doesn't show on your pants. What's wrong? Find a woodchuck in your wine ration?"

Morrison waves his arms. "Well, Jesus! I go a million miles out of my way to arrange us some entertainment and immediately you start making social disease jokes and armpit jokes and all kinds of shit like that. Where's the old respect for motherfucking nature?"

"Huh?"

"Crabs are organic."

I shift as I accelerate and miss the frigging gear again. I swear the gears are moving around just to tease me. Car stalls for the millionth time. Start the car as a stream of cars go detouring around us.

"We'll never get there!"

"Look, you wanna drive, you're welcome. I'm doing the best I can. I can't help it. Somebody dropped a midget in this gear box and he's moving things on me."

Finally I get organized and we progress. After two centuries, one of them pregnant, we finally pull up to the two chicks who are thumbing. I manage to pull over without hitting any parked cars or the two hitchhikers. Morrison opens the door for them and they crawl into the back seat.

One of the girls is a real looker. Maybe sixteen or seventeen. Blond the way girls can get only in the California sun. Tall with wicked long legs you could sense through her tight blue jeans. Thin and high-breasted, face set in that phony cover-girl pose.

But her friend is a place called hunger. She looks like second place in a two-man hatchet fight. Overweight, mouth two sizes too big and too too much in the chest, if that's possible. Putting your head on her stomach would be like putting on a pair of soft pink headphones.

I smile at the good-looking one in the rearview mirror but she's smiling at Morrison, who's turned in his seat to face her. I turn and look at the other one and she's staring at me the way a shark stares at its next bite of swimmer. I close my eyes and sigh.

"Hey, where are you guys going?" asks the pretty one. She shakes her head, throwing her long blond hair off her face like a wild horse tossing its mane. Morrison smiles at her and she smiles back. "My name's Sandy."

She points at her friend. "And this is Gail."

Gail asks again, "Where you going?"

I look at Morrison and he shrugs. Neither of us know.

"Probably to jail," I answer, "the way I've been driving." I forgot to tell Jim I didn't have my driver's license yet. I had one but the picture only looked a little bit like me and the name was nothing like mine at all.

"I'm glad no cops saw that U turn. I'm glad no cops saw anything, period." Suddenly I feel superparanoid.

Morrison ignores me, offers the bottle of wine to the girls in back. "Uh, we haven't exactly decided where we're going. We're just kinda going. You chicks got any ideas?" Morrison's forgot the unlit joint, now very wet from wine, still hanging out of his mouth.

"Far out," says Sandy, blinking her cat-cold green eyes. "Me and Gail were just out cruising. We were thinking of maybe going down to the Strip to see if anything is happening."

"We'll go anywhere you want," says Morrison as I start the car moving.

I just pull back into traffic when I hear the sirens.

"Oh shit! I knew our luck was too goddamn good to be true!" Guess we did one too many intersections. That last U turn had to be the clincher. Kiss our collective asses goodbye. Wine in the car, beer in the car, dope in the car, underage chicks in the car, me underage in the car and without a license. Also one central bad-news secret too depressing to mention let alone think about. Dream a little dream of reformatory blue.

"I hear sirens," I say, starting to ease the car back over to the side of the street.

"Christ!" says Morrison, draping an imaginary noose around his neck and hanging himself with it. "I forgot we should have put wax in our ears so we'd be safe from the sirens."

Morrison starts grabbing up dope, booze, slamming

the window down for instant ejection.

"Let us out!" That's Gail, the furiously fat one with too much of everything. She starts to open the door before I even get stopped and I have to swerve to avoid depositing the opened door on a parked car. Gail shrieks and nearly falls out.

Me, I nearly pass out. We streak across the center line. Too enthusiastic about saving the door, I miss an oncoming car in the other lane by such a short distance it's almost molecular.

Morrison drops all his illegal goodies, nearly falling under the dashboard. Both chicks in back scream bloody murder.

That's when I say the hell with it. I fasten on to the wheel with a death grip and whip it around. Gun the engine and we do a stunt-man turn.

"I'm running!"

As U turns go, it almost didn't. I slammed into the side of a parked car, zigged crazily off of it, zagged back across the center line, shot back into the right lane.

The fat chick with the open door is really screaming now. My turn caught her by surprise and this time she damn near falls out of the frigging car. Not that I would miss her.

My wild-ass turn doesn't quite make it up on two wheels but I come close. If Gail's boobs hadn't got caught in the door she would have went out.

Morrison's tossing out bottles of beer, eating the joint in his mouth, yelling something at me from his green mouth. Everybody's yelling at me but I'm too busy for conversation.

I wiggle-waggle across a couple of lanes, trying like hell to straighten out this runaway crap pile of Detroit metal.

Sirens getting louder and louder and I respond by slamming the gas pedal into next week. For once, I get the shifts right. The front end lifts up, the tires squeal like scorched demons and we go whipping along.

Everybody's pushed against the backs of their seats

and I'm trying to keep us there.

I'm hoping I can get going so fast toward them that by the time the cops know it's us, we'll be so long gone they won't be able to turn around in time to catch us.

Accelerator buried, I get up to eighty-five miles an hour and the car is vibrating like two mating chain saws.

Then the sirens go screaming by . . . on an ambulance.

"Shit!" I don't know who says it but it sums up the whole thing pretty well.

I ease up on the gas, ten years older, downshift and miss a gear. Jesus! Here comes another intersection! Engine sounds like it's going to go into orbit! Shift again. Miss it again. I duck.

There's a big grey blur like a World War Two torpedo streaking across our bow. We just miss the tail end of a black car by the width of two and half molecules. Just ran another stoplight. Becoming habitual.

One of the girls is screaming. I don't know which one 'cause my head is under the dashboard, looking for religion.

I pull my head up. Morrison's got the wheel and we're still going straight, beginning to slow up. I rise up, believing in miracles and wondering if maybe there is a God who is betting on our team.

Morrison gives the wheel back to me and I'm okay. Had enough of this street though, so I turn down a one-way street, luckily going the right way and plenty slow. I shift, miss it and stall the car again.

"Do you always drive like this?"

I look back in the rearview mirror. It's Gail. She looks like yesterday's menu is forcing itself back up today's throat.

"Usually I'm not this good," I say, looking at the fat marks under her chin. "Maybe you'd like to drive? I'm having a little bit of trouble with the video portion of this broadcast." Understatement. Only thing I'm doing well at the moment is heartbeats. About three million of them a minute.

"Sure. I'd feel a lot safer. Besides, I really dig driving. If I had me some wheels, I'd be cruising all the time."

What a relief! So glad to get to let go of the reins. Besides, I've just done something brilliant on an intergalactic scale.

Gail, bursting with youth, several thousand pounds of it, can drive and sit next to Morrison and ooze her fat out at him. Me, I'll be in the back with Sandy (Let's-pick-her) Peaches and (see if she knows how to) Cream. My time to get lucky. Maybe I'll get to be the juicer and she can be the juicee.

The car doors fly open, and before I can orient myself, Morrison is climbing in back with the looker and doughnut overdoser is slamming me across the front seat with a hip that Moby Dick would have been proud of. Oh, Jesus!

I'm not saying this chick is fat, understand, but if you saw her running around naked and you were a little nearsighted, you might think her clothes badly needed ironing.

I look back at Morrison. He's grinning like a Cheshire cat discovering downers. I look at the whale beside me and she gives me a look that makes me shudder. I think they once made an Edgar Allan Poe movie about her: *Masque of the Overfed Death*.

She winks at me and gets some sort of expression on her face. Either a provocative look or gas pains. With her, how could you tell and why would you want to?

Morrison's happy as a cocained cobra. Me, I feel like putting my head in the glove compartment and slamming the lid.

Gail shifts, eases out the clutch and we take off smooth. No jumps or false starts. When I was driving you got the feeling you were riding a five-dollar epileptic Mexican whore.

The car runs down the street. I think even the car is

relieved now that somebody competent is behind the wheel.

"Jesus!" yells Morrison suddenly, scaring the shit out of everybody. *"Fire!"*

Everybody turns and looks at him, frightened.

"Fire!" That's me shouting, for a few seconds even feeling the flame on my back. I'm staring at the back seat. The idiot! I'm sliding down the other side, trip wise, mellowing out on Cream Ale. So why am I screaming fire?

Morrison holds up his wine-soaked joint. "We need the secret of fire."

"I just wet myself," I said, looking down at my lap.

Gail laughs. "No you didn't. You had a bottle of something between your legs and when you moved over on the seat it spilled. I saw it."

"Oh," I say.

"You got matches?" That was Morrison talking to the chick in back.

Sandy starts digging through a rabbit-fur purse she's got slung over one shoulder. Really digging deep. Must be twenty pill bottles in there. She comes out with a silver cigarette lighter. "Will this do?"

"All right! All right!" Morrison takes the lighter and fires up the joint. Has a hard time getting it lit. But does. The sweet, tasty smell of dope fills the car.

The chick who's driving turns off Van Nuys onto Victory Boulevard and we start going toward Laurel Canyon. Smoke begins filling the car. Morrison lights another joint, puffing like crazy to get it going.

A joint gets passed and I take a hit, a big one. I'm drifting out of my acid state, going into that speed-like energy glow that you get on the down side. I look back at Jim. That maniac is lighting up a third joint. Enough smoke in the car to stone a troop ship. Morrison's got to be getting a real burning glow by now, a real acid roller-coaster rip, if he doesn't drown it completely with wine and smoke.

I end up with two joints in my hand, hyperventilating like crazy. I pass one to Gail. She smokes weird, puffing on it like an amateur, surrounding herself in a cloud of smoke. Doesn't matter. There's enough smoke in the car to get the upholstery stoned.

I suck in a wind tunnel full of smoke, look back to see how Jim is doing. He and the chick are trying to occupy the same space in the back seat.

Whispering secrets to each other's tonsils with their tongues.

There is a big bump under Sandy's T-shirt. That bump is Morrison's hand. The squeeze that pleases.

I sigh. Stare back out the front window. Not going to get the good time this time around. I look over at Gail the Whale for a second and turn away quick before I go blind.

I wind up with two joints, put them both in my mouth and take a hit that destroys my chances of ever becoming an opera singer. Inside of my throat feels like a scratched record. Maybe I'll get lucky and pass out.

I feel something creeping up my leg. Feels like a tarantula wearing overshoes trying to give me a knee massage.

I look down and a hand that's probably been a tradition with sailors since 1946 is creeping up toward my better half.

Poorly hidden behind the smoke from two joints, I feel like crying. Take the joy sticks out, cough half a lung out.

"Where are we . . . uuuuuh . . . going?" I ask, afraid to take her hand off of my leg. Touching her intentionally would be like kissing a mad dog.

As the hand slides up toward my lap, I keep creeping up the back of the seat until my head is touching the roof of the car.

My voice keeps cracking. I'm as nervous as a virgin trying to give a hickey to a rattlesnake.

"Hey!"

It's the girl in back, momentarily resurfacing.

"We know where there's a party down by Sunset off Laurel Canyon."

"That's right," says Gail. "Let's go there. Okay with you guys?"

"Sure," says Morrison, speaking for us both.

A traffic light turns red and Gail lets go of my lap to handle the gear shift. Thank God for small favors and manual transmissions!

I seriously consider jumping out of the car and running like hell. I get my hand on the door handle but the light changes and we start rolling again. Damn! Missed my chance.

Maybe just as well. I haven't told Morrison my one special secret about this car. Don't want him biting the bullet. The chicks could go hang but I kind of admire him. He is crazier than I am. But with more style.

Morrison says something. I think it's French. I turn around, thinking he's talking to me, and see a tight T-shirt disappearing over a honey-blond head.

Squeals of delight. Throaty breathing. Clothes coming undone. Oh flaming frigging frying flying horse-shit!

I face forward, quietly bash my head against the dashboard.

Sounds of struggle, clothes resisting. Lip sounds, hip sounds. Rip-her-zipper sounds. Inhibitions leaving and hot breathing.

I open another cream ale, warm as piss by now, and down it all in one gulp. Tastes like donkey whiz. Open the window and throw it at a parked car. Miss the windshield, bottle smashes against the roof.

This is gonna be one of those nights. If I want decent action tonight, I'm going to have to take advantage of myself.

Fat chick driving, still shifting, thank God. She's got one eye on the road and the other eye on the action in the back seat. She's getting hot, licking her lips nervously.

Heading down Laurel Canyon, a mean twisting snake of downhill road. Beginning to whip down some steep turns. Soft pleasure moans from the backsexcycleseat.

A pair of black lace panties drifts out of the beginning of a nudist convention in back, landing on my left shoulder.

My fault, I tell myself. Shouldn't team up with this kind of guy. He gets more ass than a toilet seat.

I can smell the sweet girl smell on those black panties. In sympathy, my lap begins to ache, my tight pants getting too tight.

Gail beside me is panting like a dog sitting on a hot plate. Getting hotter all the time too.

I slide as far away from Gail as I can get without actually falling out of the car. I open another Shoenling Little Kings Cream Ale. Rim of the bottle breaks on the edge of the ashtray. Get glass in the beer. Shit. Drink it anyway.

Like a horror movie that follows you home in your nightmares, I see Gail's hand begin creeping across the seat toward my crotch.

I think about opening up the window and diving out.

I'm beginning to sweat, half frightened, half frenzied. Glance in the rearview mirror. Everybody back there has gone horizontal and parallel. Two of the nicest girl legs I've ever seen. Look like two swizzle sticks made out of pearl. Wicked-looking legs thumping against the car roof.

I have to look away, resist the impulse to dive into the back seat and mingle like a mad dog. My blood is racing like the Grand Prix. Soft pleasure sounds come from the back.

Gail is so excited she's gunned the accelerator. We're flying. She's just barely watching the road. Big hills coming up and tricky curves.

I can see us at the bottom of a hill, a tangled mass of bleeding meat. Me on the bottom, flatter than a circus strong man's paper drinking-straw and the Betty the

Boop blimp stretched out atop me like a beached whale. Morrison and the beach baby on top, still fucking like bandits.

"Watch what you're doing!" I yell, batting her hand away. We glide into a curve marked thirty-five miles an hour doing about seventy. Gail hits the brakes, hard. My head smacks into the dashboard. I say something obscene, collapse back against the seat.

Gail's got her hands off me, concentrating on getting us through the curve in one piece.

A leg appears as if by magic across my left shoulder. A soft, warm girl's leg. I figure they're doing Numbers 17 through 26 in the *Kama Sutra.*

Hot leg brushes across the side of my face, like touching a live wire. I almost got to sit on my hands to keep them from grabbing onto the leg and dragging it up front. My pants are so tight on me my eyes are swimming.

Somehow we whip through the curve, still on four wheels, straighten out and ride into another one. Driving is tricky here, takes her mind off me.

A cop car goes by going the other way. Morrison groans. I quietly go mad. I'm hornier than a hot rabbit with socks on.

A very married looking couple in a blue car pull up level with us as we slowly dip into another turn. Mr. and Mrs. Straight America.

They stare at us. Both about fifty and constipated. He's driving, both are staring. He's pop-eyed, looking at our colorful back-seat window display. He must catch them changing position or something. Mr. America's got his mouth open in an imitation of the Grand Canyon.

We make the turn, then make another one. Mr. America, eyes still on our traveling exhibition, plows straight ahead. Misses the curve completely. I turn around just as they leave the road.

Don't see the crash but have lots of fun imagining it.

"You're frightening the horses, for chrissakes," I mutter under my breath.

Then Sandy starts having an orgasm. Excited, throaty little bursts of pleasure. Jesus! I can't stand it! I should have jumped out the window and lacerated myself to death.

Can feel her pleasure pumps all up and down my spine. That same hard kick you get from rock and roll. That same hard kick I first got on the seventeenth hole of the Northmoor Golf Course, me fourteen, her thirty-eight. Ah, sex, where is thy stain?

Why didn't I move faster in getting into the back seat? Could have been me back there. Should have been me. I open another bottle of beer, lift it to my mouth, making a mock toast.

"And here's to the boys in the back."

Gail squeezes my lap, most painful grip I've ever felt. Damn near went through the roof. Head slams forward, crotch spasm. Tears in my eyes. Who was the bastard who invented tight pants?

Gail is panting, face flushed. Somehow she's managed to unbutton the top three or four buttons of her shirt. Three hundred pounds of her is hanging out.

"Maybe I should pull over," she says, reaching for me.

I sit up straight, beating her hand away with a frantic flurry of blows. "No!" I shriek, hysterical. "I mean *no!*"

"Let's get down!"

I have to do something quick. "I . . . I . . . Hey, listen, we'll be at the party soon. I'll get you at the party! Yeah! See I need lots of room. I don't like quickies either. Uh, yeah, get you there, then I promise I'll screw all night long!" I'm talking faster than a Speed Queen dishwasher.

Gail blinks a couple of times, processing the information through her fat or something.

"Okay. Beds are better anyway," she says finally.

Background, those tense hot little come sounds. *Unnnnh! Unnnh!*

Gail looks feverish. "I can hardly wait. We're only a couple of blocks away." Another crotch squeeze and I double up.

Unnnh! Unnnh!

"We get to that party and . . ." Gail leaves the sentence hanging, just pants at me, looking like a bullfrog with hormone problems.

The loudest one yet. *Unnnnnnnnnnnnh!* Sounds like the big casino.

I quietly tear my fingernails out. If I get any hornier, I could defy gravity.

Silence from the back seat and exhausted breathing.

Let's hear a big wet cheer for Saturday Night L.A. Sex in cars and topless bars. Big-breasted chicks who dance taps on the tops of tables in the back rooms of racing stables. Chicks who drink and smoke big cigars and get it on in double-parked cars. Let's hear it for too much dope, too much booze and all the chicks you'd make if you could choose.

Horny! If I tripped trying to get out of the car, I'd pole-vault clear across the street!

Morrison reappears. A hand comes out of the back seat, taps me on the shoulder. "Got a joint?"

I turn around and look back at them. Two intertwined bodies like a pink worm farm.

"Go fuck a biscuit!" I say, opening the glove compartment. I get a bag and pull out a couple of joints. I pass them back, keeping two for myself. I light them both. I need it.

"I just did," says Morrison, putting a joint in his mouth. "Did somebody mention a party?"

The car, still full of smoke, gets fuller.

Gail, the fearlessly fat driver of our moving violation, makes a turn off of whatever street we're driving on and we go up a drive with big mansions. We are among the habitats of the rich and playful.

I toke furiously on my joints. I've got a definite plan.

I'm going to pass out and to hell with everybody else. Gail especially. Let's see the dumb bitch messing with me when I'm in a coma. Maybe I'll even throw up on her just before I slip into unconsciousness. That'll teach her to maul my family jewels.

One mansion at the top of a hill is lit up like a Saturday night drunk. Cars parked every which way, on lawns, driveways, sidewalks and a couple of dented ones sticking out of hedges. One parked on top of a rock garden, a jazzy-looking Jaguar with the windshield smashed, has half of a tree laying across it.

Loud noise masquerading as music blasts out into the late night air, probably sterilizing everybody and everything in its path. This looks like my kind of party.

Gail pulls up somebody's driveway, trys to edge in between a blue Alfa Romeo and a Thunderbird. Catches the Alfa Romeo on the left front fender, practically tearing it off.

"Oh, shit," she says, turning the car off.

"Nobody'll notice," says Morrison, lost somewhere in a thick cloud of dope smoke. Everybody's eyes are stinging. Even the oxygen in the air is stoned.

Gail puts on the parking break and turns to gather me up in her arms.

The thing is, I'm already ten steps from the car and still moving.

I look back to see if Morrison is coming. Car is so full of smoke, I can't see anybody in it.

Suddenly the ground rises up and hits me in the face. I am waaaaaasted!

The door is still open where I've exited and Morrison stumbles out after me in a cloud of smoke and a hearty "Hi Ho, Silver."

The ground rises up and hits him in the face too. He is waaaaasted!

I lay there on my stomach, trying to stand up without using my legs. Not easy.

Morrison crawls toward me, near-empty wine bottle

in one hand and some of his clothes in the other. He's wearing nothing but his pants. How he got them back on is one of life's great mysteries.

I can hear his chick cursing about something in the car. She's looking for something, probably can't find her clothes, or one of her legs is missing. Maybe I smoked it, thinking it was a pink joint.

"Mluck," says Morrison, glassy eyed and mentally keelhauled. "Far . . . out!"

I'd agree but I can't get my mouth off the ground.

Smoke is pouring out of the car. Where's it all coming from? Looks like we arrived in a forest fire.

Morrison drags himself up to me, nudges me with the wine bottle. "Geeet . . . upppp."

I roll over on my side, just so I can get the grass out of my nose. "That's . . . easy for you to say."

Somebody must be standing on my tongue.

Morrison gets to a sitting position, reaches down and pulls me up. We lean against each other to keep ourselves from falling over.

Morrison looks around. "Where the . . . hell are we?" He's so high he's almost glowing in the dark.

"Shit!" he says, sort of on general principle.

"Did you . . . you . . . uh . . . I forget."

"What?" asks Morrison.

"Did you . . . you . . . uh . . . I forget."

"I don't know," says Morrison, staring at the wine bottle. "You were there . . . wasn't you?"

"Was I? Where was I where?"

"I thought one of us was," says Morrison.

"Oh," I say. Then I remember. "Did you . . . you have a smooth ride?"

Morrison nods, slipping off my shoulder and falling over on his back. "Oh, yes," he says. "Pretty neat. Pretty neat." He drags himself back up, falls over on me, almost knocking me down. "I am in love . . . from the waist down."

I can hear Sandy in the car, still cursing about something. I vaguely remember that there is somebody I should be escaping from. I remember Gail the Whale, panic and look back to see if she's after me. Some of the smoke is out of the car, enough for me to see her still in the front of the car, struggling with her shirt buttons.

I put my arm around Morrison's shoulder. "You gotta help me. I got to ... to ... to ... I forget."

"Trust me," says Morrison. "I can keep a secret."

"No. No. S'not a secret. Except to me. I can't remember."

Morrison looks around. "Where the hell are we?" Confused.

I shake my head. "We already did that line."

"Tell me the secret." Morrison bends over so I can whisper in his ear. I slip and fall over on his legs.

I look up at him. Now I remember. "I gotta escape. Like Ish ... Ishmael and the ... the Great White Whale."

Morrison nods. "All right!" Lifts the wine bottle and kills the last of it. When the bottle's empty he turns it upside down and stares into it suspiciously. "Somebody stole it," he says.

"You gotta save me!"

Morrison nods. "Commit suicide," he suggests.

"No, let's get up and ... I forget."

"Get up and dance?" suggests Morrison idiotically. "Get up and get down?"

"Run!" I remember. "Jesus! I got to get the fuck out of here! If I don't, I may become the first elephant rape victim in the world."

"Right!" says Morrison, putting a hand on my shoulder. He pushes off me, staggering to his feet. The hand that steadies him pushes me into the ground.

"Salvation!" cries Morrison, raising his arms to the sky. He takes two steps back and falls over a bush.

"Shit!" says Morrison. "Earthquake!"

"You're no help." I drag myself over to a tree and be-

gin clawing my way up it. Somehow I get to my feet.
My head keeps wanting to kiss the ground but I'm
standing up nevertheless.

"Resurrection!" yells Morrison, rising from the
trampled remains of the bush. He raises his arms and
falls forward over the same bush.

I stagger over toward him. I reach down, grab him by
the shoulder and help him up. "Far out," he says, as he
regains his feet.

We stand there, falling against each other to keep
from falling down completely. My head is spinning,
dancing around on synaptic legs. My crotch is in-
flamed. Those tight pants haven't let up on me at all.

Morrison holds out the wine bottle. "Empty," he
says.

Then he pitches it over his shoulder. There's a crash
as it smashes the windshield of a Mercedes. "More,"
says Morrison. "I'm not off yet, not . . . not high yet."

"Huh?" I stare at him. "How do you know?"

" 'Cause I'm still standing up," he says.

I look back at the car, trying to see how much of a
running head start I've got on the human hippo. She's
still in the car, still buttoning up the front of her shirt
so Mount Rushmore doesn't catch cold.

"How do you like the chick I picked for you?" says
Morrison, giving me a polar bear laugh. The cool bastard.

"Eat shit and die!" I tell him.

"She looks like the place where Moby was Dicked!"

For some reason that strikes me as being funny. So
funny that I try to hit him. I miss and we both fall flat
on our asses.

"Twenty-mule-team Borax!" says Morrison, wild-
eyed. "The fucking wind is gale force tonight!"

We both begin staggering to our feet.

"Oh, no!" says Morrison. "Here come the Cos-
sacks!"

Morrison grabs me and pushes me toward the party.
Stumbling like paraplegic marathon runners, we get

our feet down on the good earth and try running with them.

Over my shoulder I see Gail the Whale coming up behind like an approaching ice age. It's like seeing a tenement lift up its skirts and run.

We race for the door, coming out tied, smash into it, and fall over ass backwards. Jumping up at the speed of barbiturated light, we both bang on the door.

It opens, five or six people hanging on the door. We push past them before they can ask us in. Once inside, as one, we both turn and help slam the door.

"Hey, what you doing?" asks one of the drunks hanging on to the door.

"Lions!" says Morrison. "Tigers!"

An old chick on the bad side of forty with a face like a collapsed universe stares drunkenly at us. "Lions? Tigers?"

Morrison reaches out, pats her on top of the head. "Don't worry! If they get in, wink your hysterectomy scar at them and they'll vanish."

The old lady puts her hands over her lap and stares down at her crotch. Morrison pinches her on the butt and staggers away, looking for the john.

"*Oh Lord! Let me make it to the next gas station before the prayer runs down my leg!*" he yells and vanishes into the party crowd.

Me, I am trying to focus an eye well enough to find the back door, the back door and the fastest way out of there.

CHAPTER 4

I start wading through the party, pushing and shoving, trying to get to the back door. I also got to piss and anything that even remotely looks like a toilet is gonna get wet.

Guess I am too enthusiastic. Somebody hits me on the side of the face. I think I stepped on his toe. I take two quick steps sideways and fall over an end table. A ceramic sculpture on the table joins its ancestors.

I shake my head. Dizzy. Not sure what happened. Maybe I better just lay here until the earthquake is over. I close my eyes, willing to sink into a coma. A couple of pairs of hands seize me and I find myself catapulted into a standing position. A couple of people I don't know are dusting me off. Somebody hands me a can of beer, says, "Hey, man, like don't worry. Everything's cool."

I sip the beer and nod.

I can't focus my eyes and I have a definite list to starboard, but if somebody is sure everything is cool, who am I to disagree?

One side of my face feels like the section of the *Titanic* that kissed the iceberg. I stagger forward, with only the vaguest idea where I am going or why. Seem to remember there is something important I got to do but can't remember what it is. Something nautical, something hazy about a whale.

Somehow I find myself with an arm around a little blond girl with pimples. Either I know her from somewhere or I don't. Can't tell.

She's talking about getting busted for possession. She sounds like a vacuum cleaner going over linoleum. Really dumb. I know she'll never get busted for possession of her faculties.

Drinking my beer, nodding my head up and down in time to the music of her mouth. She's speaking B flat or something. Morrison's gone. I remember enough to remember that he's disappeared. Probably he fell in the john and drowned in those little white bowls they always got in those kind of rooms.

Am just getting to remembering that I ought to get out of there and why when something like fifteen pounds of raw meat puts the vice grips on my shoulder and spins me around.

My eyes just about pop out of my face and I spill beer all over myself. Oh, no! Gail the Whale has arrived. In my spinning vision, looks like six of her standing there. Maybe a dozen. All in the same pair of ready-to-split-and-spill-fat tight pants.

"Remember me?"

Before I can claim to be dumb, deaf and blind or pretend to go into a coma, she puts her arms around me and gives me a hug.

The little pimple-faced blonde is still chattering away. Don't think she notices that I am gone. Probably didn't notice I was there in the first place.

I feel something wet in the middle of my chest, something wet creeping down and getting inside my underwear. Gail crushed my beer can and I'm getting Miller High Life on my swizzle stick.

I feel my face getting red as all the air squishes out of me. I try to push her away and she tries to kiss me.

"Let's find a bed." I can't hold her off. She kisses me and I choke, half a can of beer trying to come up from my stomach and say splash to the floor.

"Gonna pass out," I say and try to fall down. She releases me and I start to collapse on the floor. But she gets a death grip on one arm and begins dragging me off. Hard to pass out when you're being dragged, one arm threatening to come out of its socket.

"Help!" I try to pull free, try to resist, but I'm too wasted and she's stronger than truck-stop coffee.

"Help!"

Somebody hands me another can of beer as she drags me across the room. Some wise-ass. "You better drink it," a long-haired freak advises me. "Looks like you're gonna need all the help you can get."

Wise-ass!

We're almost across the room, almost to the hallway that leads to the bedrooms. I am trying frantically to get away. I grab hold of a tall guy with beads and a black beard. Grab him by the leg as I am dragged by. "Help!" I say, pulling him over on top of me. "I'm being raped!"

He's unsympathetic. He takes one look at Gail the Whale and beats a hasty retreat, throwing my arm off.

"Better you than me," he says.

In desperation, I put one leg between Gail's legs, trying to trip her. She hits my leg, damn near breaking it, and I fall on my face, hard. It doesn't slow her in the least. She's dragging me by one arm like I am a six-foot sack of cotton.

"Tote that bale, lift that barge!" says the bearded bead wearer, an unnatural-born comedian. A couple of people are looking at me, laughing. Terrific. Just arrived at the party and already I'm a social success. Shit!

Out of the front room and down the hallway, managing to get to my feet at least. We approach a door, the downstairs guest bedroom door, and she tries to open it.

Locked!

Saved! She lets go of my arm and bangs on the door. "Hey! We wanna use the room! Finish up in there!"

A muffled shout comes back through the door.

I start creeping away, on tiptoe, backing away ever so softly. Somebody runs into me, pushes me forward and I collide with Gail's back. She thinks I'm trying to give her a hug and she puts an arm around my neck and gives me an affectionate squeeze. Almost swallow my tongue.

The bedroom door opens up. A fat guy and a thin guy hurry out. The fat guy is dressed in a Sears and Roebuck plaid shirt, Montgomery Ward plaid slacks, and has hickeys all over his neck. He's also dead drunk and limping bow-legged. He comes out first, stumbles past muttering something that sounds like *"Incrediburble!"*

The thin one, smelling like a brewery vat, staggers uncertainly in the doorway. Has to lean against the door frame to keep from diving forward on his nose. He's got a long-haired wig hanging at a crazy angle on his head. He stares at us, eyes barely focusing, and steps sideways through the door, stretching the fabric of his dress with his knees.

He turns his ankle and falls, high spike heels striking out like rattlesnake fangs.

Sharp pain in my knee as his heels catch me.

The guy shakes his head, wig slips even farther.

"How simply silly of me," he says, adjusting the falsies under his dress with one unsteady hand. He puts his other hand out to me.

"Would you help me up, young man?"

Weird-looking guy from another planet. Got lipstick on his nose and one false eyelash hanging free at one end. Half of his face needs a shave and he's got a tattoo on his right cheek, the words "Lovechild" in old English script.

I haven't got anything else to do except get raped so I reach out one hand and drag him to his feet. He falls all over me, trying to put his arms around my neck, forcing Gail to let go. This guy smells like Saturday night under the bleachers at a Fire Island football game.

"Thanks, darling." Tries to straighten his dress by jerking on the crotch of it. Doesn't much.

He's still blocking the doorway. Gail's impatient.

"You're a dear," says the guy. "And so strong." He runs his hand up and down my chest.

"He's not interested," Gail says, pushing him roughly away from me. He bangs back into the door frame, cracking his head against the wall. His wig slips down over his forehead and he has to reach up and push it back so he can see.

He draws himself up straight, absolutely furious.

"Up yours, honey!"

He marches up to her, puts his hands on his hips, and thrusts his pelvis out in what is meant to be a seductive gesture. He runs his eyes up and down her body, moving his head from side to side as each incredible slope of her appears before his eyes.

He looks back at me, I suppose wondering what the hell I could possibly see in her. Looks at me, looks back at her, then looks back at me and says, "Well, lover boy, if you're strong enough to mount the human el-

ephant here, you're probably so hot I'd have to pay you
for it."

He's staring at my crotch. "You'd have to be hung
like a moose to get through the first layer of fat."

"Get out of the way, you . . . faggot!" says Gail, really pissed off.

He reaches out and grabs one of her skyscraper
breasts, pinching it to see if it's real. He bounces the
end of it in his fingers. "Honey, you've either got a camel sitting on your chest or you pulled into a gas station
to get air in your tires and got it in the wrong place."

Gail slams his hand away, karate style. She screams
at him, kung fu style. Stepping into him, she knees
him in the crotch, redneck style, and clips him in the
jaw, lumberjack style, as he folds up in a genitals-prob-
ably-crushed style.

He smashes back against the wall. She karate chops
him twice, slamming him violently against the wall.

He doesn't know what hit him. He slides down the
wall slowly, bony knees pushing up the dress until it
splits. Almost in slow motion, he slips over sideways,
out cold and not knowing how lucky he is.

Gail, the fattest SS trooper in the world, doesn't even
look at him. "Lousy fag," she says and drags me into
the bedroom. Like a fool, I was so busy watching the
fight I forgot to escape. I want to cry. How do I get into
these things?

Gail starts to shut the door and lock it when a hand
reaches through the door and grabs her by one big
breast, giving her a big squeeze. Stunned, she backs
away from the door and Morrison pushes his way into
the room.

I'm looking around, trying to find a window I can
dive out of.

Morrison's got a can of beer in one hand. "Heeeeey!
What's happening?" He looks like a wild horse.

Gail's touching her breast where Morrison has
squeezed her. She's got a dangerous look in her eyes.

She's hotter than a cracked radiator at Death Valley.
Don't know what Morrison's thinking. I know Gail is
thinking threesies. Me, I am thinking windowsies and
dive-outsies.

Morrison hands her the can of beer, kisses her on the
cheek and winks at me. Gail lights up like Las Vegas.

"Hey, pretty lady! You strong enough to get it on
with me and my partner?" Morrison motions toward
me. I am trying to crawl out the window. Too screwed
up to get my leg over the windowsill. Now I know
what Morrison's thinking. Obviously he isn't.

Is he out of his frigging mind?

Yes.

He is.

Gail drinks some of the beer, sloppily, getting foam
all over her face. She hands the beer back and, using
both hands, begins tearing her shirt off. Huge mountains of her begin appearing in the air, polluting the environment with their amplified grossness.

Do I have the desire to stay and put the pork to the
Magic Mountain? Insane!

Am I out of my frigging mind?

No.

I isn't.

If I cannot raise myself over the windowsill, I shall
lower the window! I shall dig a tunnel with my bare
hands through the floor! I will crawl through an elec-
trical outlet! I am gonna get the fuck out of there is
what I am gonna do!

I fall down by the window, one leg half out, and
crack my head on a wicker chair. Morrison comes over
and picks me up.

"Don't panic! Save your engines. The situation is
under control," he whispers to me as he helps me up.

Hell with him! I lean over the windowsill and start
to crawl out. Morrison grabs me and pulls me back in.

He stands me up. I shake my head. Feel something
warm on my neck. Cut it against the chair. I stand

there, brain fried, but not that fried. Don't think I could ever get that fried. "I don't wanna . . . uh! Let me out of here!"

Morrison restrains me, digs his elbow in my side, shuts me up.

Gail's excited, all tangled up in her shirt, a ring on her finger caught in a hole in the material.

Morrison winks at me again. Makes a be-cool motion at me with one hand and moves over toward her. He puts his hands on her arms. "Take the beer can. Finish it off," says Morrison, holding the beer can for her between two fingers.

"Drink up and let me get that button for you," says Morrison.

The whale lady is so thrilled she's almost giving birth to babies. Obediently, she tilts the beer can back and belts down half of it. Sloppy bitch. Some of it runs down her face.

When she puts her head down, Morrison's finished with the buttons and is pulling her shirt out of her pants. He seems intent on what he's doing. Me, I figure he's a sickie and I'm making for the door and the hell with him.

A joke is a joke. But no sense going for the laugh of the century.

I'm at the door when Morrison turns and looks at me. "Hey, man, trust me. It's cool." Again the sly wink. "Come and give me a hand." He's having a hell of a time getting the shirt out of her pants past her fat.

I pause, the bedroom door unlocked and my hand on the doorknob. What the hell is he up to? I let the lock fall back into place. Well, shit, I can always run in a couple of seconds.

"This beer tastes weird. Tastes funny." Gail stares at the can, cross-eyed. Her face looks like a sinking ship.

"Finish that beer, foxy lady, and we'll get down. Get it on!" says Morrison, face red as he tugs on her pants. He can't get his fingers down inside to reach the button above the zipper. She's just too frigging fat.

"Help me," says Morrison, struggling with the pants.

"You're frigging crazy! You're out of your mind! I wouldn't . . . I couldn't . . . I . . ."

Well, shit, I go over and start pushing on her stomach so he can get his hand down far enough to reach her top jean button.

Gail staggers back against the bedpost as I shove her stomach in. She's got a real strange expression on her face.

"Finish that beer, girl," says Morrison, sweating from the exertion. Christ, she's fat!

The button comes undone like a dam breaking and fat spills out like an Indian attack.

"I . . ." Gail staggers, almost falls forward on her face. "I feeeeeeeel . . . straaaap . . . stranmp . . . straaaaaaaaaaange."

She weaves in front of us like a punch-drunk fighter on Nembutol.

"Hey! What's happening here?" I ask, staring at her.

Morrison yanks and the zipper comes down, liberating another mountain of flesh. Even her pubic hair is fat.

Gail stumbles forward. "Hooooooornyyyyyy!" she says, bellowing like a pitchforked cow and raising her arms, trying to grab us. She misses us by about four yards. She doesn't look too healthy. She looks like somebody who just lost a sledgehammer fight.

"What's wrong with her?" I ask, moving back to get out of her way. She seems in danger of falling over on me and breaking my bones.

Morrison is pushing on her chest, pushing her back against the bed. The bedpost groans under her weight.

Jim holds up one hand. "Downs." He spreads his fingers, numbering them. "A handful of them in the can of beer. She's just entered Phenobarbsuburbia!"

"What are we taking her clothes off for? You're not

really gonna . . . gonna . . ." It's too horrible to even mention.

Morrison straightens up, puts his hands on his hips and gives me an unreadable stare. "Didn't you hear this beautiful specimen of blushing girlhood proclaim she was horny?"

"You're out of your frigging mind!"

Gail lurches forward. Morrison grabs her by two or three tons of one of her breasts and pushes her back against the bedpost again. She tries to grab his arm but he brushes her love-starved hands away.

"Help me get these frigging pants off."

Gail's slobbering all over herself, staring wildly around the room.

"*Hoooooooooooorrrrrnnnyyy!*" she says, in case we forgot.

I sigh. How do I get myself into these things?

"Like to help you out but I just can't get involved," I say. "See, I've got the clap and crabs and syph and hemorrhoids and shingles and tonsillitis and and and . . . and hangnail." I shake my head, being definite about it. "I'm pregnant too."

"Help me with her pants, you pregnant asshole! This is gonna be the event of the century!" Morrison's getting pissed at me.

Like the fool that I am, I get on one side of her and get hold of her pants. Morrison's on the other side.

"If I were a time traveler," I mutter, "I'd skip this century altogether. This time zone is too exciting for me."

"Ready? Now!" says Morrison.

We yank simultaneously, me harder than him. Guess I don't know my own strength. Gail throws her arms out like an executed peasant. Slobbering something incomprehensible while her pants ride at half mast, she tilts toward me. Realizing the danger too late, I can't get out from under. She falls over on me and breaks every bone in my body.

Ever have a meteor with breasts fall on you? How to become one-dimensional in one easy lesson.

I try to say something, try to attract Morrison's attention. I got five tons on my windpipe and all I can do is gasp.

He reaches under, grabs one leg and yanks me out from under her. My tongue is five foot long and my chest is sixteen inches thinner.

I just lay there beside her. Moaning.

"Somebody bury me. I just died with my boots on."

I get dragged to my feet and stagger around like a gut-shot gunfighter trying to steal a scene in a B movie.

"Help me get her on the bed." Morrison's pulled her pants off already, is now trying to lift her up onto the bed. Like trying to raise the *Titanic*.

I get hold of one of her arms, Morrison grabs the other one and we somehow heave her up on the bed. At least the top half of her. She's so heavy we have to throw her in sections. Finally we get her all the way on the bed. She keeps making feeble grabs at us, keeps mumbling, "Horny horny horny."

We get her in the middle of the bed, which sags a lot. This is one girl who does not defy gravity, she agrees with it.

"Well," I say, beginning to edge away, "I just remembered they're having a surprise autopsy in my neighborhood and I'm invited. I'll see you around."

I start for the door.

"Cool it," says Morrison. He waves me back to the bed. "The scene is set, man. Do you not dig the theatrics of it all? This is Grand Guignol! It is an escaped Rorschach blot with a bad case of the get-it-ons!"

"Me, I don't want to get involved."

"Me neither. I ain't crazy!" says Morrison with a laugh. He goes over and begins unscrewing the light bulb in the lamp near the bed. "But don't you think the blimp would be a good gang-bang gift from me and you to the rest of the party?"

I look at the hippo moaning "Horny" on the bed, think about it for a couple of seconds and the enormity of it all hits me. This Morrison cat's got style! He's got the power! He's even crazier than I am. And I am pretty friggin' crazy!

"Man oh man! I like your act!" Got to admire this guy. Terrific stunt. I pull a chair out, stand on it and start unscrewing the overhead light bulb.

"To see it," says Morrison, throwing a hot light bulb under the bed, "is to refuse to believe it."

"Let us hope the dark is dark enough. Ouch!" Burn my fingers on the hot bulb. Bulb comes loose, scorching my palm. Drop the bulb and it breaks with a pop on the floor beneath my chair.

"Clumsy," says Morrison.

Room is now pitch black. I step off the chair, miscalculate the distance to the floor and fall forward on my face. Crash over the top of a wicker chair and crush an aluminum wastebasket into lopsided flatness.

"I'm not clumsy," I tell him, dragging myself up off the floor. I can feel blood on my face. Feels like I broke it. "I'm just athletically inclined toward pain."

From the bed, Gail yells, "Hoooorny!"

I stumble around in the dark, feeling around for the door. Trying to aim in the opposite direction from the moaning sounds coming from the bed. Get a little freaked out, stumbling round in the dark. Can't find the door, can't even find a wall

Morrison catches me by the shoulders and suddenly the door is open and we go through it.

Life is like that. You're struggling in the dark with elephants who are out to do you in, and then suddenly the door is open and you're going through it.

Outside the bedroom the party is going full stroke. Everybody's getting drunk, train wrecked and dizzy on the end that blows bubbles. Also enough coke going up noses to fly a small country to Cuba.

This is one of those all-types, all-talking, all-singing,

all-dancing parties. A little bit of everybody is there. Geese and the goosers. Macrobiotic munchkins eating bread, wine and cheese and shoot-'em-up drug abusers. All the tried and true not-so-beautiful losers. Everybody is everybody.

There's also a lot of very straight looking types wandering around. People with suits even. Rich people with bad bodies and great clothes to cover them up.

"Wow!" I say, staring at the human wreckage. "Who looks like a likely candidate?"

Morrison nods toward an Ivy League type leaning against a wall. An escapee from a college frat house and obviously embalmed in beer.

This guy's got one arm around a lamp and a glazed expression that looks like someone has buttered his eyes.

"We gonna let it all hang out," says Morrison as we zero in on our target.

"Hey, man!" Morrison slaps him on the shoulder, almost flooring him. "Long time no see! How's it hanging?"

"Woooowee, man! I'm druuuuuunnnnkkk!" says the mental midget in the Sears and Roebuck suit.

"Getting any poontang?" asks Morrison.

Our new friend shakes his head vehemently, smashing one cheek into the wall. He lifts his head away from the wall, surprised that he is that close to it. Stares at the wall suspiciously.

Morrison comes around him and lifts him up, one arm around his shoulders.

"Hey, old buddy! How'd you like some poontang?"

"I ... uh ... no thanks. I don't ... don't do no drugs." An enormous belch, about four point five on the Richter scale, splits our friend's face almost in half. " 'Scuse me. Just drink ... boy, do I drink!"

Morrison shakes his head. "Idiot! Poontang is pussy! Smoke muffins!"

"You mean girls?" asks Squirrel-eyes. "Oh, that's

different." He nods his head, painfully thinking it over.
"Yas . . . girls is different. Much."

"You wanna get laid?" asks Morrison conspiratorial-
ly.

"Me?" He seems astounded. "Who? When?"

Morrison turns him around and aims his head
toward the bedroom door. In front of it a tall blond girl
stands talking to a couple of guys. She's a hot looker.
Long wicked legs trying to burst a hot little miniskirt
that just barely covers the central goodie. Two high
breasts like baby ducks pushing against a thin tie-dyed
T-shirt. She's got to be all of six foot tall and sharp the
way only California girls can get.

"See that girl over there?"

Our friend nods idiotically.

"Well, she's horny," says Morrison. "She wants
you."

Our newfound friend giggles. "You're putting me
on," protests Booze Boy. "She wouldn't want . . ."

Morrison smiles like Satan witnessing the signature
on a contract. "Hey, listen. I used to date her. Man, ear-
lier this evening she was telling me she didn't like the
looks of the studs in this room. Till she saw you, that
is. I don't know what you got but she's been watching
you out of the corner of her eye all night, man!"

"No shit! Jeeeeeeeesuuuuuus!" He licks his lips in
anticipation, straightens up his shoulders and sticks
out his chest. He looks as masculine as a deflowered
Burma Shave sign.

You sure . . . sure she's . . . that she was talking
about me? Jeesuus!"

I want to join the chorus, want to add some corrobo-
ration, but am too busy sinking into fits of internalized
hysteria. I am swallowing laughs like fraternity goldfish. Trying to hold them in, I am wheezing like an up-
hill somnambulist with asthma.

Morrison starts marching him across the room. "Listen, prick, she wanted me to come over and get ac-

quainted with you so she could find out who you were, find out if you're connected up with anybody! Know what I mean? This chick wants to get down with you."

"Screwing? You mean screwing?"

"A rose by any other name," agrees Morrison.

"Huh?" Confuses his five-watt brain.

Morrison waves his hands in the air, ready to scream. "Yes, goddamn it! *Screwing. I mean screwing!*"

A couple of people stare at us. Morrison moves past them with a phony smile on his face.

"No shit?" Booze Boy has all his lights lit up like a pinball machine dispensing free games. He's seeing heaven on two legs. "She really wants me?"

Morrison sighs. "How many frigging times I gotta tell you! She's ready to rape you on the spot!"

Our friend giggles again. An irritating snigger.

Morrison looks like he'd really like to smash this guy in the face. God, what a simp Booze Boy is!

"What should I do?"

I'm following them. The girl's talking to a couple of surfer types, all blond and blank between the ears. As our entourage gets near her, she excuses herself and begins going off somewhere.

I follow her with my eyes like probably fifty other guys are doing. She's got a body that won't quit and doesn't even have to try.

Morrison turns our friend around and we push out after her.

I'm getting confused. Thought we were going to send our candidate in to bang away at our own personal elephant.

Morrison stops abruptly, bringing all of us up short. He puts his arm around our victim's neck. "Hey, listen! You don't want something like that!"

"Yes I do! Yes I do!" Our friend is positive. Jesus is he positive! Beginning to drool and everything.

"You can do better than that."

Panic in his eyes. *"No! No I can't!* She's okay by me! Jesus!"

"What kind of friend would I be if I let you jump something like . . . like that!" Morrison shakes his head.

Almost in tears. "My best friend! Honest! I like her fine! I don't want any . . ."

Morrison begins turning him around.

He resists. "Please! Really! Hey, I wanna—"

Morrison holds up a hand. "Be cool. Man, my partner and I are watching out for you. We don't want you catching hold of some second-rate poontang."

"Yeah," I say. "Nothing but the best for our friends."

Our friend looks like the end of the world.

Over his shoulder he watches the girl of his unreachable dreams heading in another direction.

This is a cruel trip we are on.

"But . . . but I . . ." Heartbroken.

"Be cool." Morrison smiles at me. "Think we should tell him?" he says to me.

He's turned around, still trying to see the golden one that got away. "Tell me what?" he asks dully, still in mourning for what might have been.

I nod. "Tell him."

Morrison smiles at him like a cat with bird feathers on his breath. "Well, this chick has a sister. An older sister."

Booze Boy swivels around, staring at us.

"And this sister of hers makes this chick look like something so dead that the dog would refuse to bring it in," says Morrison.

"Huh?"

"She's good-looking, asshole! She's good-looking!" This guy is pretty frigging dense.

"Pretty?" asks the fool, as Morrison begins pushing him toward the bedroom and his date with obese destiny.

"She was a foldout in *Playboy* magazine. She's got

such a terrific body they had to use five staples to cover
up her snappy," says Morrison, hurrying him along.

"And guess what?"

"What? What?" Jesus, is he eager!

"She's here and she's even hotter for your body than
her sister was!" says Morrison.

"Jeeeeeeeesuuuuuuuuussss!" He looks all around,
trying to spy heaven with two legs, the older version of
it.

"She's so hot for you that she's already in the bedroom. She's got her clothes off, just waiting for you to
come and get her. She told me, 'Eddy Pusswrecks'
(that's my name), 'you go over and tell that handsome
stud I'm in here waiting for him and I'm hot to trot.' "

His eyes are wide open, mouth dropped down to his
navel, and he's sweating like the Boston Marathon.

"Waiting for me? Jeeeeessuuuuuuuuuus!"

We get him up to the bedroom door. Morrison opens
the door. Beer Brain looks into the darkened room,
can't see anything at all. There's a moaning sound
coming from inside, sounds like a buzz saw in heat.

"Go in and get one for God," says Morrison, slapping
him on the back.

Our boy is in his own forest fire. Panting, eyes glazed
with amplified lust, fingers jumping around at the ends
of his quivering hands. Hovering in the doorway, puls-
ing with high energy of low degree.

Morrison gives him a push. Our boy staggers into the
room and we slam the door shut behind him.

We listen at the door.

"Hooooooorny!" Sounds like an elk whispering the
"Star-Spangled Banner."

"I'm coming, baby!" That's our boy. Sound of
clothes being ripped off, shoes coming off and thumping against the floor. Patter of feet as he runs toward
the bed.

Thump, squeak of protesting bed springs, a squeal of
delight. Then sounds too frightening to think about.

A mountain making a molehill.

Morrison looks at me victoriously. He licks the tip of one finger and makes an invisible number one in the air on an invisible tally sheet.

"That's one," says Morrison, with that wicked laugh of his. "Only forty more to go."

Well the dark was big
Where your cars went through
What you thought
You thought you knew
And there was a clock
Attached to birds
That explained you and me
Without any words.

Jim Morrison and Craig Strete

CHAPTER 5

"Don't step on no snakes," Morrison says and then disappears into the wreckage of the party. Me, I wander around dazed, bouncing off people, walls, things like that.

I'm all banged up on the outside like a human fender bender. I feel like the loser in a demolition derby. Some brown-haired girl with sympathetic eyes leads me into a bathroom and washes my neck.

I just barely understand what she is doing. She leans me up against the sink and I stare blankly at a sign over the toilet that says "Vietnam Is Only 3000 Miles

Away. Is It Safe to Cross the Street?"

She rummages around in the medicine cabinet, then goes through the drawers under the sink. She comes up with a tin of bandages. Then I remember cutting my neck, falling down on a wicker chair somewhere, seems ages ago, and can't remember where. In any case, I'm still bleeding.

"You've had a rough time," she says, tearing the wrapper off a bandage. "Let me slap this on your neck and maybe it'll stop bleeding."

I start kissing her, both of us leaning crazily against the sink. Nice-looking girl and stoned stoned stoned. She's laughing as I grapple with her, still trying to get the bandage on my neck. She's ticklish.

I get my hands down inside her pants and she jumps. The bandage gets crumpled and sticks to itself.

She giggles hysterically and drops the bandage.

"Beast," she says but doesn't seem to mind.

I'm fingering her and her hands are shaking as she gets out another bandage. Her back arches and she leans against my hand. Clumsily I make my hand that's still free attempt to unbutton her tight blue jeans.

The bathroom door bursts open and a drunken Mexican staggers in. Says something in garbled Tex-Mex Spanish, unbuckles his belt and drops his pants. He isn't wearing any underwear.

"Hey!" cries the girl, startled, and moves closer against me for protection. My feeble brain can't quite grab the scenario. I just stare at him stupidly. He weaves toward us, pants at his ankles, chattering away in garbled Spanish. Neither of us understands what he's saying. This guy's really blitzed, practically oozing beer from every pore. He shakes his head at us, shrugs and turns his back on us.

The Mexican sits down on the toilet and lets go. He must have been saving it for a week.

The stink drives us out.

We walk out together, her still struggling with the

bandage, me forced to follow because I got my hand rammed down her tight pants and I got a signet ring stuck in a hole in her underwear.

"Let go."

"I'm stuck."

"C'mon! Get your hands off. People'll see."

"I tell you I'm stuck."

"*Get it out of there!*" She's pissed off. A couple of her friends have seen us.

I feel like a little boy caught with his fingers in the cookie bowl.

"I'm stuck on your underwear. My ring—"

She slaps me. Pisses me off royal. I rip my hand out of her pants. Come away with my whole hand, her underwear in shreds and some of her pubic hair. Looks like she dyes her pubic hair blond.

She screams and bends over double, clasping her crotch.

"Sorry! I tried to tell you. I had this ring—"

Somebody grabs my shoulder and spins me around. A guy about ten feet tall puts a fist the size of a Ford station wagon up against my face. It's like watching a train run over your head.

I feel my bones loosen as my back slams into the floor. Before I can figure out how the floor got so close to my back, I get a couple of good hard kicks in the stomach. Then I kind of fade out. Not knocked cold, sort of just stunned semi-frigid.

Then I see a shoe come toward my face and I pass out before it gets there. Maybe it's an imaginary shoe. Too out of it to know. Anyway, I go on a snooze cruise.

Don't know how long I'm out. Maybe ten minutes, maybe a couple of hours, just know that I've got a swollen jaw that hurts like hell and big nasty bruised places all over me. I feel like a golf ball a drunken golfer has been slicing with all day. Real groggy. Feel something wet on my forehead, something warm. My eyes focus and I see the girl who had lost her underwear. She's got a warm washcloth on my forehead.

"You all right?" She's worried. "That stupid fucker. I can take care of myself."

"Who was . . . who was that guy?" My throat so dry I can hardly talk. Have a vague idea the entire National Football League just walked across my tongue in their socks.

"That was my husband. He's such a jerk. I'm sorry."

"Wow!" I try sitting up but it hurts just about everywhere. She helps me, holding my shoulders.

There's pressure in my stomach, crotch. Jesus H. Flaming Christ! I gotta go to the bathroom. Got lots of cream ale inside somewhere, aching to come out and go splash. I mumble something, trying frantically to scramble to my feet. She grabs my arms and helps pull me up.

"What?"

"Bathroom! I gotta get to the bathroom." I stumble, almost fall flat on my face. She embraces me, half carries me, and we stumble off to find the bathroom.

Get to the bathroom. Locked. Oh, shit!

She bangs on the door with one knee. "Emergency!"

Some guy inside tells her where she can put her emergency. She keeps banging on the door.

I am bent over double, trying not to get religious and send prayers down both my legs and turn my socks yellow.

Finally the door opens and we stumble in, as some fat guy with pimples stumbles out.

She locks the door behind us as I fumble clumsily with my zipper. I kind of notice I am not alone in there but am too polite to mention it to her.

My hands don't want to cooperate. I'm leaning against the wall, tugging like crazy on my zipper. Can't get it down.

"You gotta pull it down, not up," she says. "Let me help."

I am in no shape to argue.

She gets me unzipped, starts dragging my totem pole

out, and I let loose a little too soon. Get a little bit on her hand but she doesn't seem to mind. Just wipes it off on a towel.

Probably I piss for an hour and twenty minutes. Seems like it to me. Probably raise the water table in L.A. by two feet when I flush.

When the pissing is over, I feel much better. Start to zip back up but she's already beat me to it in reverse.

She's got my pants down around my ankles and is working on peeling off my underwear.

"Hey, what's—"

She pushes me against the wall, one-hands the toilet lid down, sits on it and grabs me with her mouth. She's got to be kidding. Wonder if she's heard the expression "flogging a dead horse."

I am long since past the mood to be in the nude.

At least I was pretty sure. I look down and see where she is beginning to create a very convincing contradiction. Mentally, I am a little stunned. Physically, I rise to the occasion.

However.

I remember a certain house-size fist with my facial expression no doubt imprinted on the outside of it.

Push her head away. "What about your husband? You trying to get me killed?"

She licks her lips. "I locked the door. Relax. He can't get in."

She moves back in, mouth centering on target. My mind may still be protesting but my body is leading its own parade. This girl is experienced. She probably entertained troop ships.

But I keep thinking about the fist as big as all outdoors. I push her away again.

"What if he comes looking for you?"

"Hey, cool it. Be cool. Just enjoy it. Told you I locked the door."

She grabs me again, clamping on me so hard with her tongue I almost shoot the rapids in one big jump.

I notice how flimsy the bathroom door is. "Holy shit! That door won't stop him! Christ! He could eat *that* door."

I relax a little anyway. You can't fight fate or fast tongues. If you can't beat them, put your hands behind their necks and help them.

I am definitely feeling something, I mean something besides my aches and bruises. Them I don't feel at all anymore. Amazing painkiller. Yes, definitely feeling something. Not going to last long at this rate. This girl is healthy, this girl is vigorous. She's gone down on everything but the *Titanic*.

My legs tighten, I rise up on my toes and I am about to have a Grand Canyon Climax. I am as hot as a rabbit on the rag.

Just edging into it and there comes this knock on the door. Sounds like somebody hit the door with a ten-pound sledgehammer.

"*Oh no! It's him!*" I panic, trying to pull away.

She locks her fingers around my back, tries to swallow me whole.

"Let me go! Let me go!" I panic, trying to push her away.

She shakes her head, tightens her mouth, and hangs on.

"I know you're in there, Marsha!" Sounds like the war cry of an enraged bull elephant.

"I'm gonna break this fucking door down and kill you both!" The door strains outward and then the doorknob falls off.

You know, I believe him. I believe every word he says. I am willing to take him at his word.

I shove her hard, losing some skin to her teeth in the process, but I get free of her. She falls off the toilet seat and lands on her back under the sink. I groan in agony, rubbed raw, half gummed to death.

There's this hammering on the door and the door is bending in like it's made of cardboard.

I'm frantically pulling my pants up, trying to stuff my erection into tight pants and not finding any room for it. I ram it in anyway, hunching forward a little with a lot of pain, and look around desperately for weapons. What I need is an elephant gun. Maybe two of them. One for each hand.

"Marsha! I know you got that wimpy little bastard in there. You hear me!" Guy is screaming with rage now. "I'm breaking down this fucking door!"

No weapons but, hot damn, there is a tiny window. Only thing is it's a size seven window and I am a size ten. It doesn't open all the way either. Oh, shit!

Marsha's standing up now, one hand rubbing the back of her head where it hit the bathroom floor. She goes to the door, shouts through it, "Jack, you stupid bastard! If you break this door down, I'll castrate you! I'll kill you!"

"Fucking bitch!" he screams back at her.

This is too much fun for me so I am not sticking around. I'm standing on top of the toilet tank, kicking like crazy at the window frame. Not all that easy to kick at something you're holding on to. Finally I connect, having already shattered the window with a clumsy kick or two. I knock the little window right out of the windowsill. It crashes outside and smashes into pieces.

I duck my head through the window and start squirming. Even with the window gone I'm having a hard time getting myself through. Mother Nature had given me a big chest, nice for the ladies but hell when it comes to windows.

There's this big crash and the bathroom door comes bursting into the room. The door catches the girl head on and sends her spinning back into the room as if she were catapulted. I feel her body smash into my legs.

Oh, shit!

She's screaming. He's screaming. I get a glimpse of him. Only thing slowing him up is a size seventeen shoe that's caught in one of the door panels he put it through.

A worm could have learned something from me. I squirmed like I hope I never have to squirm again ever in my life, short as I know it's going to be.

My belt gets caught on the little crank that winds that window open and shut.

Oh, shit!

A hand grabs my leg and practically yanks me in two.

I get my hands around the frame of a TV antenna tower that's outside the window. Get a death grip on it, but Hercules is reeling me in like a goldfish on a line baited for shark. My fingers ache, strain and begin to slip. He twists me around. Now I'm on my back and can see him. You could reconstruct a dinosaur along the lines of this guy's physique.

He gives a tremendous yank and I lose what little grip I've got, already twisted out of position.

This fucker is gonna kill me.

Now, almost back inside the room, I make one last desperate grab and hang on to the top of the windowsill with both hands. Now he's got me pulled out straight like a witch on the Inquisition rack.

Everybody's got to die someday. But who wants to die in a toilet? Ain't gonna look like no crucifixion of Christ, is it?

My fingers are slipping. The bastard is laughing. He knows he's got me. He's laughing 'cause he knows he's gonna kill me.

Suddenly the girl is in front of him and gives him a shot in the eyes with an aerosol can of hair spray from the medicine cabinet.

He screams, drops my legs and claws at his eyes. I fall down with a bang, my back crashing into the wall. I slip down, one leg going into the toilet.

He's still screaming, hands clamped to his eyes.

His wife's dancing around, absolutely delighted.

"Bastard!" she shrieks at him. She's still spraying

him, covering his face and hands and getting it in his mouth.

He's choking, gasping for breath.

Some marriage these two got. I haven't seen anything like it since the Roman Arena where the early Christian got the hungriest lion. And I don't want to see anything like it. It's too much fun all at once.

I get up as quick as possible, try to edge around them both and get the fuck out of there. I stumble around. Suddenly the big guy lunges forward, rams into me, and I get shoved back. Off balance, I teeter on the back of my heels and fall heavily into the bathtub.

Hot burst of pain in my right shoulder as it slams into the bathtub faucet.

The girl is still dancing around him, emptying the can on him. He's blindly reaching out with one hand the size of a basketball, trying to grab her.

They are both still screaming obscenities at each other, having a lovely weekend, I guess, L.A. fashion.

I crawl out of the tub, wait for an opening and a clear shot at the door. I got a profound urge for distance.

I duck under his arms, stumble over his feet and fetch up against the side of the door, past them, if not completely on my feet.

She sees me go. "Wait! You and me can—"

Her husband centers in on her voice, grabs her. She screams. She tries to wriggle away but he gets a hand on her throat and starts choking her, his other hand still covering his dripping flame-red face.

I stand at the door for a second on legs so shaky they are barely able to hold me up. I feel I ought to help her or something. He takes his hand away from his face. I can see in the medicine cabinet mirror that his eyes, still shut tight, look like two pieces of raw red meat.

He starts slapping her. Hard, vicious blows. Blood bursts from her nose, her lips get cut open. He's literally beating her to a pulp as I stand there. Think he's gonna kill her. I step toward them, for a second there thinking I'll come back into the room and help her. But stop myself. I have never been much of a human being and have always been a little less than kind. The hell with her.

I turn around and walk out. I don't look back.

I stumble through the party wreckage, stepping over stunned and stoned bodies. I shut the front door behind me, take some real air into my lungs for a change and stagger off to find my car, just one big bruise.

I don't think about the brown-haired girl getting pounded by her husband, probably getting killed. I just climb in my car and drink a warm beer. Real tired. Tired.

There is no sign of Morrison. Think I'll split without him. Beer tastes like bear piss, but I drink it anyway.

Some asshole left a six-pack of beer on the hood so I crawl out and throw it away. All empty bottles anyway. Weary, I get up on the hood of the car and rest. Can hear music from the party very clearly from where I sit. Just sprawl there, tapping time to the music and feeling the ache in my shoulder where I hit the bathtub faucet.

The night is going down to defeat. Me too, starting to crash. I finish my beer and try to throw the empty bottle through the front window of the house where the party is, but miss by at least ten yards. Shoulder too sore.

Sit there for a while, glad to be alive but wishing it wasn't so painful. Asking myself what my next move is.

I'm on my last bottle of beer. No wine left in the car either. Think maybe I ought to go back inside and try to put the snatch on some booze before I split. I ought to come home with something or other. Probably the chick I am living off of is getting worried about me by now anyway. I haven't seen her in two or three days.

Might find Morrison, that weird dude. Figure he might know some good parties to go to for next week. Sitting here is just making me tired of being tired, so drag my ass off the car, aching everyplace, and head back to the party.

I better put the snatch on a whole lot of booze. Chick I'm living with gets on my nerves. I like her better when I'm loaded and I try to stay loaded.

Truck back inside. Being careful. Don't want to meet up with old whatsisname with the Ford station wagon fists no matter how blind he probably is. Shouldn't probably even be back in here taking this chance, but I got this firm rule. Never go to a party unless you rip something off.

Inside, looking around, don't see Morrison anywhere. Ask him if he wants a ride home, wherever that is, maybe even get him to drive me, 'cause I am pretty wasted. Could fall asleep standing up.

Ask this fat dude, in a suit no less, where the booze is. He tells me to go into the kitchen, so I do.

Jesus H. Retail and Wholesale Christ! Enough booze to refloat the Spanish Armada!

I tuck a quart of rum and a six-pack of beer under one arm. Snatch up a huge bottle of Chianti and two more six-packs with the other arm. But then hesitate. This whole frigging table full of goodies. Too much good stuff to waste on these assholes. I put down two six-packs and the Chianti and grab up a pint of fine old bourbon. Force it down into my tight back pants pocket. Snatch a pint of Southern Comfort and stash it down inside my pants. Put another pint of rum in one cowboy boot, a pint of scotch in the other. Stuff a bottle of white wine down my shirt.

Then grab up the six-packs of beer and the Chianti again and start making tracks. Get out into the living room, clanking like an overloaded milk delivery man, feeling self-conscious at all the bulges in my clothes. Get through the crowd and then there's some kind of commotion at the door. Can't get through so I step back against the wall. Don't know what's going on, probably some frigging fight or other.

The front door booms open and suddenly the room is
full of blue uniforms. Cops pouring in the door like
hordes of army ants. Seems like a hundred of them but
that's only 'cause they're moving fast and my eyes are
seeing slow.

Turns out there's just four of them. Too few for a
raid. Too many for a friendly warning about the noise
level. Somebody is in trouble.

I try not to panic, wondering if it is me.

Lots of reason why it could be.

I start looking for a place where I can get rid of the
booze and fast. These jerks just may be looking for me.
They had reason enough, but how could they have
found me this fast? Did someone see me? Oh, shit!

But the cops don't look around for me, they go on
through the living room and on out of sight into the
interior of the house.

That settles it. I am definitely getting out of here.
Just gather up my goodies and get the hell out of here.
Any party with walk-in cops is a party that is too com-
plicated for me.

Start pushing through to the door, but have to stop,
get pushed aside again. This time it's the ambulance
crew, carrying a stretcher. Don't have to wonder too
much about what's happening. Maybe somebody
OD'd, or suicided or old mad Jack, the irate husband
and all that jazz, did his number and went too far.
Probably the son of a bitch killed her.

Some guy is standing next to me, explaining to a
pimple-faced girl exactly what happened. I listened in,
couldn't help overhearing.

"Jesus! He really beat her up! She might die." He
looks righteous, taps himself on the chest proudly. "I
was the one called the cops."

The cops come out with good old Jack, all nicely
handcuffed. Being led away like a prize hog at the fair.
His eyes are still fire red, looking like raw meat that is
beginning to spoil. He stumbles along like he is blind.
He probably is. Cops are none too gentle in guiding

him through the crowd. One fat cop with a thick neck keeps jabbing him in the side with his nightstick.

As for me, I'm not interested in this whole scene.

The pimple-faced girl turns away from the cop caller and looks directly at me. "I think that's terrible, really terrible, don't you?"

I shrug. "Don't ask me. White people are all in an obstacle race with themselves as the biggest obstacle."

She frowns at me, decides she thinks I'm terrible too and turns her back on me.

I mean it, though. Are white people human beings? I know what their civilization is all about but my jury is out on whether or not I'm gonna join it. A secret part of me stays Indian, no matter how hard I try to lose it.

But this is rock and roll, this is L.A. summer, this is the dreamland we all run to, and you don't have to act like a human being if you don't want to.

Right?

CHAPTER 6

Eventually I get out the door, ignoring some nasty looks as a couple of people see me exiting with all that booze.

I stash it all in the back seat of the car. I'm ready to crash. Too much of everything. I lean against the car. Feel like I'm going to pass out.

Dawn is coming. Don't know how long it's been since I've really slept in a bed. Last night I was at the beach. Maybe I was at the beach. Vaguely remember but I'm not sure.

Think maybe I'll just get in the car, crawl into a comfortable coma. Too tired to drive. Music from the party still blaring, people passed out all over the yard, couples, several threesomes he-ing and she-ing it.

Got to be speed freaks. Who else would be awake at this time in the morning? I am ready to concede the night to the cocaine crew.

I slide down the side of the car on my knees. Such an effort to get the door open.

Course back of my mind is telling me that if I cash in here, I'll wake up tomorrow in the slammer. Hell with that. I've no fondness for becoming conscious in the nick.

So like the maniac that I am, I make myself get up and busy myself. Another trip back to the party. Cop some more booze and maybe pop a bennie so I can get wired enough to make it home.

I crawl back to the house. Crawl is the right word. I'm real wasted, whole body threatening to shake to pieces.

Get to the front door, only somebody's been screwing around since the cops have been here. The door's knocked off its hinges, and some guy's stretched across it snoring in three-part harmony.

Inside, lots of people sprawled out on the floor, about half of them naked and some of them not too competently trying to be. Looks like one rock-and-roller is trying to take his pants off over his head and is succeeding. Everything's busted up. Place looks like ground zero at Hiroshima or Keith Moon's birthday party, whichever comes first.

A tall white cat in a white robe staggers up to me, carrying an ax. He looks at me, cross-eyed, takes a step back, and then falls solidly on his ass.

"I'm Woody Woodpecker," he says, holding up the ax. With those words, he tilts over on his back, out cold.

Surprisingly, there's still a few people standing, leaning against walls, shattered furniture.

I go up to four guys rapping intensely in the corner about quality control on acid manufacture, something heavy and intellectual, you know.

"Anybody got a Christmas tree? A bunny? I mean a bennie?"

They all ignore me.

Somebody puts an arm around my shoulder, leans on me from behind. I almost fall flat on my back.

I turn around, stumbling.

There's a chick with blue face and blood around the corners of her mouth. She's wearing black lipstick. Hair dyed white on one side, red on the other. Looks like the Sudden Death Queen of New Orleans.

She's dressed in a black 1930s-style ballroom gown that's slit in the middle down past her navel. In the center of two of the whitest breasts, like two lumps of flaccid butter, is a tiny tattoo, a death's-head.

Her face is painted blue, with her eyes outlined in blazing blood red. She's the kind of chick you meet at a weinie roast in hell.

"You want some speed?" She has her arms around my neck, facing me. A thin dead voice that would have scared God (if he existed).

I'm so stunned I almost choke, my tongue jamming up against my teeth. "Uh, yeah. I'd, uh, like to buy a hit of—"

"No." She puts one hand on my face, running inch-long green fingernails up the side of my face caressingly, moving up toward my eyes. "I don't sell. Give. But no selling."

"I could use some." I'm glad I'm not tripping. If I met her under acid I'd be checking into the first padded hotel for the Mentally Bewildered.

She's got her fingernails under my eyes, lightly scratching the skin, scaring the shit out of me.

"Who are you?" I ask.

"You don't know me? This is like, you know, my party, you dig? So you crashed my party."

She drops one hand and digs her fingernails into my chest. I jump, surprised.

"Did that hurt?"

"Yeah." She damn near drew blood.

"Good," she says with a strange smile. "I like it when it hurts. That's the part, the best part."

"Uh, you said I could have a bennie . . ."

"You'll get one if you do me a favor."

"Uh, well, maybe I don't really want—"

"It's my party, right?" She's suddenly angry, fingers of one hand tightening against my face.

I don't argue.

"Yeah. Sure."

"I'm not asking you to kill somebody or something," she says, looking around the room, "although that might be fun. Just do something for me."

"Like what?"

She takes her arms off of me, eases one of her breasts out of her dress, pointing it at me. "See this."

How could I not see it?

"Yeah."

She moves up against me, rubbing it across my chest. She lets go of her breast, uses both hands to pull back on my lips, looking at my teeth. "Lovely," she says.

"I'm, uh, too screwed up for screwing. Kind of partied out, if you wanna know the truth. So maybe we just better . . ." I start apologizing.

Jesus! It'd be like climbing into a coffin to make love to the worms.

"I don't want that."

Suddenly she grabs my hair and slams my head forward, bending me over. My face collides with her exposed breast.

Her arms wrap around my back, her body arches tautly against me.

"Bite it until it bleeds!" she shrieks.

I try to pull free, but she's wrapped me up completely and has the strength of a maniac.

I got no choice. I get her breast in my mouth and bite down. She clutches me convulsively, moaning, "Harder! Harder!"

Her hands push the back of my head, drawing me tighter up against her.

My mouth is full, I bite harder, tasting blood, gagging a little.

She screams in ecstasy. I push against her stomach, trying to push free. She jerks convulsively, having an orgasm.

I get loose, shove her off me. She staggers back, coming against the wall, shuddering with delight.

I'm numb, shocked, strung out like a cocained chicken.

I look at her. Her breast is all bloody and I can feel blood dribbling down the corners of my mouth. I wipe my mouth off, staring at the stains on the back of my hand. I tell myself, well, here you are, having just another party night in bitch goddess L.A. and it could be worse. So you turned cannibal, that's not the worst thing in the world, is it? It took you a little sudden is all, before you had a proper chance to really get into it. But don't be depressed, 'cause there's still a few perversions you haven't tried yet. There's still dogs, ducks and donkeys. And grandmother rape.

Okay, cannibalism is no fun.

I look at the chick, slowly coming off the wall, strapped up in a hideous rapture, face contorted with pleasure-pain, one breast looking like a sacrifice to a lawn mower. A dead woman a vampire wouldn't have claimed, or maybe once did.

Maybe I spoiled the fun of being a cannibal by mixing in, considering the way she looks, too much necrophilia.

The hell with her!

I start marching off. Green fingernails dig into my arm, spin me around.

"Don't you want your up?"

"Uh, well . . ."

She releases me, digs into a small fur purse dangling by a long cord from one shoulder, comes out with a white envelope.

"How many?" she asks. "I got some good acid. Want some belladonna too? How about some M.D.A.?"

"Just an up," I say, wiping the blood on the back of my hand off on my shirt.

She opens the envelope, and I see inside. Must be fifty pills in there, all kinds, shapes, colors, sizes.

"How can you tell them apart?"

She digs her fingers in and comes out with a fat white pill. "I got a good memory. I know what each pill is."

"An up." She holds it out to me, two-fingered, blood on her arm. A fat white pill, rectangular, the giant economy size.

"You're really bleeding. Maybe you ought . . ."

She smiles. "I know. I love it. It really hurt. I got off." She looks at me longingly, licking her lips.

"We could go into the other room. I'd give you all the drugs I got if you'd whip . . ." Her teeth are black from her lipstick.

I back away, not even taking the pill.

"No!" Time to run. This girl wants to have too much fun.

She shrugs, seeing she's lost a customer.

"Okay. Here. Take it." She pushes the pill at me. "A favor for a favor."

I take the pill, turning it over in my hand, looking at it suspiciously. "You sure this is an up? I never seen this big an upper in my life. Looks like an elephant tranquilizer."

"It's an up." She's positive. "Hey, c'mon. You treated me nice. So swallow it."

I put it in my mouth, nasty taste, struggle to swallow it dry, finally get it down. My mouth still full of blood, salty taste.

"Uh, thanks." I nod at her.

"See you around," she says, massaging the torn skin

around her breast, shuddering deliciously from the pain it causes. She's absorbed in what she's doing, hurting herself. I back away, getting the hell away from her.

I get halfway across the room when she shouts something at me. I turn and look back at her, sitting on the floor now, in a little puddle of her own blood.

"I lied!" she yells at me, waving one bloody palm at me. "That wasn't an upper! I don't know what it is!"

She laughs hysterically, and begins licking the blood off the palm of her hand.

"Oh, shit! I'm gonna die!" I shake my head. It's my fault. I'm too kind to people and they're always taking advantage of me because of it. It's the nice, normal ones like that girl that always give me the most trouble. It's the crazy ones that never bother you. Right?

I stagger off through the wreckage, expecting at any moment that my head will explode with some kind of wonder drug as yet unknown to science, turning me into a lightning bolt. I manage not to trip over anything or step on anyone, almost a magic act in itself.

The cannibalism number kinda woke me up. I head for the kitchen, with a little more energy than I came in with. Terror is good methedrine.

I have to move a girl's legs away from the kitchen door. The legs are attached to a body that has said a firm goodbye to Saturday night in L.A. She's passed out with an ashtray on her forehead, and cigarette butts all over her face. When you can't have any more fun, you can at least be useful.

Open the kitchen door and find something new there. Morrison is under the kitchen table. Dead drunk. Or drugged out. Or maybe just dead. Hard to tell.

Some girl in a Mexican poncho is trying to take his jacket off. Having a difficult time of it with him sprawled out under the table like a cold-cocked matador. He's just a dead weight in her arms and she's no tow truck strength-wise.

I bend down and watch her. She tugs the jacket off finally. I wonder if maybe I should applaud but don't because persistence is its own reward.

Her head almost bumps into mine.

I shake a finger at her. "Naughty! Naughty! Shame on you!"

She sees me, jumps, banging her head against the bottom of the table.

"Thou shalt not steal. Unless you are white and have signed a treaty." I hold out my hand. "Gimme!"

"Screw you!" She folds her arms protectively against her stomach.

I can see tracks on both of her arms. Just another junkie chick trying to pick up some loose change. Probably went through Morrison's pockets too.

She starts backing out, trying to get away on the other side of the table. I reach in, grab her by one arm and yank her out from under the table.

She struggles against me, slips and then falls forward on her face. She tries to crawl through my legs so I grab her by one leg and hold on. She coils up in a ball, protecting the stolen coat with her scrawny legs.

"My friend isn't going to like waking up to find some little junkie's made off with his coat. So better let go of it."

"Let me go, you stupid bastard!"

She reaches up and tries to jab me in the crotch with her fist. I lean back, knocking her hand away and letting go of her leg. This one plays nasty, believes in dialing direct.

She tries again so I grab her by the hair, holding her out at arm's length, protecting my lap. She tries to pull her head away, wincing with pain.

"You're hurting me."

"I'm not trying to."

"Owwwww!" I give her hair a little yank, so she knows I'm not kidding around.

"C'mon, play nice. Give it up. It doesn't belong to you."

"Screw you! It doesn't belong to you either," she says, looking around wildly as if looking for reinforcements. She seems to be thinking, holds that pose a few seconds and then tries this one on me. "Hey, look, he's dead. Okay? He don't need the coat no more. Okay?"

I don't believe her, though this is the kind of party where it's not that unlikely. "That makes you a grave robber and that's even worse."

She spits in my face suddenly, taking me by surprise.

The spittle is stinging my eyes and it makes me madder than hell. I let go of her hair, put my arms under her armpits and drag her upright. She tries to roll herself into a ball like a porcupine protecting its belly. I end up holding her in the air 'cause she won't put her legs down to support herself. The weight almost tumbles me over backwards on my ass. Jesus H. Christ!

I stumble forward, can't support us both, and her back bangs hard against the edge of the table. It hurts and her legs come down like aircraft landing gear. The coat drops out from under her poncho.

I smile at her sarcastically, and with exaggerated politeness say, "Thank *you!*"

I bend over to pick up the coat and she kicks me in the face. Hard.

I fall over backwards, my head slamming into the kitchen floor. She makes a dive for the coat and starts scooting for the door. I have just enough presence of mind to reach out, grab her by one bony ankle and yank it out from under her.

She falls over on me and comes up yelling, kicking and going for my face with her fists. I slap her once, trying to fend her off and hit her harder than I intended right across the eyes.

Stunned, she rolls off me.

I get up slowly, holding my nose, my hand getting sticky with my own blood. Think a couple of my teeth are loose.

Feel my front teeth. Think one is definitely loose. I tell her angrily, sincerely, "I ought to break both of your goddamn legs."

"Bastard!" She tries to slap me. I don't believe her. She must have seen too many John Wayne movies or something. I catch her hand and twist it until she gasps with pain. Not trying to be cruel, just trying to hold my own. I don't put on much pressure, just enough to make her feel like quitting.

I let go and she slumps to the floor.

She's crying now. Probably not because I hurt her but because she's afraid she's not going to have enough money for a fix. I don't understand how we do the things we do to each other and to ourselves.

I back off a few steps, holding the coat, just watching the tears flowing down her half-starved cheeks. Her wrist is turning purple. Guess I was a little too heavy-handed. Didn't mean to savage her. Christ! What am I, a fucking cop?

Still I find myself standing over her, holding my aching face, asking, "Is that all you took?"

"That's all, you crummy bastard," she sobs, holding her wrist. Save me from junkie children who've slept in all the rooms of hell.

She gets up slow, starts to move around me. I see she's still got a suspicious bulge under her poncho, tucked down behind her shirt. Not being no cop, I should let her go, but my face feels like raw meat and I haven't wasted all my anger yet. I should let her go but I don't. I reach out and grab her by the throat, but not trying to be too rough. I tilt her head back far enough that it hurts a little, just a little. "I think you're lying."

I tap her stomach with my other hand. Something hard under there.

"What's that? You trying to give birth to a night bank deposit box?"

Her fingers come up, sharp claws going for my eyes. This is my night to get ripped to shreds. Well, screw it! I lose control. I turn away but not quick enough. Feel her nails go under my right eye, raking down the side of my face. Feel the blood welling under the skin.

"Why, you bitch!" I shake her like a dog shakes a dead rat, her head flopping back and forth like a broken doll's head. Near feel like killing her but I see the madness in her eyes, the drugs dancing down deep inside her and making her what she is, and you can't fight against that.

Besides, I never hit a girl before. Till now. Don't like the feeling at all. I must be a little flipped out.

I push her away from me, understanding for the first time. She's really just a little girl who's dead inside. Accidentally, my hand tangles in her poncho, brushes against her cold little-girl breasts. A cascade of wallets and watches comes tumbling out. This little zombie's been busy tonight.

She falls on the pile on the floor, eyes glazed, blood dripping from a tiny cut on her chin. "That's mine," she mutters. "Mine! Mine! All mine! Mine!"

She slumps over her pile of stolen goodies, clumsily trying to protect them with her knees and with her arms.

I shake my head, step back, a little dazed. What the hell was I doing anyway, this insane cop routine. I came into the kitchen to steal stuff myself. I must be flipped out.

"Okay. It's yours. Keep it."

I let her grab up her stolen goodies and stuff them back inside her shirt. When she gets them safely stowed and gets up on her feet, I'll be damned if she doesn't try to deck me again. She's really insane. I duck her swing, spin her around by one arm, aim her for the kitchen door and give her a friendly kick in the ass to get her going. She crashes into the swinging door and goes on through.

"You should have wasted her, man."

I turn around, surprised. Morrison is sitting up under the table, staring at me with a glazed look on his face.

"I seem to have been trying to. Guess I'm a little flippy. Taken too many licks tonight, too much drugs. Almost off the deep end." I shrug. "Never hit a girl before. Don't like the feeling. Guess it's the drugs. You take them and things happen."

"You let her mess you over. She couldn't have been more than fifteen or sixteen," says Morrison, crawling slowly out from under the table.

Morrison gets to his feet, staggering, having to lean back against the table for support. I throw his jacket at him.

He flips up a hand, catching it.

"What was it all about?"

"Your coat. She was stealing it."

Morrison's still staring at me, as if he's never seen me before. He shrugs. "Coat wasn't worth much."

I felt the need to explain.

"You're with me, or at least we came here together. It was yours. Somehow, at the time, it seemed important."

I wave my hands in a forget-it gesture. "Besides, what's it matter? We're all just killing time until they get our graves dug."

"You should have wasted her, man."

"What? Why?"

"For the experience, man."

Morrison rubs his face with one hand, trying to wake his face up, looks thoughtful a second. "You got to be a lord, man. A fucking lord. You don't suffer. But other people do. The creatures are to be beaten, they exist to suffer for us."

"What the fuck are you talking about?"

"The lords and the creatures, man."

I just look at him. Is this a put-on?

Morrison gestures with his hands, suddenly feverish about explaining it all. "Look, man, life is like some giant game. It's a connect-the-dots game for a race of giants. We only see the dots, one by one. We gotta rely on the world out there to see the connections between the dots. We don't even own our own fucking lives. It's being lived for us. Don't you see it, man?"

This is some kind of rap he's laying on me. I understand about half of it but that half sounds interesting.

He goes on, still using the table to prop himself up, swaying drunkenly in front of me. "Look, it's like some kind of huge perceptional journey and we only perceive a little bit of it. I mean, that's what the creatures get. Just tiny pieces of the whole bit. The lords see it all. They don't suffer. They stand above life, but trapping themselves with all these secret exits, entrances and disguises, man. Like you and me, man, we're both in disguise."

"Disguised as what?"

"As human beings."

"What does that mean? And why are we disguised?"

"We hide ourselves 'cause the creatures don't like the lords. It's like historical. We are the real strangers, the lords. In the old times, see it was the primitive societies in which the stranger was always the greatest menace."

"Why?" I have to ask, not disagreeing, just curious.

"Because the only fucking power in the world is . . . the *only power* is . . . enslaving others in your own designs."

I think I understand. He's talking manipulation, at which I am past master. "You mean trap people, taking them into the fantasies we project on them? You mean like putting lies over on people?"

"Exactly, man."

I scratch my neck, touch my nose to see how bad it's bleeding, thinking about what he's saying. Hard to think when you're bleeding, but I'm listening, interested.

I shrug. "So okay, Adolf Hitler was a lord."

Morrison comes away from the table, raising his voice. "*Atilla the Hun was a lord!* All men who enslave others are lords!"

"Shakespeare, adept plagiarist, liar and lord," I say.

"Assassins are lords, public lovers are lords, politicians, pimps, madams and all artists are lords! Art is the greatest enslavement of all. Art obscures and blinds the imprisoned, they never see the walls of their frigging cages because art keeps them silent, awed, distracted, and finally, indifferent." Morrison's delivering a speech he's given someplace before. "Art is the exercise wheel in the cage that keeps the rat from going crazy and dying too soon, thereby depriving the ruling lord of his fair share of amusement."

"So we, us, you think we are both lords? Right?" I ask.

Morrison gathers himself up, standing taller. Begins quoting from something, a solemn voice that would chill a grave:

"I want to stifle my longings in the increased mechanization of apes.
I pose impossible selection.
Sex without limits.
Death without touching . . . cold girls I want you.
I want your kind. I want you all to become creatures who stumble into darkened rooms without windows.
To celebrate the hideous!
Penetration!
Sometimes by force, the mind takes place in an unclosed world.
Penetration!"

I'm hooked, somewhat mystified, but hooked. Trying so hard to understand I get it committed to memory so I can stack it up later for myself, sort it all out.

"You and me," says Morrison, no longer reciting. "The wind on the beaches of drug Venice brings us together."

"Lords come to collaborate in darkness," I say, liking the sound of it.

Morrison goes on. "Drugs are the weapons, the appointments of power. They fester in our burning bodies. In the summer, man. Terrible summer."

"Drugs are . . ." I stumble in my thinking, hesitating. "Drugs are the new eyes of the world."

Morrison nods, approving. "Man, it's a French Revolution of the flesh, if you can dig it. All the books of the world are closed. Our bodies in disguise record eye movements." Morrison seems excited, evangelical.

"Who the hell are you anyway?" I have to ask him, curious as hell. For the first time he makes me feel as young as I am and that he is as old as he is. That's unusual. I was born a cynical thirty-year-old with death in my eyes. "I mean who the fuck are you really?"

Morrison starts laughing. "If I told you anything, you know I'd lie. Same way you'd lie to me if I tried to find out who the fuck you really are. We are lords in disguise."

"Maybe I'm Jason and you're the Golden Fleece."

"Bullshit! Neither of us are heroes, 'cause heroes are too simpleminded to be creatures of deception. We're spies! Two spies in the house of love! We're horses in a hotel of sheep."

I got to disagree somewhere. "I always wanted to be a hero."

"Bullshit!"

"Then what am I?"

"You're a genuinely fucking *evil* villain, just like me, and you know it."

"Ah, you're just higher than a kite."

"So are you and you know I'm right. You want to be a villain and you know it. We both do 'cause we're making the same leap into lies!"

I want to disagree but can't. I know myself too well, and sense he knows me for what I am too. What was I, all of fifteen or sixteen, passing always for someone much older? The years all blur together and I walk through them in my constant play-pretend. Just faking it, all burnt out inside, taking drugs and chances. This son of a bitch knows me. A fake.

A bullshit rapper, hanging out with the rock and roll bands, with the druggies, balling the ladies, world weary and jaded at fifteen. Arrogant sex, flagrant display. Fantasy this, fantasy that, one pose building on another, all kinds of supposed torture, self-inflicted.

And this bastard was right up there with me, running along ahead of me, already wise in certain ways, having seen too much and felt too little.

"You want to know who I am?" he tells me.

This whole incredible rap, all about Jim the Admiral's son, parents dead, alone in the world. Lies. Almost all lies. Just like my life story if I'd have told it. All lies.

I forget everything he says as soon as he's said it. It's my kind of lies and not worth committing to memory. He and I are in the same performance on the drug beach.

He's good at it, though, you gotta give him that. You listen a little and you get the feeling this is the master, this is the cat who went around originally making it all up.

"You're right," I tell him. "Every word a lie and every lie a word."

Morrison moves toward me. "Let's split this funeral. Did you come back for me?"

"Uh, yeah."

"Liar. You probably came to get some pussy or to steal something. But who gives a shit. Let's blow."

We stagger out of the party, head for the car. Daylight is kicking the shit out of the stuff they call air in Los Angeles. Getting hot, to stay hot, a real L.A. summer hangover day.

Both of us are wrecked. Brain-whipped.

"Let's drive out to the beach, crawl into the shade somewhere and crash," suggests Morrison. He slings his coat over one shoulder, blinking and staggering under the merciless California sun.

He leads the way, I follow.

I stop for a second, look back at the party. It's all over, like it never happened. Maybe it didn't.

What is it that race car drivers say?

If you can walk away from it, you haven't had an accident.

CHAPTER 7

We argue. I'm for Malibu. He wants to go to Venice. Think maybe he's got some lady he wants to see there. Mainly, though, I think I want to check into my living situation. Supposed to be living with this girl, old whatever-her-name-is.

I open the car door, regretfully remembering the junkie chick episode which got me so wrapped up I forgot to snatch some more booze.

A fat head flops out of the open door, connected to a neck (fat), connected to a body (fat). Familiar fat. I've seen this fat somewhere before. Herman Melville's inspiration.

"Oh, shit," says Morrison, opening his door and discovering the other end of the monstrosity.

The head opens its eyes, the mouth comes open in an imitation of the back end of a garbage truck and slowly begins slobbering. Another head appears over the top of the back seat. It's Sandy, the good-looking blonde, now not so good-looking waking up in the back seat. Semi-waking up anyway. She looks like the loser on the last day of a six-day bicycle race.

"I thought whales migrated," says Morrison.

The whale in question turns slowly in the seat, no mean feat in itself, and crawls up to a sitting position on the front seat.

"Hey, where you guys been?" asks the blonde in back, rubbing her eyes. "We was looking for you, waiting for you."

"We were directing films in hell," says Morrison. He looks at me, shrugs. Gives me a what-do-we-do-now look.

I signal him back. What should we do, you decide?

He waves his hands, shrugs again.

"We need a ride home," says Gail, fuzzy eyed. "Jeeesuuus! What a great party! It was . . . the greeeeeeatteessttt!!"

Morrison stumbles into the side of the car, bends over double, cracking up. Laughing like a horse under nitrous oxide.

I start laughing too, can't control it. Both girls look at us like we are both insane. We can't stop, just rolling on the ground.

Gail looks at the girl in the back. Both are puzzled. Gail says, "Hey! What's so funny?"

Morrison crawls up, bends over on the hood of the car, weak from laughter. "Pimps!" says Morrison.

"Adolf Hitler," I add.

It sets us both off again.

"They're just really wasted," says Gail by way of explanation, looking really wasted herself.

Morrison slides to the ground again, convulsed with laughter.

I have to help him up and that kind of straightens me out a little.

We start climbing into the car. Guess we are going to give them a ride home. What other choice we got? Morrison gets into the back with his blond beach baby. Gail slides over behind the wheel, speaks to me, pats the seat beside her.

"Get in, stud. I'll drive."

I look at her, look at Morrison in the back seat. Morrison's sprawled out like the King in Yellow, trying not to laugh himself right into the grave.

"Oh, sure," I say, dive in the car and crawl into the back seat with Jim and the blonde.

Gail turns around, pissed off.

I avoid her eyes, slump in the seat, looking out the window at nothing in particular.

Gail starts the car up—guess I left the keys in the ignition. Car hasn't gone anywhere yet. Gail just sits there glaring at me in the rearview mirror.

"How come you're not sitting up here with me?" she asks me.

Morrison opens one eye, leans forward with a confidential air. "Listen, he's horny for you and he's afraid he won't be able to keep his hands off of you. He's afraid he'd grab you or something and maybe make you wreck the car."

"Son of a bitch!" I say and try to swing at Morrison, who ducks behind the blonde, dissolving into laughter again. The glib bastard!

"You gotta be kidding! Still horny!" She looks really shocked. "You're incredible! You was all over me last night! Jesus! I never had it so many times in my life! It was like there was ten of you!"

Gail has the dangerous look of a convert who's just met God, personally. She gives me an affectionate look, a loving look that makes the hair stand up on the back of my neck.

She says, "Honey, I don't think we could make it even if you wanted to! We made it so many times last night I'm so sore I can hardly move!"

Sandy leans forward, pats Gail on the shoulder with a way-to-go gesture, says, "Far out!"

Morrison is choking, red-faced, laughing his muffins off.

I hope the silly son of a bitch swallows his tongue.

"Funny, Morrison! Real fucking funny!" I tell him.

"Yeah," he agrees.

"You're some lover!" says Gail.

"Far out!" says Sandy, staring off into space.

"It runs in his family," says Morrison. "Everybody in his family is densely populated."

"Far out!" says Sandy, communing with the car upholstery.

Gail gets the car rolling, eyes occasionally straying back to me, visually drooling all over me.

Morrison tunes out, eyes glazed. I settle back in the seat, half mad and half laughing. The blonde jammed in between us is falling all over Morrison and he could care less. I sneak a feel, touch her breasts, and she doesn't seem to mind.

She puts one arm around my neck, feeling me mess with her chest, looks at me and says, "Far out!"

She's a terrific conversationalist, dead from the neck up. I let go of her breasts, settle back in the seat, too tired to be interested. Instead, I just lean back and pretend to be a corpse. Doesn't take much pretending. I'm pretty banged up.

"It's a nightmare," I say to no one in particular. No one seems to hear.

Gail makes a couple of turns, and we're heading up Laurel Canyon, heading back toward North Hollywood.

"Where we going?" I ask, not really caring.

"Back to my house," says Gail.

"Terrific!" I say.

"Far out!" says Sandy.

Jim opens his eyes, looks at her. "I think your record is scratched."

The car dips and dives, swooping awkwardly up the curves of Laurel Canyon. Gail is driving like somebody who's had too many downs. Like a snow-blind, epileptic kamikaze pilot, in other words. Trying to be in every lane all at once and sometimes succeeding.

This isn't doing my stomach any good. Also, I'm getting some kind of strange shot-in-the-guts sensation. I seem vaguely to remember a certain white pill that . . .

Oh, shit! Feel my stomach trying to bring some beer back up, so I open the window on my side and stick my head out. The whole universe is shaking and baking me. My nose is full of clotted blood, I ache in a thousand places, and oh, Jesus, my guts now feel like wild dogs are dancing around in there, practicing hydrophobia on each other.

I try to hold it all back but no way. I toss my cookies in one long monster stream. I give that side of the car a better vomit paint job than Earl Sheib can do for $39.95.

Morrison is half asleep and doesn't see it. The blonde is draped all over him, eyes closed in her own private oblivion.

Only Gail is really awake and she's not watching me. She's got her eyes fastened on the rearview mirror, watching something behind us.

I am just about falling out of the car, upchucking like the puking Sphinx Tuli Kupferberg used to sing about.

On the positive side, I retain maybe half of my stomach lining. But now I got the dry heaves, pumping long after there's anything left to pump.

"Holy shit! You dumb ass, get back in the car!" Gail's talking to me, all shook up. What's the big deal? Ain't she never seen somebody blow their lunch before?

I'm done anyway, so I pull my head back in the car, really worn out. Compared to the fun I've had today and yesterday, World War One was a picnic sponsored by the Home for the Criminally Insane Glee Club.

"Can't a guy have a little fun outdoors once in a

while?" I ask, of no one in particular. Then I hear this loud noise. Where have I heard that noise before? A loud blaring noise. It's coming from behind us and I turn and look out the back window.

Oh, yeah. Now I know where I've heard that noise before.

"Oh, shit!" Official bad news. We are about to sail off the edge of the known world and get eaten up by the boys in blue. You know, sirens, nightsticks, guns and all that heavy social-consciousness jazz.

There's this patrol car with two cops in it right back there, siren blaring, lights flashing, just chewing up our tail pipes (figuratively, since they are long gone).

Suddenly I am as sober as Carrie Nation, only a whole lot more scared shitless than she ever was.

I punch Morrison on the arm, hard. Morrison jerks awake with a start. Balls his fists at me, rubbing his arm. Looks really pissed off.

"Hey, what the fuck you trying—" he starts saying, then flashes on the siren song and turns and looks out the back window.

"Oh, fuck!" he moans, looking at the interior of the car. "We got dope, open booze and underage chicks in the car! Our asses are grapes! We're gonna get enameled!"

If Morrison knew what I knew, he wouldn't be so fucking optimistic.

"Fuck!" he says, scrambling around frantically in the back seat, doing nothing but doing it very fast.

"Don't panic," I caution him. "Just do what I do, don't question me. Just do what I do."

He ignores me.

"Maybe your father is a police commissioner?" he suggests, without too much hope.

"Far out!" says Sandy, resurfacing from her own mental tar pit.

"I knew you'd say that," says Morrison, pushing her off his shoulder. "You always seem to know the right thing to say."

I push the blonde forward, get her away from him so

I can whisper something to him.

"Far out," she says, bent over, staring at nothing.

In a whisper I tell him, "When the car stops, open the door and run like hell!"

Morrison smiles. "You better check your pants. I think you just shitted your brains away."

"Hey, I got a special reason for running. Unless you want to shoot it out with them or are really hipped on ten years in prison, my choice is the only choice."

Morrison has to nod, knowing what I say is true but still not happy about it.

"The ladies can—"

"Find their own road to salvation," finishes Morrison. "We're psycho. We're both gonna get a warning shot in the back of our heads!"

Gail slows the car up, weaving all over the place, and begins to pull over to the side of the road.

I get my hands on the door. "You going or staying? Me, I'm running like hell!"

Morrison runs his hands through his hair, lifting it off his face, thinking it over. Gives me a penetrating stare, trying to figure me, maybe. Hesitates, then abruptly pushes Sandy off of him, giving himself some launching room. It's like pushing away a bag of Jell-O.

Totally zipped up, the blond girl slides off the seat and falls on the floor, legs all tangled up, aiming at the ceiling. She's got attractive pubic hair. She must have left her underwear and her jeans back at the party, probably in some pervert's mouth. Anyway, she's a natural blonde all over.

She's dangling upside down, eyes unfocused. She seems to take it all in stride. "Far out," she says.

Morrison gets his hand on the door handle, pulls it down, unlocks the door and holds it flush with the door frame. I notice what he's doing and do the same thing. A pretty good idea. Should speed up our takeoff. We may need every inch.

"Far out!" says Sandy, discovering her legs waving above her head.

"Who said the art of conversation is dead?" I mutter.

"If we get the shit shot out of us, I'm gonna come back and masturbate on your grave," says Morrison.

"I hope it gets caught in your zipper."

Our car slows, almost stopped. The patrol car slides in behind it, car doors banging wide open. They aren't even going to wait until we come to a complete stop. Cops have already got us pegged as a bunch of dope perverts, sex fiends and armed necrophiliacs. Popping out of their car with drawn guns.

"Oh, shit!" says Morrison, seeing the guns. "Let's move!"

Our car is still moving when we hit the doors and go flying out. We land running like hell.

As if we rehearsed it, both of us zip past our car, cut across the same yard, and duck into the first alley we come to. No time for either of us to look back to see what the cops are doing.

Never ran so frigging fast in my whole frigging life. Every step expecting a warning shot in the back of the head. Morrison and I edge up on the sound barrier. I'm pumping my arms so hard I rip the elbows out of my shirt.

We hear the cops yell and one of them must have put his gun up in the air—'cause we hear a shot but no bullet goes streaking past us. Maybe the only time a warning shot by a L.A. cop was not fired directly at somebody. We must have lucked out, got a couple of new recruits or something.

The shot is like one enormous boost of crystal meth. Our stride almost doubles. We boom down the alley, cut across a couple of backyards, dash down a side street and keep right on screaming.

We hear the roar of a car engine, screaming siren, and know at least one of the cops is pursuing us in the patrol car.

"Where?" I gasp frantically, as we turn a corner. Morrison motions to the left. We pound up to a tall cedar fence. Morrison grabs the top and vaults over. I do the same, or try to. Get over but fall on my ass, damn near becoming a boy soprano on the top board.

Morrison yanks me to my feet and we run around some fat bastard's swimming pool. We know it belongs to a fat bastard because the fat bastard is in the pool on a black inner tube and he yells something angry at us as we pound by him. We got no time to pay him much attention. Morrison trips over a lawn chair and goes sprawling.

I'm halfway across the guy's backyard when a little poodle the size of a good spit comes running out and bites the shit out of my right leg. Off guard, I end up plowing into a concrete birdbath and wind up wrapped around the birdbath with this fucking dog attached to my leg like some kind of crazy fucking flag.

I try to kick the frigging dog loose and get bit about four times in the process.

Try to reach down and deck the little shit with my fist and almost lose the fingers part of my hand.

"You leave my dog alone!! *You . . . you . . . you punk!*" screams the fat guy in the pool. "*Kill him, Snappy! Kill him!*"

Morrison thunders up and the dog turns to attack him. Guess the frigging poodle underestimates Morrison's speed because Morrison runs right over the silly son of a bitch. His foot smashes down on the dog's back and damn near pushes the frigging beast right into the ground.

Shit! Why couldn't I have done that. My leg feels like an ear of corn at a farmer's picnic.

I let loose of the birdbath, Morrison grabs me and pushes, getting me going again. We tear across the yard.

"*Murderers! You killed my—*" screams the fat guy in the pool, trying to stand up, forgetting where he is, and falling backwards off of his inner tube. He sinks with a soggy *phump*, cutting himself off in midsentence.

We hear him thrashing around in the pool, hopefully drowning.

We run into a chain-link fence, bounce off and try to

pull a gate open that has to be pushed. We figure it out eventually and go breathlessly stumbling through.

Despite all our ducking and dodging, we hear the police car getting closer and closer. We run toward a big hedge and duck down behind it, an alley at our backs. Suddenly the siren's screaming in our ear, we both turn and see the cop car zipping into the alley at our backs.

"Yaaaaah!" says Morrison.

We practically shed our skins like snakes as we both explode through the bottom of the hedge. I lose some skin, some shirt buttons and about two pounds of perfectly good flesh in the process.

The patrol car crashes by us.

We come out under a bunch of tall bushes and kind of collapse there. We've had it. If that cop saw us, he's got us. Neither of us could run the length of a coke spoon.

Sound of brakes, tires squealing.

"Oh, shit!" says Morrison, on his stomach. "He saw us! He's coming back!"

Before the words are completely out of his mouth, there is a rending crash, sounds like a kamikaze pilot crashing into an aluminum can factory. The siren goes *WHEEEEEEEEEEEEEEEeeeeeee ... eeee ... ee ... ick ... eee ... ee ... ick ... ick ... ick.* And then fades, as if mortally wounded.

We're both panting like two long-haired dogs with sweaters at Death Valley in the summertime.

"You think he saw us?" I ask, scared crapless. If Morrison knew what I knew, he'd be equally crapless. Instead, son of a bitch is almost laughing. Beginning to enjoy this razzmatazz.

"Well, this is certainly another fine mess you've gotten us into, Stan," he says.

"Blow it out your swivel, Ollie." I look around, scared. "Maybe we ought to run some more." I'm too tired to breathe but I want to lift legs for the horizon and get the hell out of there.

"Let's homestead this claim, what say, old partner?"

says Morrison, from a bad cowboy movie. "Ah! The
wide open spaces." He brushes the leaf of a bush out of
his ear.

I start to get up but my running equipment seems to
have a truck parked on it. I flop back down, let my
tongue hang even farther out and just concentrate on
gasping for breath.

Morrison's out of breath too but semi-pretends he
isn't. You never see him unposed.

Neither of us has exactly been in training for a marathon race. My stomach is doing loop-the-loops and
Morrison, despite the jokes, looks as green as a frog's
bottom. I probably look even greener.

Nobody seems to be coming for us. Down the alley
we hear angry shouts. I guess the cop in the patrol car
zigged when he should have zagged.

"Looks like we won the race," says Morrison. "I
think the cop car raced somebody across an intersection and only came out tied."

"Lucky for us," I say. "That car we just ditched . . ."
(trying to talk between breaths) "was *hot!* I lifted . . .
lifted it this morning!"

Morrison rolls over on his back, thrusts his startled
face in mine, isn't sure he heard me right.

"*You what?*"

"I stole it. . . . Keys . . . keys were in it. Found it
parked just . . . just down the street from where I was
crashing . . . so I boosted it!"

Morrison looks stunned. "You mean we've been doing all that wild-assing in a stolen car! You stupid turd,
we could have went to jail for eternity!"

That pisses me off.

"Why is it that whenever I go out and try to have a
little fun somebody is always bitching and complain-
ing and telling me I shouldn't do it?"

"Asshole!" says Morrison.

"Oh, yeah. Well, you can just screw that horse shit!
If you're gonna get parental on me, you can just fucking well *walk home!*"

Morrison rolls his eyes. "We don't have a car anyway, shit head! We're *both* walking!"

"Oh, yeah. I forgot," I admit. "Well, if I did have a car, I'd make you walk!"

"Shut up," says Morrison.

"Make me."

"You're not my type."

I roll over, turn my back on him. The hell with him. I'll go unconscious on him and wait for a meteor to hit him.

Now that all the fun's gone by, my whole universe is demanding sleep. *Sleep!*

Morrison's saying something. Something about Jean-Luc Godard and a weekend.

Me, I could have cared less. I was Philip Marlowe, doing a Dick Powell scene from Raymond Chandler's *Murder, My Sweet.* You know the one I mean.

Somebody saps him with a blackjack and Marlowe/Powell says, "A black pool opened at my feet and I dove in."

Me, I hit the bottom of the black pool before Marlowe even got off the diving board.

CHAPTER 8

Thou shalt never sleep under bushes.

It was raining and it never rains in Los Angeles.

Flavored yellow rain.

I open my eyes. What the hell is going on?

Son of a bitch! A goddamn poodle with upraised leg is hosing the bush I am sleeping under.

I kick out at him from under the bushes where I'm lying. The dog yelps and runs away.

I stare up at the thick bushes over my head, wipe the dog piss off my face and try to remember just where the hell I am.

It all comes back, the eyes focus, the head stops spinning around like a top and I roll over painfully, expecting to see Morrison passed out beside me.

He's gone.

I get up on my hands and knees and crawl out from under the bushes. Force myself to try standing up. I make it but I am pretty shaky. I stagger around, blinking in the chill of the Los Angeles night. I hurt everywhere. I've got blood all over me, ruined clothes, aches and pains in every part of me. Sore throat, splitting head and a nose that is so sore it hurts to breathe through it.

Moonlight feels like a razor cutting into my eyes. Feel like I just want to roll up in a ball and die or like I already did that. Keep asking myself how I got here, where I am going to land next. I never seem to know. No direction leads home.

I'm thousands of miles from the home I don't have.

Home.

That's what the rock and roll world is instead of.

I had one once. Sort of. I didn't start out here, in this dreamland of snow-white beaches, this L.A. nowhere. I traveled to get here from my own personal nowhere. Fled in the beginning of the summer, another Indian taking the highway the white man has driven across the world's heart.

I'm out here on the streets, fifteen but passing for older, owned by no one and owning no one. I am an escapee from White Christmas, a despiser of holidays, of birthdays, of all official celebrations of love and caring. I hated them all because I never got them.

I am one of the people your parents warned you against. How I got here, it's not easy to tell. But they say some are born to sweet delight and some are born to endless night, and it's been dark ever since my world began. If you could cut me open with a knife, you'd find all the love I didn't get and all the tears I couldn't cry.

• • •

I had been this adopted creature who lived in a cold house with two white people who didn't love me enough or at all.

Doctors had told my adoptive parents when they were trying to have some children and couldn't that they should adopt a child. Something was wrong with the woman, some kind of hormonal imbalance. The doctor said caring for a child would cause some kind of physical, psychological change in her and she could then get pregnant.

So they went shopping for a child. Anyone would do, but white was their first choice. Thing was, white wasn't available. I wasn't white, I was Cherokee, full-blood father and half-breed mother. They had to take what they could get and I was all they could get.

My real parents were killed in a car wreck. And the few other relatives I had were either indifferent or in the process of dying from being Indian in a world that didn't have much use for Indians. As far as close relatives go, I had two uncles, but they didn't live long enough for anyone to say they even existed. One died in a bar fight and the other committed suicide. So there wasn't much of my own people to hold on to.

I had only a small child's memory of a tall man who drank too much and a dark-haired woman who took the beatings he gave her in silence. And always traveling, always moving from one nowhere to another. The three of us wearing a reservation face, some external brand that marked us, that set us apart from the white people. We were tattooed by our way of life as surely as if we were inmates of a concentration camp and had numbers on our arms.

Then there was that train that was as inevitable as history and the car driven by a man who drank too much. Then it was just me, a survivor in the back seat with blood all over me, all over everything. I still remember their screams as the train crushed the front of the car, sheering it off. It's a nightmare that waits for me when I sleep and never goes away. I can't seem to get their blood off me, not in this lifetime.

After the train, I didn't belong to anybody.

I got put in a home where we were lined up in rows and hopeful people came and looked at us. We were taught to smile and wag our little tails like puppies in a pet shop.

I guess I smiled good 'cause I was a little too old to get chosen but I got chosen. My new parents didn't meet all the qualifications for adoption, couldn't get a white baby through legitimate means. Least that's what they told me later. So they made a deal somewhere along the way and money changed hands and they took me home with them and they taught me just how empty empty can be.

It worked out for them if not for me. The old lady got used to the idea of caring for a child, she got pregnant and they had a kid. It took them two years but it worked out for them. Almost worked out for me too. Almost. 'Cause those two years were the only two years of my life I ever remember anybody being kind or loving. Two years of love, just long enough to begin to understand what it is to be wanted.

And then there was a boy, their first and only natural son. Suddenly I didn't exist anymore. I was only a device, a dose of medicine once prescribed by a doctor and now no longer needed.

They fed me, gave me enough clothes to keep me from running around naked and very little else. Christmas and birthdays were the worst.

Christmas mornings, when we were older, my brother raced down the stairs to that wonderful world of packages and ribbons and strings and toys and surprises.

I was told to stay in my room. For me, no toys, no surprises from the heart. Only an empty room and silent walls without arms to hold me. Love went away without explanation. I felt like a toy that had been broken, that no one had any use for anymore.

I had become an embarrassment, a dark-skinned

stranger who had overstayed his welcome. Only my little brother was kind to me, late at night, when nobody would know.

An escapee from White Christmas, a gift to the world with nothing inside, I hit the streets, seeing them as the only home I was ever going to have. And those cold dark streets led me to L.A.

I had begun my journey to L.A. just a few steps ahead of the cops. I'd been living on the streets of my hometown, destined for trouble and had found it. Found it where no Indian has a right to be, on the streets where the rich white people live.

I had walked past all those big houses and all those fat well-fed citizens safe and warm inside. I guess I got the idea I should break in and steal something. Stealing was nothing I hadn't done before. All the last couple of months I'd been living off what I shoplifted from supermarkets. I am good at stealing.

I pick the biggest house. I know who lives there. Everybody in my hick town knows the people in the big house. They practically own the town. The husband, already rich, made optical lenses for bomb sites in World War Two and made a fortune out of the death business.

All I ever hear is talk about the parties they throw, the jets they catch to here and there. Servants and fancy cars and all that trash.

The big rambling house is dark in every room.

Maybe they are off somewhere. Nobody home.

I don't know why I think nobody is there. It just seems right to me. Maybe I'm a little too drunk to think clearly. Goddamn, I guess I had been drinking some, I admit that.

I don't have any burglar tools, just an old screwdriver with a broken handle, but that ought to be enough to get me inside.

I get over the stone wall easy. And just as easily into the house. They didn't even bother to lock the patio doors. Only poor people lock their doors 'cause they know how loose their grip is on the things they own. There's so many ways the few things they have can be ripped out of their hands. It's different with rich people. It's too hard to steal from rich people. They hold on to their money too tightly.

It's warm inside the house and I like it. I go floating around inside, touching and feeling all the surfaces of things. All the chairs feel like bales of soft cotton. Inside, the house is richly furnished, like a fancy movie set about millionaires, and everything I see or touch says *wealth, comfort, luxury.* Even the paintings on the walls drip money. The carpets are so thick they bury anything dropped in them like quicksand. It's the kind of a house I'll never live in and it drives me crazy. How could they have so much when I got so little?

I just kind of wander through the rooms, a little drunk, a little bit awed, looking for something worth stealing. The thing I really want to steal, the right to live like this, in a house like this, is too big. It won't fit in my pocket.

I look for something else. Something that the black dude who lives above the pool hall on Magnolia Street will give me cash for. A radio, TV set, silverware, tape player, something like that. The currency of the black market.

I'd like to have some money in my pocket. Ten or twenty bucks is enough to get me where I'm going, wherever that is. It don't take much money to go nowhere.

I get lucky. I find a small reel-to-reel tape recorder, an expensive one, on a fancy table in a little room that must be some kind of den or something. Also a small movie projector. Also expensive. I could get more than enough cash for these two things to feed myself for a couple of weeks.

The projector fits into a little carrying case. Putting it in the case, I damn near break my arms. Feels like it weighs five hundred pounds. The tape recorder is only maybe two hundred pounds light. I ought to get that

black dude to pay me by weight. Christ! I get them off
the ground, one in each hand and start back the way I
came. I haven't made any noise and I haven't heard
anybody stirring in the house.

I get in the center of one of the big rooms, making
my way very carefully through the semi-darkness.
This is no time to knock something over in the dark
and wake everybody up.

I don't know what gives me away. Maybe nothing.
Maybe just bad luck.

Suddenly the light comes on and there's a scream,
half frightened, half angry. I turn around quick and
there's this white-haired woman dressed like a witch
with a gun in her hand.

The projector falls from my hand and crashes against
the floor with the sound of lenses smashing, parts
breaking.

I am going to drop the tape recorder too, to get free
for flight or surrender, but the old woman is too fast for
me. She holds the gun up in front of her face like she's
never seen it before.

She screams something at me I don't understand and
pulls the trigger. No chance to think, no time to react.
Just terror as the bullet goes past my face like an angry
bee.

I scream, try to run, try to get away. Unthinkingly,
my hand freezes around the handle grip of the tape recorder. The gun crashes again and I stumble back
against a chair, falling to my knees.

*"Please don't! Please don't! Don't shoot! I'm not
armed! I give up!"* I scream at her but she doesn't hear
or doesn't want to. The arm of the chair I hold with
one frantic hand splinters almost under my fingers, the
bullet smacking into the hard wood.

"Please!"

This is the way I'm going to die.

I stagger up, like a slaughterhouse cow the hammer
just missed, trying to back away, trying to escape.

There's no way out. I'm like a Jew backing away from the insanity of the Dachau oven. How could this happen to me? What did I do to deserve it?

I move toward her, down on my knees, crawling. "Please . . . please don't. Don't kill me. I . . . give up . . . please." The tape recorder bumps against my knees. It's the price of my life. I'm going to die for it.

My eyes don't find any reprieve in her face, just a smile, savage, triumphant. The gun wavers unsteadily in her hand and I realize she's pretty drunk. So drunk she almost drops the gun.

"Son of a bitch!" she says and fires point-blank at my head. Her being drunk is the only thing that keeps the bullet from pulping my face. The bullet tears through my long hair on one side like an angry wind.

I am in my final nightmare. I am trapped in a wrecked car with the blood of my father and mother all over everything. The train that missed me then comes for me now. I already can feel the bullet slamming into my face, feel the brains and blood exploding outward, splattering the wall.

I'm not fifteen years old. I am seven years old again and I scream, like my father and mother screamed.

The woman staggers in front of me, reeling drunkenly.

"Stand still, you thieving little bastard!" she says, aiming the gun, holding it in my upturned face.

She has all the cruelty of the world in her face.

I'm on my knees in front of her like a human sacrifice, kneeling before an angry god. I fall against her legs, ready for death.

Still have the tape recorder in my hand and I swing it toward her, purely reflexive, as if trying to stop the bullet with it. The heavy machine slams heavily against her legs, throwing her back.

I am seven years old, screaming, covered with blood, waiting for a mother who never comes.

The gun explodes in the room like the end of the

world and I writhe on the floor like a dark-bodied spider fallen in fire. I feel the bullet driving through my back, pinning me to the floor in my own blood.

I roll over on my back, screaming, untouched by the bullet.

My eyes stare up at her, hating her, hating this life, hating this world.

The woman stands above me, toppling backwards with her ugly mouth open in a forever kind of surprise. There's a red stain under her chin, the beginning of a flood pouring from the gaping hole in her neck. The bullet took her under the chin and came out where her right eye should have been.

It's almost slow motion. Her knees bend and she goes over backwards. Dead before her body slams against the floor.

The bullet meant for me, deflected, the gun thrust up at her face as she fired.

I crawl toward her. Feeling nothing. Not sorry. Not even surprised. Just feeling nothing. Who am I to feel anything?

There's people in other parts of the house shouting now, doors banging, the sounds of panic and confusion.

I stagger to my feet, standing over her body. The tape recorder rests between her outstretched legs. The gun rests against my right foot. I kick it toward her.

She can keep it for a souvenir.

The door opens and a man rushes into the room. I turn and start to run, not thinking, just acting by reflexes. I make it to the patio door before a heavy weight pulls me down from behind. Her husband climbs up my back, fingers tearing at my face, gouging my eyes. Screaming insanely.

I throw him off, try to roll out from under him, get out the door. There's no stopping him. He's got the strength of a berserker. We roll across the floor like two reptiles mating. I don't want to hurt him, just want to get away, just want this nightmare to end.

His hands go round my neck, squeeze, cut off my air.

I hit him. Again and again but I can't get him off me. My eyes feel like they are going to pop out. I roll over, trying to twist out of his grasp. My chest rolls over something sharp and hard. The broken-handled screwdriver that had been in my back pocket.

I am frantic, beating at him, trying to get free. Our faces are together and his eyes bore into me as if stealing my soul. In a rage, he screams at me, words I can't make out. I can't hold him off. He's killing me.

My hand closes on the handle of the screwdriver.

I can't breathe. My head is exploding, eyes bulging in their sockets. He's killing me!

I swing the screwdriver up and hit him in the head with the handle. His eyes widen but he doesn't let go. I hit him again and again.

His hands loosen from my throat and I tumble him off of me, his blood flowing out on my hands.

He flops off of me, twisting away, ripping the screwdriver out of my hand.

I jump up, weak, dizzy. I fall forward, half in and half out of the door. His eyes stare up at me, murderous, hateful. "Get you . . . get you . . . get you, you bastard. Gonna . . . *gonna kill you!*" Foam flecks his lips and he breathes in harsh gasps.

I get to my feet, holding on to the door, pulling myself upright. There's other people running into the room. Servants.

His arm reaches for me, tries to catch my ankle, but I kick back at him and my foot strikes his face, pushing him away from me, knocking him over on his back. He moans in pain, bleeding on the floor.

I stumble out, the shouts of the servants chasing me across the yard. I get to the stone wall somehow and start up it. I'm half dead, my strength gone.

Somehow I get up the wall, exhausted, hanging halfway across, trying to breathe, trying to get my deadened body into motion. Someone rushes out into the yard. A shotgun roars and birdshot slams into the wall. Fierce hot stings bite my legs and back.

I lean over the wall, shoving myself forward, and then drop head first. I try to somersault, land on my feet, but my body is like a puppet with cut strings. I land painfully on my back and side.

I hear police sirens screaming in the night.

I stagger to my feet. Anger comes back to me, and with it, new strength. Nobody's going to put me in a cage. Nobody's going to kill me. The train misses me again.

I run.

Blindly, not knowing where I'm going, I run.

Out into the angry night, blood on my hands and murder in my heart.

This is the strangest life I've ever known.

CHAPTER 9

I run down street after street, legs and back stinging from the buckshot, running scared. My sides ache, my lungs are on fire.

I got no place to go, no place to hide.

My shirt's torn, jacket ripped. I got blood all over me. The way I look, the way I am, who's gonna adopt me tonight? Who's gonna give me shelter from the storm? There won't be any home in any face I see.

I'm on my own and no direction leads to sanctuary.

There are squad cars out looking for me, sirens screaming. I figure they probably know my name, know my face, figure they'll find me too. Just a matter of time. I've already dodged a couple of patrol cars already. Can't do it forever. They are gonna catch me sure as hell. I've escaped from the slaughterhouse but it's only temporary.

I hear loud music coming out of this old warehouse-like building and I pound up the alley toward it. It's a place I've been before, the local rock and roll club. Maybe a place to duck into, catch my breath.

A siren screams behind me. Oh, Jesus! A frigging cop car turning into the alley almost on top of me, coming right up my backside. I run to the back of the building, just a dozen steps ahead of the cop car. I smash into the building, grab the handle to a heavy metal door and pull.

If it doesn't open I got nowhere else to go. They got me.

The door isn't locked and I swing it open and crash on through. My back is exposed and I wince, almost feeling a bullet in my back as I go through the door.

I hear the tires squeal, the cop car skidding to a stop outside. No doubt about it. They saw me. They are right behind me.

The backstage door clangs shut behind me and I lean against it, dead tired. I gather myself up, looking around frantically for some way to bar the door against them, but the padlock and bar that should be there are gone. I hear the cop cars slam and the cops yelling at each other.

"He's inside!"

That clinches it.

It's dark where I am and the noise from the rock and roll band onstage is thunder loud. I move away from the door, in a panic to find someplace to hide.

I run down a dark hallway, colliding with half-seen things as I go. At the end of the corridor there's a dimly lit john, door hanging loosely by one hinge. I rush inside and try to close the door behind me. The door won't move.

I have a little time. The cops don't know if I'm armed. They aren't about to rush through that back door until reinforcements get here. I thrust my hands into the sink, try to turn the tap on, thinking maybe I can get some of this blood off of me, and maybe then I can slip out and hide in the crowd. There's a chance, a real small one, they don't know exactly who they are looking for, but I doubt it.

There's lots of people here, enough to get lost in if I'm lucky. It's the local Saturday night rock and roll crowd. My only hope is to lose myself among them.

There's no water. The faucet's rusted shut. Desperate, I run my arm down into the toilet and yank the lever. The toilet flushes, soaking my arm. I peel my blood-soaked jacket off and throw it under the sink. My shirt's blood-soaked and I rip it off too. I got to get me some new clothes somewhere or steal a coat or something.

I look at myself in the mirror over the sink. I don't look so good. I bump into the sink with my hip. There's an empty beer bottle sitting on the rim of the sink and it falls over and breaks in the sink.

A hand closes on my shoulder and I almost go through the roof. My hand goes into the sink, seizes the broken bottle and I spin around, swinging. If he wants me, he's going to have to kill me. I don't want to get caught any other way.

Only it's no cop. It's Russ, a not too close friend of mine, the road manager of the band doing a gig here.

Russ ducks under my crazed swing, the jagged fragment of glass just missing his face. His hand strikes against my shoulder, flinging me back hard into the sink.

"Holy Christ! Hey, man! Be cool! You almost took my frigging face off! It's only me, man!"

The bottle fragment drops from my hand. The jagged edges of the glass have cut deep into my palms. I am bleeding like a broken piñata.

Russ grabs my hand, turns it palm up. "You did

yourself up, man! Remind me not to sneak up on you in the dark. My face could have been your hand! Christ!"

"Sorry, man. Didn't know it was you. I thought you was a cop."

"What did you do? What the fuck happened to you anyway, man?" Russ points at the pile of bloody clothes on the floor. Russ is cool, stoned, not even shook up about almost getting his face carved. He's that kind of guy. Nothing ever shakes him out of his tree.

Russ motions at the pile of bloody clothes on the floor. "Jesus! Did you win the war?"

"I'm in real bad trouble!" I look at him, searching his face, unable to read it. That half-stoned smile that's always there. Can I trust this guy? Can I ask him for help? He doesn't owe me anything. I just barely know him.

"Trouble is when you can't go to the bathroom," says Russ. "Then you got trouble." Russ studies the backs of his hands, cool, unconcerned. Does anything ever move him? He's kind of like I want to be. Nobody can touch him, nobody can get to him. You can bleed all over him and he hardly notices you're there. You get the feeling he doesn't even know he exists let alone you.

"What did you do? Forget that the difference between rape and seduction is patience?"

"Hey! I'm not shitting you! I got real trouble! I wasted somebody! An accident, but no cop would go for it! They are crawling all over the place, looking for me!"

A nervous reaction is setting in. I'm shaking, near hysteria.

"They saw me coming in here! What am I gonna do? *What am I gonna do!*"

Russ smiles his smile. "This ain't no time to hit the chicken switch. Can you drive a truck?"

"What?"

"Can you drive a truck?"

"Uh, yeah, sure. I can drive anything with wheels. You got one?"

"I don't but I know somebody who does. What you need is a job."

A *job!* A job when I'm about to get blown away or put away forever. This guy isn't playing with a full deck!

"I ain't old enough to drive legal. I'm only fifteen."

"That don't mean shit. There's ways around everything. Besides, it could work out good for everybody." Russ nods at me. "Stick with me, man. I'll do you up righteous. The cops can go screw themselves! Follow me, man. I'll hide you until the cops are gone."

I got no choice but to trust him.

We both hear feet pounding along the hallway, cops yelling. Russ grabs me and shoves me under the sink, shielding me with his body. He bends over the toilet and makes loud throwing up sounds. A cop sticks his head in the door, sees Russ being sick and ducks back out, not seeing me.

Give Russ credit, this guy is fast on his feet.

Russ grabs me, drags me to my feet, and hustles me to the door. My hand is beginning to throb, beginning to really hurt. I really cut myself up. There's blood running off the tips of my fingers.

Russ thrusts his head out the door, looking both ways to see if the coast is clear. It is and we go running up the stairs to the backstage rooms. He's got one arm around my shoulders, helping me run. I'm a little shaky on my feet.

We burst into the equipment room full tilt.

"Get behind this spare set of Sun amps. I'll stack them up in front of you."

I rush to obey, crawling around in back of the amplifiers.

Russ wipes the floor with a rag, blotting up some of my blood, and then tosses it over the amps at me. "Wrap up your hand. You're bleeding all over the place."

I lean against the back wall and jump forward. I forgot about my back. I still got a few shotgun pellets in me. I'd been too scared to remember until now. I'm a mess.

"This isn't going to fool anybody for long! Cops search this place, they'll find me!" I yell out at Russ.

"I'm way ahead of you, man. This is temporary until I get to the main game. Just stay cool. Let Russ handle the fuss. I'll get you a disguise. Hang in there and I'll be right back."

The door opens and I hear Russ run out.

It's dark behind the amps and I lean against them, never felt so tired in my life. I'm out of strength and I ache all over. I wish I had a cigarette. My head feels so heavy I don't know how I keep it up. Feels like it's falling off.

The rag is dirty, has some kind of oil or maybe gas on it. It stings when I wrap it around my hand but I got to have something to stop the blood. It's not bleeding as much as before. Maybe I am too tired to bleed.

I sort of collapse, drift off, trusting Russ. What other chance do I have? I hear voices, doors slamming, people shouting.

The door bangs open and some cops burst into the room. I tighten up inside, awake now, and so tense I almost can't breathe. Maybe Russ is going to be too late.

The manager of the rock and roll club is with the cops and he's screaming at them. He's one of those intense middle-aged types trying to be hip as a nineteen-year-old and never quite making it.

"Fucking pigs! Where's your motherfucking search warrant?" I hear the club owner scream at them. "You got no goddamn right to burst in here and . . ."

One of the cops says something I can't hear and there is the sound of a scuffle. Then the sound of something hard smacking into flesh. The club owner groans and I hear a body hit the floor.

"Jesus!" says one cop. "You really boogered up that scum bag! You shouldn't have hit him so hard."

The other one says, "The fucker's not gonna lay his hands on me and get away with it." I hear another sound. I think the club manager just got kicked while he is down. There's a muffled gasp of pain.

"Let's head for the stage. Maybe we can see him from out there. I know he's in here somewhere. I'm sure I saw him go in the back door."

I hear them walk across the room and go out the door that leads to the stage. I hear the manager groaning on the floor. The dumb bastard! Did he think they were gonna kiss him or something?

It gets quiet. The thunder of the rock and roll band ceases. Must be the end of their set. I crouch down behind the amp, just waiting, no place to go. I almost pass out. So tired.

The sound of people coming into the room brings me back. Sounds like a whole lot of people coming into the room. Sounds like a party.

"Come out, man. It's me, Russ. I got you some clothes."

The amps get moved away from me and Russ is standing there with a whole bunch of people, the guys from the band and some chicks and assorted hangers-on.

There's a tall girl standing next to Russ, big chested, no expression on her face. Dressed up like a lamp-post—leaning girl you can buy for ten bucks any night of the week. She doesn't look like she would be worth it.

I come stumbling out, dizzy. I look at Russ, standing empty handed in front of me. "What clothes? I don't see any clothes."

"Strip," says Russ, turning to look at the girl. She's not much to look at. I think she belongs to somebody in the band, somebody with poor taste.

Obediently, the girl starts stripping. She doesn't

even have to think about it. The clothes peel off. The wig comes off with the dress.

This isn't a girl. It's a guy.

The clothes tumble to the floor at my feet. Complete strip-off, even the tiny red cotton panties that weren't meant to cover the kind of equipment this guy is carrying. This guy is hung like an elephant.

If he isn't shy about stripping, neither am I. This isn't any time to get delicate. Besides, although there's chicks in the room, nobody is even paying any attention. Naked is not something people in this room haven't seen before.

I get my clothes off and awkwardly begin putting on the dress. I'm going to feel like a total idiot but I don't give a shit. Better dumb than dead. I'd dress up like the Queen Mary if it would help me escape the cops.

I'm only halfway into the dress and really having some kind of trouble trying to find where and how I'm supposed to fit into it. The manager of the rock and roll club is still on the floor, his face swollen on one side and his nose bleeding. He's moaning, kind of rolling around on the floor in real agony. Nobody pays much attention to him either, except a really stoned groupie who offers him a beer. He's too screwed up to respond to the offer, though.

Nobody makes a fuss about anything. What happens, happens. Your pain belongs to you, your nakedness, whatever. It's your trip. The message is clear. This rock and roll world is a place where nobody interferes with anybody else.

I'm struggling with the frigging dress, trying to find where the frigging snaps are that hold it all together. A couple of guys from the band come over and stand beside Russ. I recognize them. I've seen them play before, hit a few parties with them, know them by name and not much deeper.

Spence, the one with the body that's studying to be a giant, stares at me like I am a piece of meat. "This the one?" he asks, speaking to Russ.

"That's him," says Russ.

Chris, the drummer, who is cut thin to win, snickers. "He looks like Bob Dylan in drag! How did he ever kill anybody? Did he vamp them to death?"

Nobody laughs. Maybe nobody is even listening.

My bloody hand gets no comment. If they notice it, they give no sign. The rag hides it pretty well. I keep my fingers balled into a fist around the rag, holding it in place. It stops the blood but makes me awkwardly one-handed.

I guess they see the difficulty I'm having getting my act together. Spence comes over and grabs the back of the dress, yanks it on, straightens it up, then works on the fasteners. "You need a frigging college education to figure out these buttons!" he mumbles. "How do chicks get into these frigging things anyway?" He jerks on the fabric of the dress. "Man, I hope I ain't establishing a frigging pattern here! I'm not going to start a second career getting you dressed in your dress every day."

"Hah!" You could cut me with a saw and get sarcasm every inch.

Mick comes in, holding a guitar in one hand and a chick by the chest with the other. "Wow," he says. "Is this some kind of new thrill?"

He comes over to watch the clothes get draped on the dummy.

The club manager is sitting up, blood on his paisley shirt. Nobody pays him any attention. Nobody will until it's time to get the money for the gig. Money is the only thing that makes this kind of guy real to anybody.

Russ waves at the band members. "There's a good chance you can ride with us. If you pass with us and can do an up-front job of driving, we'll keep you covered."

Spence backs away. "There you go, man. It's on."

The dress opens up and falls forward on my arms.
Spence doesn't have a college education. He isn't very
straight either.

There's a disturbance at the door. The door opens
and two cops burst into the room. Suddenly there's a
lot of people standing very close together right in front
of me. It is automatic, like a steel trap closing shut.

Jungle law. Predators uniting against the outsiders,
against the intruders. No cop gets anything given to
him here. Cops are the enemy and the wall closes
against them.

The rock and rollers don't have to know me or care
for me to do a number for me. They aren't doing it *for*
me, they are doing it *against* the cops. Whatever reason, I duck down behind them, trying to get the dress
on right and hoping the wig is on straight. I'm glad as
hell to have these cats fronting for me. I lucked out.

There is a silence as deep as a beer can and about as
profound. One of the cops finally steps forward, snarling, "Did any of you see—"

He shuts up. There are no answers on any of the
faces here, just outright hostility, and he recoils from it
as if physically struck. He's got no friends here and
knows it. If looks could kill, the cops' shriveled
corpses would be all over the floor. The cops know that
too. They hesitate, but not too long, and beat a hasty
retreat.

The manager, on his feet now, and looking like
death made a house call, stumbles out after them,
cursing them under his breath. Maybe he's gonna get
lucky twice and get laid out again. He ain't shackled by
the fetters of intelligence. Dumb bastard!

The dress is tight around my back and the places
where the buckshot kissed me hurt like hell. Somehow I get the mess all hooked up, one-handed. The
dress—minus the falsies, which I won't even touch, let
alone wear—doesn't fit me too well. The dress on me
looks like a bowling shirt somebody left out in the rain

too long. I don't have the breasts for it and I'm not about to either.

The shoes don't fit, about seven sizes too small, and I don't even bother with them. Good thing I'm from an Indian family tree. No beard to contend with. I probably will pass as a girl if nobody looks too close, or makes a grab at a curve I'm supposed to have and don't.

"Now what do I do?" I ask, feeling as awkward as a pregnant linebacker. This is my first time in a dress and it better be my last. I hate it.

Russ shrugs. "Just be cool, babycakes. The cops couldn't catch cold on their best day. You're covered. You just come out front with me and sit down, catch the rest of the show. The dudes got one more set and then we tear down and we're off."

Chris touches the sleeve of my dress. "Is he gonna wear a dress all the time? Frankly, I don't think he has the knees for it."

"Fuck off!" I tell him.

"Sensitive, ain't he?" says Spence. "Especially for somebody who just wasted somebody!"

Russ looks at his watch. "Christ! You guys are ten minutes late for the last set! They'll tear the place apart if you don't get out there! Hustle your asses out there!"

"Slave driver!" says Spence, squeezing a girl where she sits down.

"Capitalistic pig!" says Chris, touching his emaciated sides. "I should have got me a cheeseburger. Look at me, I can't go out there! I'm starving to death!"

"Get out there, you assholes!" says Russ, jerking his thumb toward the stage door. "*Now!*"

"His mother didn't love him enough," says Spence, chewing on a guitar pick. "She sent him out Little Lord Fauntleroy and he came back Adolf Hitler."

The guys in the band begin dragging themselves reluctantly toward the stage door. None of them seem overly enthusiastic. Mostly they just seem stoned.

Randall, the group's bass player, is already there ahead of them, never having left the stage. He's like that. Treats his bass guitar like a second skin, never lets it out of his sight.

"What do you think of them?" asks Russ, watching them leak out of the room. "A bunch of animals, aren't they?"

"They are kind of laid back, aren't they? I mean not much shakes them up, does it?" I say, moving around experimentally in my frigging dress. I think about the band for a minute, then I say, "Doesn't it bother them I wasted somebody? I mean it was an accident but they don't even seem to—"

Russ held up his hand, warding it off. "Hey! Save it. I ain't asking, okay?"

It bothers me a little. "But don't they even care? Jesus I . . . I can explain how it happened . . . see it isn't like I—"

"Screw it, man! Ask them, not me. I ain't interested, you want to know the truth. You're going to be our driver and that's all I care about. Let's go up front."

I shrug, out of my depth, surrounded by strange fish from a new cave. This is their world and I seem to be welcome to it. Why question it?

Russ and I go through the side door and down the steps and on out into the rock and roll crowd.

There is a moment where I almost jump out of my skin as we walk past a cop. He's giving all the people up front near the stage the eye, searching for me. But the cop doesn't even so much as glance at me as Russ and I walk by. We sit down in the third row between a couple of drugged-out space cases. The big speakers are right in front of us. You can always tell the heavy druggies. They sit right in front of the speakers where the bass rumble can hit them full blast and scramble up what little brains they have left. It's a great rush if you like brain damage.

The band leaks out onto the stage, moving apathetically. They seem clumsy, awkward. I get the feeling these guys have never seen a musical instrument before in their lives. They are taking their own sweet time getting ready. The crowd's real restless, upset by the presence of the cops and the long delay between sets. Everybody is stamping their feet and shouting, demanding some action.

Somebody sticks a joint in my mouth and I take a toke. Russ's hand tightens on my arm and I look in his direction. A cop is standing there, frowning at me.

I choke. The joint shoots out of my mouth and lands in the long frizzy hair of a girl sitting in front of me. The smell of burning hair comes back to me.

The cop points his finger at me and waves it at me in a "naughty, naughty" gesture. His hand goes down and touches his gun and then comes up and he drags one finger under his chin in a throat-cutting motion.

I am so freaked out I faint into consciousness. I am so zapped with fear I feel the hair leaving my head. If my pump hadn't been dry, I'd have wet myself.

The cop licks his lips, gives me a fierce glare and then stalks off. I figure he is going for reinforcements, that he has spotted me and I am a gone goose. I jump to my feet, start to run, but Russ grabs me by the rear end and drags me down into the seat so hard my wig goes forward over my face.

I'm all bent over, ramming the wig back in place and giving some thought to crawling under the seats or something stupid like that. I am out of control and know it.

"Be cool, asshole! The cop was only commenting on the dope stick! He's got bigger fish to fry than busting a breastless chickie for joint sucking! Will you fucking-A relax!" Russ is as close to pissed off as he ever gets. "See, you frigging maniac! The cop's walking down another aisle, still looking for you. You're safe. Just relax and don't do no more dope until it's safe, okay?"

"Well, how was I to know that he—"

Russ sighs, cutting me off. "You keep this up, you're gonna be more trouble than you're worth!"

I sit back in my seat, tight lipped, angry. Russ is about as sympathetic as a rattlesnake.

The band is playing the song every rock and roll band in the world knows. It's called "Tuning Up" and it's never played the same way twice and it's never anything but boring.

My mind isn't really on the band. My mind isn't really on anything. Things have been happening so fast, I'm not sure my brain even functions anymore. I know I ought to be sorting this nightmare out for myself but I don't have any control over any of it. I am a kamikaze pilot without a plane.

Suddenly the band cuts loose and the world around me catches on fire. The music rises up and it's another world, a rock and roll movie, an unholy flat-face opera.

Primal energy, body-shaking, world-breaking waves of sound rolling down on all of us, so good you hear it only when you hear it, 'cause it's right now and right now only, and when it lets up on you, you can't take it with you. This is a one-time and one-time-only feeling, a continuous heartbeat that the whole crowd shares, an electronic mass sacrifice, and I let myself get swept up in it.

Sitting there in my new and false skin, sitting there halfway between my old nightmare and a new one, maybe sensing I'm going to be a part of all this, I get free of my troubles. I get free and get into the music. I forget the cops and the woman who'll never have a face anymore. I forget the blood and the years of pain and faces that all say I am a stranger. The houses that are not my home, the things that are not mine, I forget them.

Here's a new world, a high-energy cave. No rules. No questions. Just a dance with the high amplified gods of rhythm. I'm sold. I've heard it all before but never as a place to go. Somehow it all seems terribly important now like it never did before.

Russ taps me on the shoulder. "If these assholes

could learn to stay in tune, they might amount to something someday. You know that?"

"Huh?" If what I heard wasn't in tune, I'll be the last to know it. I know about music from nothing. Going to have to learn.

"Set's ending and the cops are leaving," says Russ, looking toward the back of the club over one shoulder. "I told you I'd get you through this mess. Fucking cops! I hate cops, man! I really hate their guts!"

Russ doesn't sound emotional about it. Sounds unconcerned. If it's hate, it's a cool kind, the uninvolved kind, like he would shoot a cop, but it's like, wow, you know, too much effort.

The band finishes the set with a riff like a hand grenade and the whole place comes apart, everyone drained, deadened from the neck up. The stonies stagger to their feet, brains blanked with music, eyes dull, faces flashing neon smiles and drug secrets.

Russ and I stand up and head for the backstage area. "Now that the piggies are gone, you can get out of that dress and into something, you know, more your own speed, if you know what I mean."

I tugged at the dress where it bulged around my breastlessness. "I know what you mean."

The guys from the band are sprawled around in the equipment room, halfway between coma and conversation. Spence is wrapped around a little groupie with pool-cue eyes and breasts like molehills that unkind genes have made mountains out of. There are little ladies all over the place. The guy who stripped for me is sitting quietly in the corner, playing with himself. Nobody pays him any attention.

Chris is sitting on the couch, nibbling in a bored fashion on a fat girl with heavy earrings that probably weigh more than Chris does. He looks like a guppie hitching a ride on a shark.

The air is thick with dope smoke. One of the chicks is doing up some cocaine from a paper plate, plastic straw up one nostril. She is making vacuum cleaner sounds, nosebleed greedy.

Spence looks up at me as I come in. He looks me up and down, as if inspecting me for termites or something. "What a drag!" he says.

"Does he ever run out of material?" I ask Russ, pissed off.

"Only when he's asleep," says Russ. "Ignore him. He thinks he's a musician and we have to humor him."

"I think I'm going to like working for you guys," I say. "I want to thank you all for saving me from the—"

"Don't go all gushy!" says Spence, pushing the girl off of him. She falls off the end of the bench and slams her stoned head against the floor. Spence pays no attention to her, stands up, almost stepping on her face. "We're taking you on 'cause we got a gig to get to, and if you work out, it's cool. We're only taking you 'cause we don't have much choice, you dig?"

One of the underfoot chicks comes up to me and shoves some clothes at me, castoffs from the band members. A little embarrassed, I start peeling out of my dress. Privacy is a luxury rock and roll can't afford.

"Still," I say, dropping the dress to the floor, "I'm glad that—"

The look on Spence's face stops me. Gratitude is the wrong song, I can see it in his face. "Forego the number, man," he says and turns and starts for the back door. "Follow me, man. We'll go outside, away from the hammerheads, and I'll put you in the picture, man. Straighten this out."

I turn and look at Russ, uncomfortable in clothes that don't quite fit me, nervous because I don't know all the rules yet. Russ motions me toward the door, gives me a wink. "Yeah. It's okay. It's cool, man. Stick with it."

Uneasy, afraid they are going to change their minds and not let me ride out of town with them, I follow along behind the giant body that is Spence. It's a little

like walking behind a tree. This is one big dude, no
mistake about it. I remind myself not to get into a
punch-out with him.

The back door opens and we stumble out into the
dark. The air outside is cool and soft with a clinging
mist, the rain softened into almost fog. The band truck
looms in front of us like a beached whale.

Spence leads us up to the back of the truck, swings
open the back door and then motions me up. "Get up
and get in there. I got something to show you."

I do as he says.

It's dark as anything inside, can't see a frigging thing.
I stumble against something lying on the floor. Whatever it is, it groans.

The truck shakes as Spence jumps up in back. I hear
him fumbling around in the dark and then a little light
flashes on. It's one of those small battery-operated jobs
and it's hooked to the wall of the truck.

There's a couple of cases of beer at Spence's feet. He
reaches down and grabs a couple of bottles. "Here,
man, have a beer. We just nicked them. The club ain't
gonna miss a few."

The beer streaks toward me and I drop it. My cut-up
hand is still wrapped with a cloth, making me a little
awkward. But the pain is gone, the bleeding stopped.
Almost forget I hurt it. The bottle lands on the floor
next to the body's head. I bend over, pick it up. Lucky
it didn't break. I don't say anything about the body,
don't even look at it too close. I figure that's why I'm
here but Spence'll tell me about it when he's ready.

Spence opens his beer and then hands me the church
key. I open my bottle with it and toss it back. The wall
light makes strange shadows on the sides of the truck.
The inside of the truck is like a badly lit sound stage in
a B movie.

Spence adjusts the light, moving it so the beam
points down at the body at our feet. He takes a long
swig at his beer. "Ya see this joker on the floor?"

"Hard to miss him. Is he dead?"

"So close to it, it doesn't matter," says Spence, and he drinks some more beer. "That fuckup on the floor is what's left of our driver."

I take a careful look at the body. I don't know who this guy was but there isn't much left of him now. Hair falling out, skin peeling, open sores on his face and neck. Yellow skin and glazed eyes. Saliva dribbles out of his mouth, rotted teeth show through a split lip. There's blood around his teeth and snot and blood crusting the right side of his face. Jesus!

The smell hits me then, excrement, sweat and stale urine, like no smell anyone wants to meet this side of hell. This guy is a self-inflicted concentration camp.

"The maggots would die on a body like that," says Spence, taking another slug of beer. He peels the label off the beer bottle with one finger, taking his time, thinking about it. He has his head turned away, keeping his nose away from the smell. "So we need a driver and that's you, okay?"

"I appreciate it that—"

"Stuff it up your giggy sideways!" says Spence. "Get it in your head we ain't doing you a favor. We don't do anybody favors. You're gonna drive for us, score dope for us, do a lot of donkey work for us." His voice is hard, exacting, edged in flint. "Do I lay it out clear?"

I nod. I understand. A trade for a trade. This is a transaction, nothing personal. "Real clear. I'm in." I drink some of my beer. Then did the next question I knew we had to do. "What do we do with him?"

Spence let the tiny bits of torn-up beer bottle label fall down on the body like snow. "Dump him in the alley before we load the truck. To the cops when they find him, he'll be just another junkie and they won't come looking for us."

"I understand. I'm still grateful. You guys saved my ass."

"Up to now. Me, I don't give a shit. Just get us to the gigs in one piece and don't fuck us up and you're covered. We'll get along real good."

"I'll help you drag his body out." I can feel my flesh crawl just thinking about touching that body.

"Yeah, I know you will," says Spence. "I'll get his feet and you get his arms. I hope we can get him out of here without puking ourselves to death."

We get hold of this stinking mess that used to be a human being and drag it to the back of the truck. We lower it as low to the ground as our arms will go, then drop it. The body flops on the pavement like a bag of dead fish.

I start to climb out of the truck but Spence grabs my arm and drags me back inside. He puts another beer in my hand and gets another for himself. We do the bottle-opening routine and we sit there in silence on the tailgate of the truck, him not saying anything and me waiting for him to.

"Tell me about the woman you wasted?" His interest sounds superficial, as if he is only making small talk.

I tell him how it happened. Spence cuts me off before I get too deep into it. "Far out! That's not murder. That's self-defense. Not that I give a shit one way or the other. Anyway, it's not important. Forget it!"

Not important! What is?

"It don't bother you?" Hard to believe anybody can be this uninvolved.

"Why should it? Man, you got a lot to learn. This is rock and roll, man! No rules! This is a world for dangerous dudes and hateful cats. Hard riders! Nobody bothers anybody else, because what goes around, comes around. You can do anything you can get away with! The harder you are, the more you get away with."

Now I understand. "Okay. You got a driver and I'm good at it."

"Underage?"

"Yeah, but Russ said—"

Spence waves it away. "No problem. I got maybe ten driver's licenses and we'll pick one that fits you. New name, new clothes, part your hair in the middle instead of the side, they'll never catch you." Spence tilts back his beer bottle and empties half of it down his throat. He wipes his mouth with the back of his hand, gives me a hard stare. "But we don't look out for you. You take care of yourself, understand?"

The guy has laid it all out cold. "Yeah. I read it loud and clear."

Spence tilts his beer bottle and dumps the rest of it on the body below us. "Here's to you, Jack! You stupid junkie bastard!"

Despite ten miles of tough, there's some sadness in Spence, buried miles deep. It's in his voice. "You know, Jack was my best friend, the dumb fucker! Well, I hope you hang in there better than that shit head did!" He throws the bottle angrily and it smashes against the back of the building.

The lesson is clear. In the rock and roll world, you also got the right to kill yourself and nobody has to care. Nobody is indispensable. If you get knocked out of the ring, there's any number of faces that can take your place, and nobody will mourn you.

Spence jumps off the truck. "Let's drag him over against the building and then you hustle in and help get this frigging truck loaded."

We lay the body against the building, next to the place where they haul out the trash. Spence and I put him there and don't say another word. It's all been said. Spence goes out and crawls into the back of the truck to begin working on a big drunk.

I go back inside, uncomfortable in the borrowed clothes that don't fit me but at least are the right sex. Inside it's a sexual circus without a proper place to happen. Nobody says anything about the guy I am replacing. It is a secret everybody knows. If there is any pain, they hide it by a frantic scrabble for drugs and little ladies. They are all dancing desperately and nobody looks in anybody else's eyes.

We load the equipment, Russ and I, getting it all

stowed away in the truck. Nobody else is in any shape to help.

The truck fills up quick. We are ready for the road.

Randall, the bass player, a straight cat who seems to belong to some other band and maybe some other planet, split hours ago, driving his own car to the next gig. Mick, too drunk to move, lies among the guitar cases in the back of the truck. Chris, so stoned he could exhale on someone and get them stoned, is crashing out in the back of the truck. Spence sits next to me in the cab of the truck, half drunk and completely wrecked on electrics, fruitcake-eyed. Russ is in the back with two groupies who promise him a trip through their own version of the funhouse.

I'm feeling pretty good, all things considered. Hand bandaged and a Benzedrine to keep me awake for the flight. The Benzedrine keeps me from thinking about thinking.

The truck's full of dope, all and every kind. There isn't a sane person in the bunch. I've got a fake I.D. in my pocket and a new name from people who haven't even bothered to learn my real one. Or maybe it's like I never had a real name and my new name is as real as any I'll ever have or get.

The engine turns over and I pull out, leaving the cops behind, leaving behind the world that hadn't ever been mine. I aim the truck down the dark streets, entering a new American night.

"Speed up!" says Spence, banging the dashboard in time to the music only he hears. "Man, you ain't even up to illegal yet!"

My foot finds the accelerator and I bang it to the floor, exhilarated by the speed in me and by my escape into the night. The truck surges ahead, roaring through the nightland.

I see my face in the rearview mirror. It hasn't changed. I am the same dark-eyed stranger I have always been. The only difference is inside. I'm thinking maybe this is the place where I belong. I don't have to

be a human being. People are going to let me alone.
This is rock and roll. This is where all the people go
who can't make it in the outside world, all the desperate ones. People like me. The hungry, hurting ones
who swallow people with their eyes and leave, still
hungry.

The truck thunders down the freeway, rain glistening like diamonds on the windshield.

"Do you know what this is?" cries Spence, cradling
an invisible guitar in his arms, tearing off a mad solo to
throw at the dark. "Do you know what this is?"

My eyes are on the road ahead. I never look back.

I don't have to ask him what it is, 'cause I already
know.

"*This is a freak show on the endless Highway of
Night!*" shouts Spence and he thrusts his imaginary
guitar toward the windshield as if impaling a dream.

And that was what I already knew.

CHAPTER 10

I'd lay back down under the bush and go right back to sleep but I don't know if I can trust that poodle. I suspect the little bugger is lurking out there waiting for me somewhere.

Man, I am tired. I am partied out. I been out on the street too long. I'm hurt and bruised and generally mangled.

So maybe it's time to go back to Tamara, the girl who lets me hide in her world for a while, to Tamara the fair and beautiful one who's made the mistake of falling in love with me.

Tamara.

Walking down some street, trying to get oriented. Don't even know where I am. But then, when do I ever?

Get out to a major street, I know I can put my thumb out and hitchhike back to her.

I guess maybe it's time to check back in, to go back to Tamara and the secret, almost human self I sometimes am and try not to be. My clothes reek of strange girls. I feel like I've traveled a faithless million miles across the cold asphalt heart of L.A.

The cars go whizzing by like angry soldiers. I got the taste of cop cars and all-night bars in my mouth.

She'll be waiting for me.

Tamara.

"I love you," she'll say, not having seen me in who knows how long. "I missed you." And I'll look at her, amazed every time, wanting to think she's so stupid I should laugh at her, but there's something fragile and unlaughable about perfect trust.

You feel like screaming at her, "Can't you see me for what I am!" because she gets to you somehow, and you can almost feel the heart you don't have breaking.

Tamara.

If I had someplace else to go, I'd go there instead.

But I don't.

Finally I get a ride that takes me to her.

CHAPTER 11

Looking in the refrigerator, I can see that I've been gone so long, everything's turned into a science fair project. Even the mold is growing mold. It's time to get on her case.

"Hey, what have you been eating? Don't you ever eat anything out of here? You got to stop eating in restaurants! Have you seen this refrigerator?"

Her voice comes from the bedroom. It's a voice easy to listen to, as if it had a smile in it somewhere.

"Forget it. I'll go to the store later. Come back to bed. I miss you and I'm glad you're back." If she had her way, she'd spend her days just holding me, just touching me.

"I'm hungry!" My ribs are shaking hands with each other it's been so long since I ate anything that even looks like food.

She comes out of the bedroom, wearing a white sheet and nothing else. Some of the good parts of her are sticking out. She's got lots of good parts. Sometimes I forget how good-looking she is. Makes me wonder sometimes why I've sold myself on the idea I like waking up with strangers, not knowing where I am. That I like not knowing the names of those blond, blue-eyed girls who all begin to blur together after a while. That I like just touching skin and going no deeper.

She's even good-looking all rumpled from sleep and lovemaking. Tamara rubs her eyes sleepily.

She puts her arms around me from behind.

"I'll make you some Cream of Wheat."

"I'd rather die first."

"You already almost did that," she says, putting her head on my shoulder as I stand there, poking around in the refrigerator. She'd cried when she first saw me, saw how I had got all banged up. She couldn't stand to see anybody get hurt.

"How about oatmeal?"

"God forbid!"

"Tapioca pudding?"

"Listen! I got teeth. I can chew. My doctor lets me eat solid food."

"How about strawberry shortcake?" she says, kissing me on the neck.

"Christ! How about some meat? You've probably heard of it. You can find it in all the stores!"

I end up with cornflakes. Stale cornflakes.

That's probably the only thing she can cook.

"How could somebody so good in bed be so bad in the kitchen?" I ask her. She kisses me, making me choke on a mouthful of cornflakes.

"Not when . . . ulp . . . my mouth is full," I gasp, red-faced from choking.

"Let's go back to bed," she says, just a big soft fuzzy animal that wants to be cuddled.

She was really falling out of her sheet.

"Didn't we do that already?" I say.

"Practice makes perfect," she says.

"You don't need any practice."

She laughs, very much in love.

I've been living with her about nine weeks now. Pretty Tamara with the honey-blond hair and big eyes that trust the world too much, eyes as pretty as her name. She loves me in a frightening all-surrendered way and I, in turn, let her pay the rent.

I try to keep her at arm's length as much as possible, which isn't too possible. I don't think it ever occurs to me that maybe I ought to love her back instead of just pretending to.

I eat so many cornflakes that my cheeks are bulging. It looks like I am storing them in my cheeks for the winter.

"You're falling out of your sheet."

"The better to attract you with," she says, laughing.

"It's very distracting. You better go put some clothes on before I lose control and attack you."

"So attack me." She gives me her impression of Mae West, thrusting out her hips. More of her falls out of her sheet.

"My lap is falling in love with you."

There's a gleam in her eyes. "You better finish your cornflakes. You'll need all your strength."

I reach out and grab her.

"Hey! Watch it! Those are attached!"

"Me too." And I pull her off her chair. We end up on the floor, rolling around passionately under the kitchen table.

She tries to push me off. "Not in the kitchen! Jesus!"

"Bonzai!" I yell, not letting her push me off.

She puts her hands on my chest, heaves hard and

pushes me off, losing the sheet altogether in the process. "Let's go into the bedroom," she says, shivering without the sheet.

"You can't get there from here," I tell her, then I'm all over her. We roll around under the table, having fun, both trying to get on top and having a terrifically interesting struggle to occupy the same space simultaneously.

It's just getting really interesting when there's a knock on the door. Then the doorbell rings.

She looks at me, eyes opening wide. "Oh, damn! I forgot!"

I look at the front door, pants at half mast. "Forgot what?"

"My parents! They said they were coming over today! That must be them now!"

"Terrific!" I'm struggling to get my pants back on and stand up at the same time.

"They're only going to stay an hour," she says and I can't remember when I've ever seen anyone who looks unhappier than she does at that moment. She has reason to be.

"Give me some money. I'll go to the store. I'll get some meat and stuff. I'll be back in a couple of hours. Soon as they've left."

She looks so lonely. "Promise you'll come back?"

"Promise." I give her a hug. I'd be back. I was too messed up to enjoy knocking around on the street, least not for a couple of days anyway.

"There's money in the cookie jar," she says, rushing to the front door, calling out, "Just a minute!" She scoots to the bedroom to throw on some clothes.

I go out the back way. I had met her parents once before and once was enough.

Tamara's mother is a forty-five-year-old alcoholic who dresses like twenty-five and looks like forty-five. She is a real bed crawler, although how she finds anyone willing to let her crawl in with him is a mystery to almost everyone. Tamara's father is an ex-professional football player with bad knees who now does all his scrimmaging at home. By that I mean he works his wife over pretty regularly. Hardly a month goes by without him giving her a pretty thorough beating. It was that kind of marriage.

And to make the chain complete, Tamara's mother used to beat up Tamara when Tamara was still living with them. Never with any reason to it, the beatings were just sort of on general principle.

They were that kind of people.

But Tamara wasn't. Tamara never hurt anyone in her life. You have to wonder how someone that good can come out of an environment that bad. Maybe it is her way of defending herself. Being good to spite the bad, being decent and trusting and capable of love in the face of the opposites of all those things. She was like that so she wouldn't be like them.

She'd left them when she was sixteen. Got a job and put herself through high school. She was eighteen when I met her, a golden, wistful eighteen. Working as a waitress during the day and going to junior college at night, trying to make something out of herself.

A true innocent. A beautiful girl who'd never really had the time to be beautiful. An eighteen-year-old virgin when I met her, an eighteen-year-old ache, aching to be loved.

I had no business even being around a girl like that and I knew it. I was fifteen and too clever. I was just the face that shows no pain. The lord, the master manipulator who enjoyed tugging the strings to see the pretty puppet dance.

She danced for me and for me only, while I, faithless, drifted through L.A. summer days tied together with drugs and strange girls that went bang in the night.

And even though I was often gone, often moving through L.A.'s unending party where strangers came together to remain strangers, she'd always be there, with her heart in her hand, waiting for me whenever I remembered to come back. She trusted in the least trustworthy of them all.

On the way to the store I've got time to think about Tamara. Sometime I wish I could explain everything to her, that I could simply let her go.

When I walk in the door, having been gone too long, and she's there and it's "I love you" and she puts her face against my neck and cries and her arms tighten around my back as if she were embracing all of creation, as if she loved the whole world, it's then I most want to tell her, to set her free. Somehow I never do it.

And she never sees me for what I am, for what I'm trying to become—a machine that tries not to think too much, tries not to feel too much. A machine that is a face with nothing behind it.

I'm paying for a steak at the supermarket. I hand over the money from Tamara's cookie jar and say to the blond girl behind the register, "Why does everybody got to be in love?"

She looks at me, steak blood dripping from the corner of the package in her hand.

"That's three ninety-eight," she says, putting the steak in a bag. "Did you know your pants are unzipped?"

I look down at my crotch. She's right.

And it's the best answer to that question I've ever heard.

CHAPTER 12

It's a new morning and some of the summer has gone by since the day I woke up under a bush to find Morrison had disappeared while I slept. Vanished in the heat of an L.A. summer day.

Not that I had been surprised to find him gone. Exits and entrances are a way of life.

But I didn't figure I'd ever run into him again. I was wrong. We kept colliding.

As if for a while we both rode the same snake to the ancient sacrificial lake. And there were days set aside by our own personal shaman for us to meet and run together for a little while.

This is one of the shaman's days, even though it doesn't begin like one.

I find myself back on the beach, having fled Tamara's snug harbor again, broke again, tired of living off the little girl that loved me too much. I'm out on the hot sand, trying to sell some righteous acid.

I know it's going to be one of those days because practically the first thing I flash on is an undercover cop trying for a drug bust. A real play-pretend fool in cutoff shorts, bared white chest and wire-rim glasses that don't fit his face very well. He's got an immaculate pimp hat, fresh off the rack, holding down his blond wig, which doesn't match his dark black unshaven chin whiskers. He hasn't shaved in about three days and thinks he fits right in.

"Like wow, man," he says, coming up to me. "What's happening?"

You can see the marks on his body where his cop suit keeps him from getting a tan. Well-tanned neck, face and hands, but white everywhere else.

"The beach is happening, babycakes! Like everyone is here, you dig?" I find myself saying, wondering if anybody really talks like that. Probably only in a Frankie Avalon movie.

"Like I can dig it," he says. "Sure is a groooooooovey day! I'm really digging up the vibrations!" He smiles like he's afraid his face is gonna break.

The idiot. He means "digging on" not "digging up." This guy stands out like a pregnant whore in an all-male police lineup.

"Hey, man! I want to cop some acid, man," he says, nodding his head as if he just said something so cool his face is gonna freeze.

"No shit! You want acid?"

His eyes flash and he pretends to be furtive, faking a dose of paranoia. The only emotion he's really managing to get across is probably constipation.

"What you want? A hundred thousand hits? Ten thousand?" I ask, enjoying the game.

Actually I got maybe ten hits of acid. Real big-time dealing! Got it buried beneath my towel in the sand in an old aspirin bottle.

"I can handle all you got, man. I want to cop heavy, man!" This guy is jumping like a fish, thinking he's just run into the big bust of the century.

Time to put a permanent crease in his ambitions. "What kind of acid do you want? You want it untabbed? Blotter? Cube? Windowpanes? Strawberry tabs? Owsley? Grosse Point sugar lab? I mean specifically, what kind of acid are you looking for?"

He looks confused, like I suddenly started talking Martian.

"Uh, whatever you got."

"Shit! Don't you know what kind you want?"

"Sure, man." He looks defensive, licks his lips nervously, afraid he's going to blow it. "But you know, um, it don't, um, matter to me. Um, I'll take whatever I can get."

I look this guy over from head to toe. What a frigging motorhead!

This human zero has got the whitest-looking feet I've ever seen. Probably the dye from his white socks has soaked into his skin.

"Well, shit! I don't sell to just *anybody*, you know!"

"Hey, man! I'm cool!" He looks frightened. Afraid he's blown it.

"I never seen you before. Where you from?"

"Uh, San Fern . . . Francisco. San Francisco," he says.

"No shit! That's a heavy place up there. You probably know White Rabbit and Frenzy. You ever cop from them up there?"

Now he's sweating. Doesn't know if I'm testing him or not. Thinks maybe it's a trick question.

"Sure. I think I got stuff from them once. I don't really remember. I buy a lot of shit, you know, man."

"Far out! Well, you look okay to me. If you got the coin, maybe you and I can do some heavy dealing."

He lights up like a two-hundred-dollar drinking

spree. "Hey, man! No sweat! I'm loaded!" He pats the pocket of his cutoff blue jeans. "Cash on the barrel head."

"Course"—I have to tease him a little, keep him off balance—"you know you asked me for the acid, so that's entrapment, so it's cool if you're a cop."

"Me a cop!" He tries to pretend he's shocked at the idea. Actually I think he's scared shitless.

"Course lots of cops pretend like they never asked, then it's just my word against theirs. When I deliver the acid, my ass is gone!"

"Hey, man! I'm cool. I can't stand pigs!"

I smile at him, reassure him. "So okay. You got vibrations that tell me you are an okay dude, so we'll do some dealing. We'll start small to get the feel of it and then take it from there. That okay with you?"

"I'm with you all the way."

"How about ten thousand hits of salicylic acid?"

"Far out! Groovey!" This jerk's ready to flip his wig, already seeing his name in the newspaper.

I hold up my hand. "Oh, shit! Wait a minute! I just remembered. I can't leave the beach. Got to meet a connection, one of my bosses. I can't leave the beach and there's a big shipment of salicylic acid coming into town today."

I tug on my chin, pretending to think (like I almost always have to). "Hey man! Maybe you can do me a favor and get yourself a big discount in the process!"

"Anything! I'll do anything!"

"How would you like to pick up a batch of acid for me? Direct from my supplier?"

"It sounds great!" This guy's so thrilled he's practically pissing himself. "Wow! Sure! I'd be glad to!"

"I'll throw in an extra thousand hits of salicylic acid. Does that sound good, just for doing me this little favor?"

He nodds frantically.

"Ordinarily, I'd be worried about maybe you'd try to

rip me off, but you'd be dealing with my bosses and nobody rips them off! You wanna know why?"

"Uh, why?"

" 'Cause they are the Syndicate and people who rip them off end up wearing concrete life preservers underwater."

"Holy fucking shit!" says the cop, turning pale, his hands shaking. He looks like he is gonna be sick all over me. Busting hippies on the beach is one thing but shaking down the Syndicate is something altogether different. He looks like he wishes he'd stayed home and played with himself.

"You got a car?"

"Uh?" Now he panics again. Sure he's got a car. Only it's got cop car plates on it and probably a couple of cops waiting in it, the rest of the undercover team he's working with.

"Good. I'll give you the address and you go pick up my stuff for me. They front it to me, so you don't have to give them any money. Bring it back here. I'll give you eleven thousand hits for the price of ten and we're in business!"

"That's, uh, great." He doesn't look too enthusiastic. Then he remembers he's supposed to be playing a role and falls back into it. "Far out, man!"

"Okay, you go west on Crenshaw Boulevard. You know where that is?"

He nods, pretending to be eager. He seems to be thinking this whole thing over. He gets over being scared. Begins imagining what it'll be like to crack the biggest drug ring in history. I can see it in his face. His eyes are practically strutting in their sockets. He's Tarzan. From the neck up.

"There's a drugstore. Thrifty Drugs. You can't miss it. It's next to Bozo's Burrito King."

"Thrifty Boulevard. Crenshaw drugs," he says, concentrating.

"You got it backwards, asshole!"

Embarrassed, he has to ask for the directions again.

"Go to Thrifty Drugs on Crenshaw Boulevard. You got it this time?"

"Thrifty Drugs. Crenshaw Boulevard. Check," he says, so frigging dumb he's answering me with radio cop car signals.

"Go in and ask the clerk for fifty thousand hits of salicylic acid. Mention my name. Say Fogface sent you. They'll give it to you."

"I'm on my way," he says and I wonder how the guy manages to be bright enough to keep himself from saying ten-four as he finishes the sentence.

"Oh, yeah. I forgot to tell you," I say, stopping him as he starts scooting away, "salicylic acid is the active ingredient in aspirin."

"What?"

"Aspirin. Yeah. See I like to take aspirin because talking to cops gives me a real bad headache."

He drops his pose, forgetting everything, coming after me, mad as hell.

"You son of a bitch! I'm going to—"

I jump to my feet, back pedaling quickly, moving away from him. The beach all around is full of druggies, stoned-out bodies getting a little sun. I sidestep and the human bull goes charging past me like a bad scene from a Mexican bullfight movie.

"Hey, everybody!" I yell as loud as I can. Everybody stops what they're doing, looks in my direction. *"This is a cop! He wants to buy some dope!"*

The cop stops advancing on me, turns and sees all the hostile faces suddenly staring at him. He looks scared enough to melt into one big piss.

While his head is turned, I see my chance and go for him. With one yank his wig pops off, revealing a real short police academy haircut.

"Let's go play with the piggie!" shouts a big black dude, and he and about a dozen of his friends start coming over to us.

"Oink, oink!" shouts somebody in the crowd gathering around us. The crowd swells until it becomes a full-fledged mob. A lot of outraged druggies have come to give the cop a real toasting.

The cop is so scared he looks like he's going to have puppies. He's only outnumbered about two hundred to one.

The cop starts backing away, getting ready to run for his miserable life, only there's no place to run to. His backward progress is halted by the chest of a massive black dealer from San Diego, a really vicious dude with very little love for cops, or for anybody for that matter.

Somebody is going to get his rear end sandblasted and the cop is the boy most likely.

Two fat guys in suits come barreling out of the beach parking lot. Guns out and everything. Hot, sweaty, overweight guys in Sears and Roebuck suits. They don't look very happy. Their undercover man is surrounded by about a hundred very unhappy druggies who look mean enough to roll him up in a *Time* magazine cover and smoke him.

With only two guns I pity them. Better they should come back with a bazooka and a flamethrower.

I pick up my towel and dig up my ten hits of acid. Time for me to melt into the background. You can't sell LSD during a riot. The vibrations get too messed up.

Somebody strikes me on the shoulder. I turn around.

Morrison's there with a blond girl in a bikini that's giving her a tan almost everywhere. She's also got a very beautiful everywhere.

Morrison says, "I don't see what you see. I see what I see. My eyes are my body. The ability to see is a viral infection. Do you have the cure?"

"What?" Oh no. He isn't gonna start a lot of crazy shit again, is he?

"Druuuuuuuuuuuuggggggsssssss." He drawls the word out theatrically, as if it were a long sentence.

"Oh." Now I understand. He's noticing the aspirin bottle in my hand and wants some bottled electricity.

Why is it I never meet people who want to buy drugs from me? Just people I want to give drugs to? There is no justice in the world.

"Sure. I got some acid. But let's get out of here. It's gonna be a riot or something."

"Oh, yeah," says Morrison, looking at the crowd, seeming interested. "I could really get into a little insurrection, you know."

The girl looks bored. "What's it all about?"

I shrug. "I started it but I forget what it's all about. Probably a child molester humped a St. Bernard or something. It's not all that interesting. Let's split."

We move on down the beach, leaving the riot to riot on its own, without our help.

We find a nice spot in the sun and tuck ourselves away. I find myself passing out, Santa Claus fashion, three free tabs of acid. One for him, one for her and one for me. Pray, who is the potter and who the pot?

I'm not really sure I'm ready for this. I've only had about ten days to recover from the last journey I made with Morrison. I'm not much more than one of the walking wounded still.

The pills find our tongues and go down and discover our bellies, to explode electrically within us.

"Well, there goes the weekend," I say.

"How heavy is this stuff?" asks the girl. Her name's Deirdre and it fits her. She hasn't got an inch of ugly on her anywhere. I can hardly keep my eyes off of her, which Morrison notices with some amusement. Guess he's bored with her already.

"Well, it's really kinda weird stuff," I answer. "It's moderately heavy but whoever tabbed it was a little bit too loose. It could be like a two-way hit or like half of one or like eight shopping days till Armageddon. All I know is sometimes it takes an hour or more for it to get you, but when you get off, you really know you are off."

"I never approved of the trial-and-error method. I wish I hadn't taken that pill," says Deirdre, but she doesn't look overly worried.

Morrison stretches out on his back, watching the clouds. That seems like a good way to jump off so I get on my back beside him.

"What are you guys, queers?" says Deirdre. "Move over." She gets between us, shoving on our shoulders, clearing a space between us for her to lie down.

We sprawl out in the sun like three lazy sea lions, waiting for something magical to happen.

The sun feels good on my body and I feel Deirdre, feel her soft shoulder brushing against mine. Her skin's like velvet warmed by a fire. I love being touched by beautiful women, love having them near me even if they aren't mine to touch.

"What do you see when you see Los Angeles?" asks Jim of no one in particular.

"A city," says Deirdre.

Morrison shakes his head. "You see a city and your lips put that name to it. It is a *city.* . . . I see a severed insect mound."

"Why is it everything you say sounds like you are writing it?" I have to ask that.

" 'Cause writing fascinates me. You can do so many things with words. People who put them in the right order or disorder can conquer the world."

"So let's write something," I suggest.

We scramble for paper, using anything we can find, digging up a battered ball-point pen. Deirdre doesn't join in.

"What a drag," she says. "Writing. Books. Reading. School, etcetera! What a drag!"

"Ignore her," says Morrison. "She's only interested in cheap thrills. But as for us, let us suppose a journey, let us bring forth one of the diseased creatures from a dollar hotel. Let us bring him forth and send him to the edge of the City where he shall discover muddied dreams and zones of sophisticated boredom. We will point the eyes of the City through his eyes and we shall hear L.A., the biggest bitch-goddess City in the world, we shall hear the bitch speak and it will say: *Look where we worship.*"

Scribbling furiously on scraps of paper, paper sacks, I say, "I'll write it all down so we can be sure to lose it all later on."

And this is the first of a few shaman's days that we will write madly in the sun, purposely and to no point. An exercise in futility. The things we wrote created no keys that would unlock doors.

For we ourselves are the diseased creatures from the dollar hotel. We have only words, and as we use them, we predict the future. Cancel our subscription to the *Resurrection!* We predict the future.

We know what the future is.

John F. Kennedy was young in Dallas, Texas.

Just once.

And so are we.

Two fantasies disguised as human who see the future, in one of those strange alchemical happenings, and blindly seek some kind of release bigger than ourselves.

"I have seen the future and I won't go," says Morrison, hunched over the scrap of paper covered with our false words.

"Yeah," I agree. "The future is crazy dancing."

"You touch your crotch and it's a dance without music. You touch some stranger and it's music without a dance."

Morrison stares at the sky as if he sees the words up there somewhere.

"And we all look for our assassins and we say one thing but mean, probably at the back of it all, *We want to be loved.* So bury us in empty swimming pools! Bury us in empty swimming pools because we want to make love to the world and die in a place that has our name on it where no one can touch us or take our name away."

And the day explodes, rocketing into a long shamanistic shared journey. Words tumble out as we write furiously, thrown together accidentally by the summer. Putting it all down on paper. Future scribbled hastily in the heat of our John F. Kennedy youth. Poems meant never to be heard except in the dark side of our lives. Stories of the yet-to-happen, fantasies that bleed and offer no comfort.

The future has been to the barricades too many times. The future has been up against the wall so many times that the handwriting on the wall is now on the future. It is on us.

We see our own deaths and the deaths of those around us.

I say to you children
Learn to close the door
Softly
Murderously
Learn to close the door
To the room
You do not return to
You must not hope to arrive
Without exile

The future is a world that trys to live without the engine of the heart (writes Morrison).

And we, being young only once, see it, for we see an enormous string attached to the puppets of the world. The string stretches out undiminished before us like a fat man climbing a light year.

And the string is the future and we cannot help but see it.

The string.

In Germany, the string begins, the string continues, passing through a large oven, as big as a house, that reeks faintly of gas. The string is coiled around a factory that makes walls in Berlin.

In America, the string ties itself into colored words that say, "You can't eat here. You can't sleep here. You can't marry my sister."

In Canada, the string is woven up in Tuberculosis-infected blankets that the Hudson Bay Company passes out to Indians.

In the courts of the land, the string is a lynch rope that keeps the mice from seeing the cat.

In South America, the string is a highway that mows down the grass that hides tiny statues made out of wind and night. In South America, the string is a ribbon that rich people cut that lets the first car drive across the broken bodies of dying animals, dying dreams.

In Spain, the string is a cure for venereal disease the natives call the INQUISITION. Everyone the string touches is ultimately cured when the grass grows back over their bodies.

In Florida, the string is a roll of tickets to the alligator farm where the last of the Seminoles lives off tips tourists give him, when he puts his head inside the alligator's jaws. He puts his head inside and prays the alligator will swallow.

How can we not see the string?

In Nebraska, the string is a rosary a Catholic priest ties to a dead Indian baby. In Nebraska, the string is a rosary that builds two churches for every Indian child, with the financial support of a God who ultimately says, "I can't see your face in my mind."

Stretched before us are the visual puppets of the future, a world gone mad, dancing on string.

And the string colors all that we see, all that we pretend to feel.

And the string touches all things. Beauty and death and hate and love are all knots on the endless surface of the string. All of it is there from the cruelty of children to the kindness of men who kill cattle with hammers in slaughterhouses.

And I write:

You and I, and those who run with us, all of us who run, soon to be dead.

Dead.
I am a killer on the highway of an L.A. night. I want
to hold beautiful girls in my arms, and when I touch
them, my hands will touch them the way a sniper ca-
resses the trigger.

"I'm bored."
The writing is stopped, wiped out as the drugs get
too intense.
"I'm bored," says Deirdre again, putting her hand on
the inside of my leg. Her hand is like a tarantula, a sen-
suous, many-legged rush, lighting a fire under my skin.
Morrison is bored of her being bored.
"You're the girl with the graveyard heart."
"I'm the girl who's sick of this writing bullshit. Po-
etry is for faggots."
"Faggots are for faggots," says Morrison, not looking
at her.
Her fingernails drag across my skin. "Let's go some-
place else," she says.
"Call your broom," says Morrison, sounding bitter.
"Fly us out of here, witch bitch."
"Fuck you," she says, putting one leg on top of mine.
I am too uncomfortable in my too-tight bathing suit.
Morrison gets up. "You gonna jump his bones right
here on the beach?"
"What do you care?" she says.
"I don't," says Morrison. "What a bring-down you
are. Let's go someplace that fits your personality."
"Like a racetrack," I say, moving my leg out from
under hers. I stand up, head aswim in the summer and
in LSD.
We are all gloriously wrecked. But bummed out with
each other's vibrations. This heavy sexual tension be-
tween us, driving us apart. Ugly situation.
Sun's going down. Soon be dark. Getting cold. Time
to be moving on anyway.
"Let's go to a cemetery. Let's invoke the dead," says
Morrison. "I want her to feel comfortable. She should
be with her own kind."

I stand up too, and pull on my pants and shirt. I'm game for anything, anywhere.

"How we gonna get there?" I stare at them, wondering if they are going to punch each other out or something ridiculous like that. "I don't have a car, and even if I did, I wouldn't trust any of us to walk, let alone drive."

"I'll go call a taxi when I go in to change," says Deirdre, gathering up her stuff. She picks up the bottle of suntan lotion that had made my hands sticky when I spread it on her golden brown body.

My blue jeans made me ache. Their tightness pressing on the hard lump that had grown when I spread the oil on her back and legs made walking no fun.

Deirdre is the kind of girl who knows what she does to those who touch her, to those who see her, and she likes it all. She is always touching everyone, promising, enticing. She likes being in a place where everyone pants.

Morrison doesn't like her very much.

"You should open up a dog kennel in the tropics," says Morrison, pulling his shirt on over his head.

"What?" She just stares at him.

"Seeing how much you like making tongues hang out with lust, a lot of overheated dogs would make you feel loved."

She stalks off to find someplace to change her clothes.

Mad as hell.

"Why do you keep picking on her?"

" 'Cause she's a bitch."

"Yeah. But what a bitch!" She's got me half crazy with desire.

"We'll let her get a taxi," says Morrison, in some drug world of his own. "Take us where we want to go, then we'll scare the shit out of her."

I don't say anything. It's his trip. I'm just along for the ride, even if I am getting scorched by some of the heat.

"Who's gonna pay for the taxi? Me, I'm broke."

"She'll pay for it," says Morrison. "She's rich. She'll buy us anything we want as long as it's something we don't really need."

The sun is a burning ocean, dreaming itself into a drug night. Our eyes have been in the sky all day, lifted there by an acid river that runs our heads.

"It's all so beautiful," says Morrison, looking at sunset-washed sky.

"Yeah."

Morrison's the only one really in control. I am drifting. So I ask him, as we sit there waiting, "When the taxi comes to get us, where is it that we want to go?"

"To a graveyard," he says, standing there in some wicked mask of his own devising. "I'm going to teach that bitch how to give birth to her heart."

I shuddered, feeling an icy wind coming from him, cold enough and dark enough to freeze my insides.

The night is going to be very dark and I am glad I am not her. She travels with two diseased creatures from a dollar hotel. She rides with two dark walkers from the nightlands.

And we ourselves are not kind.

CHAPTER 13

It's an ugly acid high, taken to the limit by a tension as deep as sex and as lasting as death.

Down on the beach Morrison, Deirdre and I are not hoping to arrive without exile. Deirdre, all golden girl in the summer, all dressed up with no place to go, has dialed us a chariot.

"Here it comes," she says, her soul on vacation, her mind all at sea and her eyes on the parking lot. "He took his own sweet time getting here, didn't he?"

A yellow taxicab pulls into the parking lot. It stops a little ways from us and the driver eyes us suspiciously.

We stumble inside the taxi's womb and settle back against the smelly seats, acid beginning to steal the world from us.

"Driver, where are you taking us?" whispers Morrison under his breath, in some drug underworld of his own choosing.

"Where do we want to go?" asks Deirdre, acting as if she's bored by wherever it is already. Her journey into electricity is a cold one. She's the first person I ever met who could be bored while tripping.

"Hey, driver! Do you know any nice graveyards?" asks Morrison. "Maybe in some secluded deserted reservation of the heart somewhere?" Morrison sounds like a killer in a bad movie, as if half of his mouth is wired shut.

The driver tips his cap back on his head and stares back at us in his rearview mirror.

"Fruitcakes!" he says, thinking out loud. "Why do I always get the fruitcakes?"

"You watch your mouth driver!" says Deirdre.

"Sorry," says the driver, not meaning it. "I didn't mean nothing personal. Where you kids want to go?"

"Let's just drive around," says Deirdre. "We'll figure it out on the way."

The driver turns around in his seat, gives us the ice-age-once-over with his eyes. "Cabs ain't cheap, you know. Takes money to go joyriding. You sure you kids got—"

Deirdre interrupts his sentence by pulling out a roll of big bills from her purse. Must be all of eight hundred bucks there and the driver opens his eyes so wide they almost fly off the top of his head.

"Here we go," he says, watching Deirdre put the money back in her purse, licking his lips. A simple soul with basic greed. He would take us to a speakeasy in hell if we had the fare.

"You want I should drive into L.A.?" asks the driver, heading there with the cab already.

"In search of ancient aphrodisiacs," says Morrison.

The driver shrugs, not understanding a single thing
Morrison's said so far, aiming the cab toward L.A. anyway.

Deirdre yawns, bored. "Nothing ever happens. Even
my hallucinations are repetitive."

Morrison laughs at her, as Santa Monica flies by the
cab windows. "That's because your breach of promise
is mixed with sunshine when you say goodbye," he
says, still living on some other planet.

Deirdre blinks, not understanding.

"What are you talking about?" she asks. "You sound
like a frigging four-year-old!"

"When you die and they make a movie of your life,"
says Morrison, "Annette Funicello will play you in the
movie."

"Well, fuck you too," she says.

"Peace," I say, wishing I wasn't sitting between
them.

"Rich girls," says Morrison. "Mentally you're always on the rag 'cause your parents are so fucking
rich."

"Wine!" I suggest, desperate for some kind of diversion. One thing I can't stand when I'm drugged up is a
lot of heavy personality sandblasting. I always get sand
in my eyes. "Let's all go get some wine! It'll mellow us
all out."

Everybody nods and I'm glad. This whole dialogue
has degenerated into a dream of Thanksgiving in steer-
age and who needs it.

"Find us a carry-out," I tell the driver.

"A what?" says the driver.

"Oh. I forgot. You don't call them that out here. Find
us a liquor store. We want to buy some booze."

We exit off some frigging freeway or other and soon
pull into the parking lot of a liquor store.

Morrison and I jump out. "I'll wait here," says
Deirdre.

"Money?" says Morrison, sticking his hand through

the cab window at her.

She shrugs, indifferent, hands him a couple of big bills.

Morrison and I go inside.

Walking up and down the aisles, watching the wine bottles in the cooler glowing with neon cold, Morrison and I become fellow conspirators in a Roman plot.

"We get cheap wine. Split up the money," says Morrison, handing me one of the bills she gave him. "Take what you can get when you can get it."

Morrison reaches into the cooler and starts handing out bottles. My arms quickly fill up. "Jesus! Who do you think we are? The whole frigging Seventh Cavalry! Custer with arrow drainage holes in him couldn't drink this much wine."

I'm ready to collapse under the weight of all the bottles he's handed me.

Morrison's got an armful too. We stagger up to the counter, dumping the bottles in front of the clerk, a skinny Mexican with knives for eyes.

"Having a party?" asks the Mexican, taking our money.

"A surprise autopsy," says Morrison, splitting up the change so that we each get half.

The Mexican shrugs. After all, why not?

We get back into the cab, with two big sacks of wine.

"He made a pass at me," says Deirdre, almost amused in spite of her professional boredom.

The driver fingers the rim of his battered cap nervously, afraid we're going to do something to him. The horny old goat.

"More power to him," says Morrison. "Maybe he's just what you need. He could mount you with his customary arthritic grace."

Relieved, the driver clears his throat nervously. "Uh, where to, from here?"

It's night now, came on us by surprise. I never even noticed it getting dark. Our taxi pulls out into a soft

dark tunnel that's lit by neon land mines on the buildings of L.A. We go cruising aimlessly past the bars and
other open sores.

Our driver's in his fifties. Red face from drinking too
much, half of a soggy cigar in one corner of his mouth,
racing forms on the dashboard. Heavy beard in need of
a shave, permanently bloodshot eyes.

Deirdre's got a short skirt on and short is an understatement. She puts one leg over mine, spreading her
legs, knowing the cab driver is looking. His eyes are
glued to the rearview mirror. The cigar falls out of his
mouth as he stares at her central goodie, struck dumb.

The cab swerves and we almost go up the ass end of a
parked car.

"Hey! Watch what you're doing!" says Morrison angrily, aware of what she's doing to the driver.

"Sorry," says the driver, sweating. Deirdre's got him
all hot and bothered. She has that effect intentionally
on almost everybody. Not that she's really interested
in the driver. She just likes prick teasing.

Morrison leans over and stares at Deirdre. "You
know something, Deirdre?"

"What?"

"If you don't get what you want, you better want
what you get."

Deirdre frowns. "What's that supposed to mean?"

"You'll find out," says Morrison, and coming from
him it's some kind of heavy, deep-down threat. He's
out for blood.

The tension in the cab is loosening my teeth. They
keep tearing at each other like wild dogs. Who needs
it?

"We ought to go someplace definite," I say, trying to
think of something definite for us to be thinking
about.

Morrison digs in the sacks, opening bottles of wine.
He starts handing them out like party favors.

"Hey! No drinking in the cab!" shouts the driver,
looking at us over his shoulder.

Deirdre lays a ten-dollar bill on his shoulder and he takes it, almost lovingly, as if she had rubbed it on her crotch first and he wants to savor its delicate aroma.

Morrison hands a bottle of wine forward, passing it to the driver. The driver scratches his chin, mulling it over in his mind. Finally, he shrugs, takes the bottle. "Be careful you don't drink none when you see a cop car going by," he says. He up-ends his bottle and takes a healthy slug. A third of the wine in the bottle is gone.

"You kids ain't so bad," he says, enjoying the wine and glancing to his right, seeing the amount already run up on the taxi meter. He's doing well tonight, very well, and getting to look at Deirdre's crotch is more than worth the price of admission. "Some of these young punks that get in my cab, I swear I could just puke. You know what I mean. I could really puke, you know. You wouldn't believe 'em."

"Yeah," says Morrison. "You could just puke."

Everybody's got their own wine bottle and we drift into it. The wine's just what we need. The cab streaks through the night, an island of warm, heated by wine, by inner electricity and a gradual loosening we all feel.

"It's drugs," says the cab driver. "These drugs, that's what it is. They get in my cab, marijuana addicts and heroin addicts and junkies of all shapes. I tell you I could just puke."

"He could just puke," says Morrison.

"I could tell you kids weren't addicts the minute I seen you. You kids are a little bit wise-asses but I don't take it personal, you know. See, I don't take it personal."

Deirdre yawned. "Why, that's ever so sweet of you."

"Anything for you, toots!" says the driver, waving his wine bottle magnanimously.

"He could just puke," says Morrison, drinking wine.

The taxi driver finishes his first bottle before I can do much more than taste mine. He lets go a little, gets very hail-fellow-well-met. "Say, I'm enjoying this!" he says. "Usually I'm hustling my ass out at the airport and my frigging fares want to go two blocks. This is all right! Yessireee!"

He points to his picture on the roof of the cab. "My name's Ralph," he says, waving the wine bottle.

"Who are you?" he asks, staring at Deirdre's tits in the rearview mirror.

"Max Ophuls," says Morrison, referring to himself. "Jean-Luc Godard." Now he means me. "And this," he says, squeezing one of her tits hard so that she jumps in her seat, "is sweet Deirdre, a former child star who made silent films for blind people."

"Pleased to meet you," says Ralph, saluting us with the wine bottle. "It's a pleasure to meet some nice young folks. I can tell just looking at you you aren't the kind to be taking drugs or smoking LSD!"

Morrison chokes on his wine, trying not to laugh, and sprays wine all over the back seat. He slumps forward, laughing and choking at the same time. I laugh a little myself. It is kind of funny when you think of it. When it comes to drugs, we three are the three most likely.

"Say, you want to hear a joke?" asks the driver.

"Oh, shit," says Deirdre. She's hitting her bottle hard. It's almost gone.

"Drink up," says Morrison, finishing his bottle. "There's plenty more where that came from." I hurry to catch up, almost choking trying to chug the rest of my wine.

The driver up-ends a new bottle, still three quarters full after one little sip out of it, and slugs it all down.

"Pretty neat! Pretty neat!" says Morrison, watching the driver with undisguised admiration. "Now there's a man that knows how to drink!"

The driver inflates like a toad in mating season. "Shit! That wasn't nothing! You should see me on my day off! I go through booze like shit goes through a goose!"

Morrison passes out new bottles to everyone. We are all getting gassed.

"Say, you want I should tell a joke?" says Ralph re-
adjusting the cap on his head. "It's a hot one."

"No," says Deirdre.

"Yeah," says Morrison. "Tell us the joke."

"Well, there's this traveling salesman, see," begins
Ralph.

"Oh, fuck that!" says Deirdre, looking drunkenly
bored, if such a thing is possible.

"Shut up!" says Morrison, pinching her tits. "Let
him do his thing."

"And he goes to this farmhouse, see," says Ralph.

"And he knocks on the door," I add.

"Yeah," says the driver, giving me a hostile look.
"And he knocks on the door!" Ralph gives me another
hostile look so I shut up and decide not to try and mess
him up anymore.

Deirdre looks bored enough to have puppies.

Morrison looks fascinated.

"The farmer knocks on the door. The traveling salesman says, 'My car broke down. Can you put me up for
the night?'

"The farmer seems reluctant. He says, 'Yeah, I guess
so.' "

Deirdre sticks her tongue out at the driver, not interested at all.

" 'But you'll have to sleep with my fourteen sons,'
says the farmer," finishes Ralph, looking back at us in
the rearview mirror.

Even Deirdre looks surprised.

The driver stops talking, takes a long pull on his
wine, drawing it out, building the suspense. It's so left
field, we all lean forward, wondering what the frigging
punch line is.

The driver pretends to busy himself with his driving,
making a turn and crossing over into another lane,
keeping us hanging.

"Well?" says Deirdre, who has no patience. "The
farmer says, 'You'll have to sleep with my fourteen
sons.' Then what?"

Ralph says, absolutely dead pan, "The traveling salesman shakes his head, says, 'Excuse me, I must be in the wrong joke!' "

He slaughters us. He takes our heads off at the knee. Deirdre dissolves into a laughing fit, spitting a gulp of wine all over everything. Morrison and I are roaring like an Arctic windstorm and old Ralph is beating the steering wheel one-handed, wheezing like a mad monk at his own joke.

"Son of a bitch!" says Morrison, riding high on drugs, wine and a nowhere joke. "It's a frigging party!"

"Goddamn right!" says Ralph, waving his wine bottle at us.

"Let's drink a toast to our driver! Good old Ralph!" says Deirdre, bouncing her leg on my knee so her skirt opens and closes. Old Ralph's blood pressure must be going into orbit by now. He sees what she's doing and it's driving him crazy. He practically bites the top off his wine bottle.

We see a lot of L.A. rolling by the cab windows, soft neon stream of color and sound, softened into something beautifully velvet by acid and wine. And the wine flows and flows. The taximeter click-clicks, like a soft woman's heartbeat. There is nothing in the world except the cab in which we ride, an island in the storm. We drive on ever deeper into the night.

Finally, it is Morrison, looking out the windows, who asks, "Hey, man? Where are we?"

Ralph puts his wine bottle down and peers none too soberly out the front window. "I don't know. I think we're lost," he says. "I think we been lost the last three or four hours."

Deirdre laughs. "I didn't know cab drivers could get lost!"

"Shit! I get lost all the time," says Ralph, taking another swig of wine. "Everybody gets lost once in a while, honey. Everyone!"

"A philosopher!" says Morrison, delighted.

"Now, you take good old Daniel Boone, for instance," says Ralph, looking out the window, trying to get oriented.

"Who? Take who?" says Deirdre.

"Daniel Boone! See, he was always going out there in the wilderness and stuff where there weren't no highways or roads or Holiday Inns or nothing. So somebody once asked him, asked him did maybe he ever get himself lost. And you know what good old Daniel Boone said?"

"What?" says Morrison.

"No, I never got lost, but I was mighty confused once for three days."

Morrison whoops with delight, pounds Ralph on the shoulder. "You're a fucking genius," says Morrison.

Ralph farts, looking embarrassed about it, hopes no one notices. He looks around at Deirdre to see if she noticed. She smiles at him, blows him a little kiss as if she was giving him a reward for producing natural gas. Old Ralph lights up like an atomic light bulb.

"If I'm so fucking smart," he says, "how come I'm lost?"

"Have some more wine," says Morrison, digging into the sacks again. Morrison's got the answer to everything and the answer is in all the liquor stores.

"Maybe we ought to go someplace definite," I suggest, thinking of the big numbers on the taxi meter, not that I really care. It isn't my money we're riding around on, after all.

"Let's go to a graveyard," says Morrison, staring out the windows of the taxicab. It's the middle of the night by now. "Seems like we been driving for hours!"

"I got to piss," admits Ralph, finishing another bottle of wine. He looks over at the meter, then looks at the mileage on the speedometer. "Jesus! We have been driving for hours!" He looks embarrassed at the amount. He's making a fortune.

"I got to piss too," says Deirdre.

"Me too," I chime in. My middle half is stiff from wine and drugs but I'm not that numb that I can't tell a gigantic piss coming on.

"All God's children got to piss!" says Morrison.

"Well, son of a bitch," says the driver, "let's go find us a place to piss."

"A graveyard," says Morrison. "Nobody will bother us there. We can sit back and drink."

The taxi driver's staring at the meter. "Well, shit," he says finally and reaches over and flips the meter off, "I made enough money. From now on it's a free ride."

I'd seen the meter turning back to zero I don't know how many times. He probably doesn't make that much in fares in four weeks' driving.

Deirdre reaches across the seat and caresses Ralph's cheek with one hand. Deirdre is drunk. Old Ralph damn near goes through the roof of his cab. "Hey, that's a really nice thing you just did," she says.

Deirdre bends over and gives Ralph a faked passionate kiss on the side of his neck. I see the expression on her face. She looks kind of disgusted, with the kind of look you get on your face when you have to kiss a funeral director goodbye, but she's enjoying the heat she's building in the old man. What a prick tease!

"Glorious bitch!" says Morrison, to no one in particular, meaning her.

Old Ralph puts a hand back over his shoulder. "Let me shake your hands there," he says, overwhelmed with brotherhood or something like that, the cab weaving drunkenly as he reaches back for us.

"Max Ophuls. Pleastuhmakeyorequaintance," says Morrison, shaking the driver's hand vigorously.

"Mumble, mumble," I say, taking the driver's hand and pumping it, not remembering who the hell Morrison said I was.

"Let's drink to L.A.," says Morrison, "and to graveyards."

We all lift our bottles, all traveling down the road that leads to oblivion.

"This is a real sombitching good time!" says Ralph, throwing his empty wine bottle over his shoulder. He just misses my face and I realize old Ralph is drunk on his ass.

The cab careens all over the road.

I look out the window, not recognizing this part of L.A. at all. Think we are out in the suburbs somewhere, just zooming aimlessly through the night.

We pass a big iron gate on the left side of the road, and old Ralph practically stands up on his brakes.

Everybody in the back seat almost ends up in the front seat.

Deirdre ends up on the back-seat floor, sideways, short skirt up over her hips. The cab skids, turns sideways, finally coming to a stop in the middle of the street.

I look out the window, glad we are in a section of L.A. where there are no cars. We seem to be in a pretty isolated section of the city. Steep cliffs and hills around us, very few houses.

"What the fuck's going on?" snarls Deirdre, climbing off the floor, crawling up into my lap. "A goddamn earthquake or what?" There's an idiotic smile on her face. She seems amused.

Somewhere between the acid and the wine, Little Miss Sunshine has lost most of her boredom. With that idiotic smile on her face she looks like a five-year-old waiting for the tooth fairy.

"A *graveyard!*" shouts Ralph. "A goddamn graveyard!"

"Hallelujah!" shouts Morrison, raising his arms until they smash into the roof. "Victory is ours!"

Ralph puts the cab in gear, accelerates, tires squealing, and we do a U turn, coming back around.

We get up to the wrought-iron gates in a big rush.

The gates are closed.

"I'll get them open," says Morrison, handing Ralph his wine bottle, and staggers out of the cab on his side.

Deirdre is kissing me on the neck erotically. Old

Ralph is grinning like a brown bear at salmon spawning time. He up-ends Morrison's wine bottle, finds it empty and looks back at me, expectantly.

Holding Deirdre off with one hand, I reach down and get him another bottle.

"Gentleman and a scholar," says Ralph drunkenly, staring fixedly at Deirdre's ass, which is up in the air while she fastens herself on to my neck.

I try to get the wine bottle cap unscrewed but Deirdre is driving me right up the wall. Deirdre drives everybody up the wall. She's got a license for it.

I hand old Ralph the bottle, unopened. He turns in the seat, really fascinated by the back of Deirdre's lap. He trys to drink from the unopened bottle, hitting his teeth hard on the bottle cap.

Morrison stumbles around outside in the glare of the headlights, trying to get the gates open. Seems to be having trouble.

He shouts something at us, which we can't understand.

"Maybe this ain't a good idea," says Ralph. "What do you think there, Deda?"

"Deirdre. Deirdre," says Deirdre, letting go of my neck to come up for air. "My name's Deirdre."

"Dee . . . dra," he says slowly, struggling to get it right.

"You got it," she says.

Ralph swells up like a toad, proud of himself. "Well, Jesus, Deirdre, there ain't gonna be no place for you to piss." He smiles, embarrassed. "I mean, there ain't gonna be no facilities for you to, uh . . . no place to sit down is what I mean."

"And no toilet paper," says Deirdre. "I don't give a shit. I could do it out the window. I could do it in the glove compartment. I just don't give a shit where I do it, just as long as I get to do it." She laughs, holding herself in, as if her hands clamped to her sides were the only thing keeping her from pissing herself. "And soon. Christ! I'm swimming in my own piss!"

Ralph sticks his head out the cab window. "Hey, Max! What's taking you so long to get that gate open? This here beautiful broad has got to piss. Speed it up out there, will ya!"

Morrison points at the gates, staggering on his feet. "Padlocked. Can't get it opened!"

"We got to get in," says Deirdre, pretending panic. "I'm dying to get in."

I groan at the bad pun, start getting out of the cab. I am not going to wait. I got to piss and right now. I am gonna piss all over the side of the cab.

Ralph gets out of the cab, reaches back under his car seat and pulls out a tire iron. "You just hold on, honey," he tells Deirdre. "Let old Ralph fix it up."

Ralph staggers away, as drunk as a sailor, heading for the gates.

Morrison sees him coming, steps back, frightened, seeing a maniac bearing down on him and the gates with a dangerous-looking weapon in his hands.

I'm pissing like the source of the Nile on the side of the cab. This yellow cab is gonna be twice yellow.

"A maniac," yells Morrison as Ralph strikes, attacking the chain and padlock holding the gates closed.

The iron bar slams into the chain. Once. Twice. The third time the padlock gives up the ghost and the chain parts with a snap. The gates swing free, one side swinging inward.

Ralph waves the tire iron over his head triumphantly, the victorious gladiator. He and Morrison grab the gates and drag them wide open.

Ralph hotfoots it back to the cab, dropping the tire iron on the front floor of the cab. He puts the cab in gear and drives through the gates.

Morrison and I close the gates behind us, and use the chain to tie them loosely, so that it doesn't look like anybody's gone through them. I'm glad we're still straight enough to be just a little bit paranoid. You live longer that way.

Morrison and I get back into the cab.

"All aboard!" yells Ralph, putting the cab in gear and slamming the accelerator to the floor. We zoom forward, tires squealing.

"Did you see me do that padlock?" says Ralph. "Slicker than greased lightning!"

"You're a hero," says Morrison, smashed out of his mind.

The cab screams up a narrow winding road, twisting and turning through the graveyard.

"This is good enough," says Morrison, opening the door before Ralph can get the cab stopped.

Ralph hits the brakes, skids off the road and we go careening off the pavement and cut wildly across the grass, knocking over a row of wooden crosses. The cab brushes up against a heavy granite tombstone, tilting it at a crazy angle, and finally comes to rest after about a hundred wild yards of cross-country jouncing around, parked sideways across a grave, somewhere in the middle of the graveyard.

I lean forward, dead drunk, to shout something to Morrison but he's gone. The son of a bitch fell out of the car before we went off the road.

Deirdre, pretty shaken up, sprawls out the door Morrison's fallen out of.

"Last stop!" yells Ralph, holding on to his steering wheel, dead drunk. "Everybody out!"

I crawl out after Deirdre, dragging the last few bottles of wine with me. We already drank a whole grocery sack of wine. Only a few bottles are left in the other one. What a bunch of maniacs! I count the bottles, only six more to go, if we don't all get alcoholic poisoning first.

I fall out of the cab, right onto my face. The moon is out and it's daylight bright. Old Ralph is out there somewhere, singing to himself, some country and western song about a girl in a bar. What else would it be about?

Morrison staggers out of the darkness, a cut on his

chin, helps me to my feet. His shirt is torn, the palm of one hand scratched up.

"Where'd you go?" I ask him.

"Rode the wind. Proved man can fly. Leonardo da Vinci," says Morrison, looking and sounding destroyed in the moonlight. "Revenge! Aviators!"

He nudges me in the ribs with an elbow. "Sometimes you find them sewing for the heathens!"

"What?" I barely remember anything. I wonder what the hell he's talking about. "What are we doing in a graveyard?"

"Gonna invoke the dead," says Morrison. "Stick with me. I'm in control."

"*Hey, Deirdre!*" That's old Ralph, yelling into the night like a lonesome coyote. "Where are you, honey?"

"I'm pissing," says Deirdre, shouting at him from somewhere. "What it to you, you horny old fart?"

Morrison and I go over to Ralph. The old man is bent over a tombstone, a wine bottle in his hand. Morrison takes the grocery sack of wine from my hand, sets it at Ralph's feet, centering it over the grave.

"I consecrate this place," says Morrison. "Forever after it shall be holy."

"I ain't religious," says Ralph. "I'm drunk is what I am."

"Drunk? Nobody's drunk in this graveyard," says Morrison, disagreeing.

"Drunk on my ass," says Ralph, not to be talked out of it. "And she's pretty. Goddamn, I'll say she is! What a great pair of knockers she's got!"

Ralphs looks at us, remembering something. "No offense, ya understand! I just think she's a terrific-looking piece of tail is what I think."

"Yeah," says Morrison. "You noticed?"

"I call them the way I see them," says Ralph. "And believe me, I've seen them and I've seen them!"

Deirdre yells, "Hey, assholes! Where the fuck are you!"

Ralph yodels at her, "We're over here, you great big beautiful hunk of woman!"

Ralph starts to move toward her, almost falls on his ass. The old guy is really shit-faced.

Morrison laughs. Standing next to him, I feel an icy wind in that laugh. A really wicked laugh.

Deirdre yells again, "Where are you guys?"

Old Ralph rises up. "Over here! Over here! You stay right there, honey! I'll come and get you! Don't you worry!" yells Ralph, the white knight in shining armor who needs a shave.

"Go get 'em tiger," says Morrison, clapping Ralph encouragingly on the back. The old man reels under the blow, damn near falling flat on his face.

Ralph stumbles off, still yelling for Deirdre.

"Love is the plan," says Morrison. "The ultimate weapon is the sound of sex on skin. Are you riding with me?"

"I'm not sure. I'm kind of drunk, you know." Besides, he isn't making much sense either.

"Don't fail me," says Morrison. "The lords will have to have their day."

"I'm with you," I tell him. "I'm with you all the way. Except right now." I hold my stomach, feeling a tiger biting me. "Except right now I think I am going to—"

I finish the sentence by throwing up all over a tombstone.

"You've got too much respect for the dead," says Morrison.

Ralph and Deirdre stagger up, weaving like two mongoloid idiots who've been dropped on their heads too many times.

"Keep your frigging hands off me," says Deirdre, giving Ralph a shove.

Ralph nods, trying to squeeze her tits. "I never laid a hand on you," he says. "You're so goddamn beautiful!"

Ralph sees me tossing my cookies. "Can't hold your

booze!" he says. "Pretty damn chickenshit if you ask me. Yes sir, pretty chickenshit!"

I wipe my mouth on the sleeve of my shirt. "So who's asking you?"

Morrison's got more wine bottles out of the sack, tries to pass them around, but there's a fine line between sanity and insanity and we already passed it a couple of bottles ago.

Nobody takes a bottle.

I'm weak, dizzy from heaving up. At least the stuff I tossed up wasn't down long enough for it to make me smell bad when it came back up. Actually, I even feel a little more sober now, losing all that wine that way.

Deirdre puts her arms around Morrison, whispering something to him. Old Ralph is practically standing on her feet, rubbing up against her like a cat wanting to be scratched.

Deirdre ignores Ralph altogether, turned on by the prospect of jumping Morrison.

I go over and sit down on the top of a cold marble tombstone, content to sit back and watch the world spin without me.

"How you feeling, old dude?" asks Morrison of our driver, not responding to Deirdre wrapping herself around him.

"Fucking-A great!" says Ralph, weaving from side to side in front of Morrison and Deirdre. "And who says I'm old! I'm a goddamn stud!" He sticks out his scrawny chest, beating it with a bony fist. Not very impressive. He's lost his cap somewhere, revealing a crewcut and brown hair heavily frosted with gray. The old man looks like his cab has been parked on his face all night.

Deirdre laughs, clinging to Morrison with wanton abandon, playing with his chest, massaging his crotch with her hands. Morrison's impassive, like a cold statue standing there in the night.

"She likes you," says Morrison to Ralph.

"I like her!" says Ralph, almost shouting. "I love her!"

Deirdre is pretty wrecked, not really listening to what Morrison's saying.

From where I sit, I tense up, sensing that something is about to happen. Something strange.

Morrison turns Deirdre around, hugs her from behind, massaging her breasts. Ralph stands there, right up against them, taking it all in hungrily.

I just sit on my tombstone, out of it. It's gonna be cruel.

"Touch her," invites Morrison. "She wants you to."

Old Ralph doesn't need a second invitation.

He grabs her breasts, kneading them like dough.

"Shit!" says Deirdre, frowning vaguely at the old man. "Cut that out."

The old man goes right on squeezing her tits.

Deirdre tries to brush his hands away but Morrison's got her arms and she's pretty wrecked, too wrecked to put up much of a struggle.

Morrison lets her struggle, trying to squirm out of his grasp, then suddenly lets her go so that she staggers forward, colliding with the old man. Ralph is practically drooling. Her arms go around the old man's neck for a second, as she struggles for balance, trying not to fall, and the old man thinks she's trying to jump him.

Ralph throws his arms around her, pulling her tight against him in an embrace. "Oh, love," he croons.

Deirdre realizes what's happening, puts her hand in Ralph's fat face and shoves him off of her. The old man staggers back, crashing into me, almost knocking me over ass backwards off my tombstone.

Deirdre angrily turns to look at Morrison, pissed off. She almost screams. Morrison's got a wicked-looking knife in his hands. I didn't even see him pull it, didn't know he was carrying one. I jump off the tombstone, afraid he's going to stab her, not sure what I should do.

Morrison sticks the knife blade under her chin, puts it up against her throat. I take a step forward, scared.

"Take your clothes off," says Morrison.

"That's not funny," she says, scared of the look in Morrison's eyes, the coldness in his voice.

"Nothing is ever funny," says Morrison. " 'Cause nothing ever happens, right?"

"Put it away," she says. "I won't do it."

Morrison tilts the knife, lifting the blade, bringing her up on her toes, almost making her scream. It hurts. The knife is almost going into her skin.

Morrison turns his head, looking at me. I don't know what to do. I'm torn. I'd kind of like to stop him. I don't really want to see her get hurt. He's only supposed to be scaring her, I remember that much of what he'd said. I kind of would like to stop him and I kind of would like to see her naked. Decisions! Decisions!

Old Ralph is out of it, so out of it he doesn't even see the knife, but what does register on him is that he's heard Morrison tell her to take her clothes off and he's all for that. "Take them off! Take them all off!" cries Ralph, using the tombstone to drag himself up to his feet. He's having trouble standing up.

"You bastard," says Deirdre. "You're serious, aren't you!"

Morrison doesn't say anything, just stands there looking like a killer, the knife pressed tightly against her throat.

I come up next to them wondering what I am supposed to do, what I am supposed to say. Maybe we're having too much fun and we should forget the whole thing.

"Take them off," says Morrison.

"Bastard," says Deirdre, hatred on her face as she begins to unbutton the top button of her shirt, moving very very carefully so the knife doesn't jiggle and cut her.

"This is crazy!" I say. "This is like rape."

"I don't want Miss Rich Bitch to be bored," says Morrison.

"You're too kind," says Deirdre, tight-lipped, struggling with her shirt buttons. She's too wrecked. Her fingers don't work very well.

"Help her. She's in a hurry," says Morrison to me.

I shrug, hesitating beside her.

Deirdre stares at me strangely. Not really angry, more as if she's challenging me, daring me to touch her.

"Afraid to?" she says, smiling at me wickedly. "What's the matter? Never raped anybody before?"

"Only on the weekends," I say, deciding to go through with it. Why not? Gonna get my kicks before the whole world goes bang-bang-I'm-dead.

I grab her shirt and start working on the buttons.

The old man comes over to us, sees the knife, sees me fumbling with her shirt.

"What's going on?" He looks at us both, not understanding. "What are you doing?" He looks upset, maybe a little bit scared.

"Having fun," says Morrison. "All God's children got to have their fun."

"Hey! Hey!" says the old man, really upset now. "I don't think you should do that!"

My hands aren't working any better on Deirdre's buttons than hers were. Frustrated, I grab the shirt on each side and yank. The buttons tear off and the shirt comes away in my hands.

"You ruined it, you bastard," Deirdre almost screams. The tug on her shirt has jerked her forward. The knife hurts her neck a little. She touches her neck.

"I'm cut. I'm bleeding," she says.

She isn't wearing a bra. What a gorgeous looker this girl is in the moonlight.

Ralph is in a sweat, so excited in spite of his fear that he damn near passes out. I feel it too.

She curses us. Ralph comes up to her and starts rubbing her breasts, squeezing her nipples.

She tells us we are bastards, pigs, but while she's doing it she's getting excited. Her nipples get stiff, thrusting out at us. She is getting hot, and that from a girl who's always hot to start with is pretty hot. We are all becoming cats in heat, even Morrison.

Ralph has one hand on her and one hand on himself.

"Oh, honey! Oh, honey! Oh, honey!" Ralph chants, face covered with sweat. "Oh, honey! Oh, honey!"

Morrison nods down at her skirt. "Take it off," he says.

"Let me do it," says Deirdre with a wicked laugh. "I don't want it ripped."

"Oh, honey! Oh, honey!"

"This is rape. You know this is rape," she says, glaring at Morrison as she tugs at the waist of her skirt.

"This is just fun," says Morrison, still holding the knife. "The kind of fun you've been asking for all your life. So you better want what you get 'cause you're gonna get it."

"Let's get naked," says Morrison, taking the knife away from her neck.

Deirdre's skirt comes undone and she bends down, stepping out of it. The first to get naked. Morrison and I strip. Ralph leaves all of his clothes on, unzipped and hanging out.

Deirdre stands between us, shivering in the night air as our hands explore her body. Deirdre slaps Morrison, suddenly, unexpectedly. "I hate you! You're an animal!"

Morrison doesn't hesitate, slaps her right back, so hard he almost knocks her down.

The knife is back at her throat again, unnecessarily, melodramatically. "Lay down, rich bitch."

"I'll break it off inside," she says, holding the side of her face, hating him.

"You always do," says Morrison.

She lays down on the grass, shivering in the cold, spreading her long beautiful legs. God, she looks lovely, like an angel in the moonlight! The most erotic girl I've ever seen.

We stand over her, SS troopers in the L.A. night.

"Who's first?" she says, mocking us.

Ralph falls on her, moaning, "Oh, honey! Oh, honey!"

She tries to push him off but he's too heavy and she's too wrecked. He struggles to get inside her, groping clumsily in the dark. They roll on the ground like two boa constrictors, one dressed and one undressed.

Ralph gets in her, ejaculating the second he gets inside, coming with a throaty moan. She rolls to her side, pushing the heavy body off of her. She balls her hand into a fist and slams it into Ralph's face, hitting him in the eyes. The old man screams, folds up beside her like an accordion, in agony. She really clobbered him. He thrashes beside her naked body, holding his eyes, moaning. One of her legs is pinned beneath him.

Morrison grabs Deirdre by the hair, dragging her painfully away from the old man. "Bitch!" he snarls, handing me the knife. "Let's see you hit me," he says.

Morrison flings himself on top of her, covering her mouth with a brutal kiss, pinning her arms to her sides. He's brutal, vicious.

She likes it.

She tears her arms loose, circles them around his back, pressing him tightly against her. I'm so turned on, I don't even know I got a knife in my hand. It slips through my fingers, falls at my feet. I want her so bad I can taste it.

Her fingers claw into Morrison's back. Her back arches and she comes convulsively, face contorted with pleasure. Her hands dig into his back, driving him deep inside her. Her hot, excited cries ring out in the night, throaty bursts of pure pleasure, total abandon.

The rhythm goes and goes. She comes again and again. Morrison groans, driving into the night, swimming to the moon.

Old Ralph lays beside them sobbing, maybe seriously hurt, no one really cares. Finally he crawls off on his hands and knees, going off somewhere by himself.

"I love it! Love it!" Deirdre screams, riding the big wave. "Don't stop! Don't stop! Don't stop!"

The world is one big orgasm for Deirdre. She bounces under Morrison like a wild horse, driving him deeper and deeper inside her. She's the ultimate erotic animal, some kind of cosmic sex child.

They come together, mutual climax, thrashing like snakes in the sand, vertebraes reaching through the skin for the stars.

I'm standing above them, on fire, blazing in the night with desire.

Morrison rolls off slowly, and she looks up at me, all sweaty, legs stretched out. Looking like every erotic vision I've ever had or ever will have. She's the fierce daughter of barbarians, a princess of flesh.

And I almost can't, almost back away, 'cause it's so different from my dreams, from my fantasy conquests. At that moment I never wanted anything more than her and it's scary. I almost step back but she sees me hesitate. Her hands come up and catch my legs. She pulls me down on top of her.

Her hands are between my legs skillfully, driving me into her. Her burning body grinds against me. It's fast, blinding, like making love to a lightning bolt. Who's raping who?

She makes love like she's making war.

Her wicked legs wrap around me, drawing me deep inside.

"Oh, love! Oh, love! Oh, love!" says Deirdre, in convulsions, fingernails biting into my back as she orgasms endlessly. A sweet ride. Sweet ride.

I ride until the dam breaks in me, spilling me into her.

I collapse in her arms, exhausted. She holds me against her, drenched in our sweat, kissing my face, lips, eyes. "Oh, love! Love!"

Morrison, lying beside us, silent, sits up abruptly, staring at us. He looks around for the old man but he's long gone, maybe crawled off to die somewhere.

"Oh, love! Love," she whispers so sweetly in my ears. So good to kiss her. And we are holding each other, lips and tongues caressing each other's faces.

Morrison gets up, disgusted, disapproving.

"You make me sick!" he says, glaring at us.

I only know I'm kissing her, getting aroused again, that I want to stay this way forever, barely aware that he's talking to us.

Her hand comes down to touch me, coaxing me. We roll over and gently, lovingly this time, I go inside her again. Her arms go around my back, caressing me.

Morrison towers over us, like some kind of angry god denied a sacrifice. We barely know he is there.

"You both make me sick!" says Morrison. "This is supposed to be a rape but now it looks too much like falling in love. Well, fuck it!"

Morrison stalks off angrily. Vaguely I'm aware we are now alone. I don't think Deirdre's heard a word Morrison's said. Neither of us cares anyway. Too interested in discovering each other.

I hold her so tight my arms ache and we make love like people in love make love. I feel things in me, feelings I never thought I had, rising in me like some kind of dam was washed away by a flood. It's crazy, it's insane, but all feelings are anyway. I think I'm falling in love, and not just from the lap down.

Dawn finds us still wrapped in each other's arms, half frozen, still naked, and as close to being in love as I've ever been.

Graveyards do strange things to people.

CHAPTER 14

I try to move my arms and they ache so bad I can barely move them. Every joint in my body aches, my back aches, my neck is stiff. I can tell Deirdre feels the same way. We disengage, roll out of each other's arms.

Didn't sleep much, either of us. Too much acid still in our systems. We held each other all night, caressing, talking about everything and nothing.

We slowly crawl into our clothes, helping each other get dressed. We stand together for a while, arms around each other, watching the first faint gleam of the sun streaking the sky. Going to be light real soon. The first

rays of the morning sun make her hair and body shine
as if they were golden. I've never felt so close to anyone
in my life.

As she had lain in my arms, I had thought of Tamara.
Wondering most of the night why I had never been able
to allow myself to love her, to release control, to just
let myself be vulnerable. As I am now.

I think I experienced a genuine regret, maybe
mourning so much time wasted pretending a love I
could have truly felt.

But now it's Deirdre, and the things I feel inside
aren't made up, aren't part of my play-pretend self-defense routine.

Deirdre puts her torn shirt on, her breasts still exposed. Her hair looks like a wild animal mane, all rumpled from lovemaking. We hug each other, kissing,
still liking the feeling of being body to body, even in
clothes. I really love the way she looks, tastes, feels.

"You're beautiful," she says, holding me tight.

"We better get out of here," I say, looking around,
wondering where everybody went.

The cab is not too far away, the doors open.

"What a night!" says Deirdre, letting me go, stepping back. "I could sleep for a week."

"With me?"

"Who else?"

We walk toward the cab, holding hands. The old
man is stretched out in the front seat, looking like a
knockout in a bare-knuckle prizefight. She really belt-
ed him in the face. His eyes look black, swollen. He's
got a couple of wine bottles, now empty, at his feet. He
really drank himself into never-never land.

Morrison's in the back, too acidized to sleep and too
drunk to move. He stares at us, not really liking us.

"It's the lovers," he says, slurring his words. "Fresh
from a deck of Tarot cards."

"We better get out of here," I say. "It's morning.
There's gonna be people in here soon and we don't
want to be here when they come."

"Spectators are vampires. We don't let them in," says Morrison, too drunk to make much sense. "We'll barricade the gate. Keep them out."

"Then they'll put us in jail and keep us in," I say.

Deirdre looks in the front seat. "We better wake him up," she says. "Hey whatsis your name! Get up!"

She pokes him in the side but he's pretending like he belongs in the graveyard on a permanent basis.

"Hey, come on." She pokes him harder. His head turns sideways and Ralph starts snoring. "What a pig!" says Deirdre, and then she really gives him a shot in the ribs.

She might as well have been flogging a dead bondage-and-discipline disciple for all the action she gets. Ralph is absolutely drowned in wine. He might not resurface for a week.

"What's matter? Old Ralph gone nitey-nite on you?" asks Morrison, staring at us bleary-eyed. He leans forward unsteadily, almost falling over, and tilts his bottle of wine over the front seat. The wine bottle's half full.

The wine splashes all over the old man's face and he snorts, coughs, the wine going up his nose, choking him. Ralph jerks his head, turning sideways, swollen eyes coming open. He falls off the seat with a dull thud, his head dropping outside the cab door.

Ralph stares up at us, totally obliterated, head angling down toward the ground.

"Wah? Wahsa?" Ralph mutters, wine streaming from his eyes and nose.

Deirdre puts her hand on the back of his head and pushes him back into the cab until he is sitting up under the dashboard.

"Wah?" says Ralph, looking around at us, absolutely no idea where he is or who we are. Really totaled.

"I better drive," says Deirdre, shutting the door so Ralph doesn't fall out the open car door on his face.

"Smy smoo," says Ralph, staring at the dashboard, nodding at it in a positive, confidential fashion. He leans against the glove compartment, having found a long-lost friend.

"That's what I call drunk!" says Deirdre. "The dumb old bastard."

Morrison's trying to open another bottle of wine, not that he really needs any more. The bottle keeps slipping out of his hands and falling into his lap. Another candidate for oblivion.

"I'll get the cemetery gate when we get to it," I say. "Are you sure you can drive?"

She looks back at me as I slide in beside Morrison. I would have got in front with Deirdre but good old Ralph is taking up too much room. "Don't worry," she says, giving me a special smile. "I'll get us out of here."

Deirdre gets the cab started, shifts and begins backing out. I look out the cab windows, noticing our surroundings for the first time in the light. Jesus. You can tell we've been here! We left ruts all over the grass, wine bottles everywhere.

Deirdre backs into a tombstone, denting a fender and knocking over the marble slab.

She frowns, takes it out of gear, puts it in first and we go forward, narrowly missing another tombstone. She cuts across a bunch of graves, leaving deep ruts as she takes a shortcut across a gently sloping hill and comes out finally on the road that goes through the graveyard. I look out the back window. Somebody's going to be really pissed off. As many wheel marks as that heavy cab left, somebody's going to get the idea a sports car rally went through there in the dead of night.

When we get up to the gates, Deirdre's driving pretty good. But somebody has already beat us there. Some old guy in work clothes is staring at the gates, holding the chain and padlock in his hands. He's got the gates open, nice of him to be so thoughtful, so we don't stop to chat with him.

Deirdre floors it and we go roaring by him. He stands there with his mouth open, watching a yellow cab racing out of the graveyard. Deirdre turns and gives him the finger as we go by, almost losing control of the car. Deirdre's tall in the saddle and her breasts are exposed over the top of the driver's side door.

The old man at the gate's so surprised the heavy chain in his hand slips and drops on his foot. Looking out the back window as we zoom away, I see him hopping around on one foot mad as hell.

"Where are we going?" asks Deirdre as the cab shoots down the street.

"To the end of the night," says Morrison from the back, maybe not aware it's already morning.

I take the bottle out of Morrison's lap and twist the top. It's hard to open but I manage to get the cap loosened. I hand it to Morrison. Morrison cradles the bottle against his chest, smiles at me. "Thanks," he says. "But you're still a drag."

He leans back against the seat. "I hate all my friends. I wish I could kill them with an ax."

Deirdre laughs at him. "You don't have any friends," she says.

Morrison smiles right back at her. "That means no enemies."

"Where do you want to go?" I ask Morrison, figuring we can drop him and good old Ralph off somewhere so Deirdre and I can be together. That's all I want to do, be with her.

"Take me to the beach. Take me to the conquistador shore," says Morrison, not looking at us. "And fuck you both."

The ride's made in silence, mine and Deirdre's eyes meeting sometimes in the rearview mirror. Ralph's passed out again, under the dashboard. Morrison's drinking, not looking at anything, just drinking.

The sun feels good, coming through the cab windows. I'm tired, a little hung over maybe, cottonmouthed from drinking, but I feel good inside. Maybe I'm really falling in love. Maybe the Pope is really Jewish. I stop thinking about falling in love because I never try to think about it. I do know I feel good even if I don't exactly know why. It's better not to think about the why.

The fog's blowing in over Santa Monica, walking across the highway down by Malibu beach. It's kissing the ground at Zuma beach and that's where we pull the cab off the road.

Deirdre and I get out. Ralph's snoring like a hibernating bear. He isn't going anywhere for quite some time yet.

Deirdre stuffs some money in his shirt pocket. "Thanks for the ride, daddycakes," she says.

Morrison sits in the back, staring at us as we stand beside the cab, holding hands.

"You getting out?" I ask him.

Morrison pushes on the door, too messed up to get it open. We go over and help him. He crawls out and we have to help him stand up. He shrugs us off, once he gets on his feet, leans back against the roof of the cab, trying to keep his legs under him. He's pretty much out of it.

"Where's my knife?" he asks. I can barely make out his words.

"I don't remember. Must have dropped it somewhere."

Morrison curses, the wine bottle slipping from his numbed fingers.

"We're gonna split. You okay?" I ask him.

"Fine," says Morrison. "Pretty neat! Pretty neat!" He is not almost out of it, he is completely out of it. I don't want to be his aching head tomorrow. His hangover is going to be a blast at ground zero.

I turn to Deirdre. "We got to find someplace to go. Where do you live?"

She smiles at me, squeezes my hand affectionately. "I've got a house in Beverly Hills."

"Great! Let's get a cab and go there." I really want to be with her and it makes me feel strange because I never feel like that.

"We could," she says, thinking about it. She hugs me, the breeze from the sea blowing her hair like a golden fan around her head. "But you'd have to be gone by tonight."

"Why?"

" 'Cause my husband gets back tonight," she says. She bends over and looks at herself in the side mirror on the cab. "Jesus! I'm a wreck!"

"Husband?" The universe spins, does a nose dive. "Husband? You're married?"

"Yeah. Been married about three weeks." She tries to straighten out her hair with her hand, smoothing it in place. "It just sort of happened. Fell in love or something."

I just stand there with my mouth open. Can't believe it.

"Married. You're married!"

"Yeah. So, big deal. He's a professional football player. He's on the road a lot. No sweat."

"But . . . but . . ."

"Don't be a drag," she says. "You want to come over or not?"

"You've only been married three weeks and you . . . and you . . ."

"Listen, if you're worried he'll come home and find us, don't." She puts her arms around me, drawing me against her. "He's flying in from New York. His plane doesn't get in until eleven tonight."

I push her away. All I can do is stare at her.

She looks at me, surprised. "Hey, what's wrong with you?"

"Nothing," I say and I feel the mask sliding back into place.

"Are you coming with me? You know you're really a great screw. Anybody ever tell you that?" she says, tugging her breasts down behind her tattered shirt. "I'll get us another cab."

"I think I'll stay with him," I say, pointing back at

Jim, still leaning against the cab, listening to us talk.

"He's out of it," she says. "Let the bastard find his own way home. Come on."

She puts a hand on my arm but I shake it off, stepping back inside myself, again becoming the machine with a face that has nothing behind it.

"Are you pissed off because I'm married? Is that it?" Now she's getting mad, puts her hands on her hips, glaring at me. " 'Cause if you are, you're a real frigging drag and who needs you anyway!"

"See you around," I say, hoping I never see her again.

"You're a goddamn drag!"

"I enjoyed raping you!"

She laughs, laughs at me, at Morrison, at all of us. "You didn't rape me. I made you feel like you loved me," she says, absolutely merciless, "and didn't mean one frigging bit of it."

She smiles and it's cold and evil and I know she's the only one who ever had control, that she's the only one who had the knife, the only one.

"And that's the biggest rape of them all!" she says, blowing me a goodbye kiss.

I watch her walking away, walking down the beach like she owns it. The sea breeze blows her hair out behind her like a flag covered with honey. She's so beautiful it makes you ache, the most beautiful girl I've ever seen, ever touched.

Morrison's standing beside me suddenly, walking somehow. He puts his hand on my shoulder, watching me watch her walk away.

"Cold girl'll kill you in a darkened room," he says.

I nod, understanding, remembering what I always thought I knew. I put my arm around his shoulder.

We start walking down the beach, away from her, to find a place to sleep in the sun. My face hurts from changing back into a machine.

"The trouble is," I tell him, "sometimes graveyards make you forget."

CHAPTER 15

The sun was too hot for sleeping, even though a cold girl had taken me into winter. Morrison went under easy, swimming in wine, but I couldn't get into it myself. Maybe I was afraid I might dream about Deirdre, that sleeping I'd think she was still in my arms, and I'd rather die than feel that again. So there was no place else to go, except back to Tamara, back to soft asylum. So I went.

Tamara looks at me strange, that same soft, unspoken mystery number she's been doing all morning, all afternoon.

"You're so restless. Is something wrong?" she says, moving next to me on the couch. "I wish you'd been here with me last night. I wanted you next to me."

It's getting dark outside and I haven't slept yet from the day before. I'm just sitting there, stiff, awkward, dressed in clothes to go out, to go cruising again. She'd watched me dress, silent, afraid to approach me.

"Where'd you go last night? What did you do? I know you haven't slept. You don't look so good. Have you been in another fight?"

"I'm all right."

"Is something bothering you?" Her hand lightly caresses my face. "Is it something you can tell me?"

I push her hand away. "I'm all right," I say. "Nothing's wrong." That's a lie. Everything's wrong. The whole world's wrong.

"Why don't you stay here tonight?" she says, that wistful look in her eyes.

I reach for a cigarette from a crumpled pack on the coffee table. She uses the beer can, with a cigarette lighter built into it, to light my cigarette for me. I draw the smoke in too greedily, have to cough.

"You smoke too much."

"I do everything too much."

"What's that mean?"

"Nothing."

"What do you do when you go out at night? You're not just selling drugs or just working for the rock and roll bands like you say you are, are you?"

"Sure. What else would I be doing?"

She looks troubled. "I guess you have to go out tonight too, huh?"

"Yeah."

"I wish you wouldn't. I wish you'd stay with me tonight." She looks like she wants to cry.

"Tomorrow night. I'll be here tomorrow night. I'm helping a band set up for a gig over in Pasadena tonight. I promise I'll be with you tomorrow night." And maybe I will be if I can remember anything by then. Knowing me, I won't remember who I am, let alone where I'm supposed to be.

"Couldn't you . . . couldn't you not go tonight? Just this once . . . for me?" It's that hurt-puppy look, please just this once?

It makes me angry. "I do what I want to do."

"Do you love me?" She turns my face with her hand, forcing me to look at her. Goddamn! She's so serious. It means so much to her.

"Sure," I manage to say, trying not to think about it.

"Are you really sure or are you just saying that?" She trembles, wrapping her arm around my neck, holding me tight.

"I'm just saying that." Why not tell her what I think is the truth. She won't believe me anyway.

"I don't believe you. I think you really love me but you don't like the idea of it somehow. I think it makes you feel too vulnerable." She kisses me on the neck.

"That's bullshit!"

"Call it what you like, I just know you love me and I love you."

She makes me tired. I remember Deirdre on the beach, what Morrison said! "A cold girl'll kill you in a darkened room." I push Tamara away from me, saying, "Then you're stupid. Love's a Japanese corpse, short and quick to rot."

Tamara just smiles, avoiding the hand that keeps her away, snuggling up to me. "You can talk as tough as you want. It doesn't fool me."

"Nobody fools you ever. You're so goddamn smart it's semisickening." She scares me and I feel like hitting her, feel like making her hate me. She scares me. I'm afraid she'll make me feel something and I can't handle that. It's Deirdre's world I live in, not Tamara's.

"Why do you always have to sound bitter about everything? There's a lot of good in the world, you know?"

"Like your parents, for instance."

She drops her head, really stung. That really hurts.

Makes me wish I hadn't said it. It's about the same as taking a swing at her.

"They've got their good sides too. There's a good side to everything and to everybody if you take the time to look."

"Christ! You'd find something positive about a child molester."

She pulls away from me, hurt. "I don't like it when you talk this way. I think it's all an act."

"Baby, if you knew what was an act and what wasn't, maybe you wouldn't be in so much trouble."

"Am I in trouble?"

"Yes." If just once she could see me for what I really am.

"Trouble with you?"

"Trouble with everything. You don't know anything about anything." Christ! Her innocence drives me crazy.

"I just know I love you. That's not trouble." She leans against my chest, putting her head close to mine. "And even if it is, it's the kind I like. The kind I want."

I don't say anything, just stare at her. She always messes me up inside. Maybe tonight I'll go out and I won't come back. Maybe tonight.

She looks down at her lap, staring at her hands. She's got that strange look again, that mystery that's surrounded her all day.

"So what's the big deal? What's with the strange stares all day long and the half-secretive, half-proud, cat-with-cream look in your eyes? What's the big secret? What do you know that I don't know?"

"It shows?"

"Yeah. What's going on?"

She looks up at me and I see things in her eyes I don't want to see. Love and hope. Anything but that. I can't handle it. Not after Deirdre. I've known too many Deirdres.

"I went to the doctor yesterday."

Oh, shit! Not that! Anything but that!

"I'm pregnant. We're going to have a baby."

"Christ!" Now what do you say? Now what do you do?

She falls against me, and I can hear her heart beating like a butterfly hitting its wings against the insides of a glass jar.

"I was scared at first. Really scared. But later, I felt like everything bright and good was happening, really happening. It's really amazing. Another life has been started, inside me."

I just stare at her. Why did I let it go this long, why did I dance this long on promises I never really meant to keep?

"I really want this baby. It's a part of you and me. It's wonderful." She hugs me like Jesus with his arms around the cross.

"Uh, you found out yesterday?"

"At noon. I wasn't going to tell you. I was going to wait until it showed."

She pushes away from me, arms around my neck, stares directly in my eyes. "Don't you think it's wonderful?"

"No. I think it stinks."

She jumps back, as if I have physically struck her.

"You don't mean it!" Eyes wide, too much trust in them.

"I mean it." I throw her arms off my neck and stand up. "I'm going out."

"Where?" She looks frightened, like she's never seen me before, until just now. "Don't. Please don't. Stay with me." She looks like she's going to cry now. "Where are you going?"

"Just out."

I start for the door. Guess I'll sneak back in tomorrow and get my stuff while she's at work. Got to find a place to stay first. That won't be hard. The world is full of empty caves and girls not too careful about who they choose to fill them.

She moves fast, gets between me and the door, puts

her back to it and holds her arms out to me. "I don't want to be alone tonight."

I turn, not wanting to touch her, stand there in front of her, with no place to go.

"I love you. I'm going to have your baby. I want you beside me tonight." Now she's crying. Her arms go down by her sides and she leans against the door, against the way out, tears running down her face. "Please."

I can't stand the ache in her voice.

"Please. Please stay with me. I don't want to be alone tonight."

I reach past her, touching the doorknob, turning it. She sees me reaching and moves toward me, thinking I'm trying to take her in my arms. Pulling the door open with a jerk, I thrust her aside. She hits the wall, not very hard, and I see that awful look, the betrayal of love in her eyes, before I go through the door.

"Don't go!"

Her cry follows me as I run through the door and down the steps. It follows me as I run down the street. It follows me all through the night, and into the nights yet to come.

CHAPTER 16

Away from Tamara, it's the beach for me and I walk the burning miles of it, looking for the next lady, trying to find the right lie.

And I find her easy enough. Sitting on her beach towel like a cat on a comfortable chair. A body mostly hidden by a one-piece bathing suit. Transistor radio blaring, suntan oil glistening, eyes properly hidden by dark sunglasses that make her look like a welder wearing a protective mask.

A dyed-blond beast, turning on the spit of her own

ribs in the warmth of the sun's summer fire. Nice legs, long like a model's legs, young looking, which is good because the rest of her isn't.

"Got any spare change? I was hitchhiking. A guy stole my pack and my money." She looks at me, the nurse novel in her hands forgotten for the moment. With one hand, she tilts the sunglasses back so that they rest on the top of her head.

I know right away from the look on her face that the look on my face is just right. I am properly pathetic.

I go into my stance, my little-lost-puppy-please-adopt phase. It works. She asks the right questions.

"Are you hungry? Is that why you want money? It's not for drugs, right?"

You don't answer right away because first you have to look angry, just a little bit, as if your pride was hurt. I do that and she notices it.

"You really are hungry, aren't you?" she says and she looks you over. She's sizing you up and you hesitate, waiting to see if she thinks you are eminently jumpable. Her eyes go all over your body and there's a flicker in her eyes and you know she's interested. Good.

So now you pretend to be terribly embarrassed by her question. "Uh, yeah. I guess I am."

Then you wipe your brow, staggering a little in the sun. "God, it's hot! I feel a little dizzy!"

"How long has it been since you've eaten anything?" She's really concerned now, all her maternal buttons having been pushed.

"Don't know." Look confused, smile at her winningly. "Day before yesterday I guess. Except I had a candy bar this morning."

She starts moving her stuff around on her towel, gathering things up, having already come to a decision. "Would you be upset—I mean, it wouldn't hurt your pride if maybe we went somewhere and I bought you something to eat?"

You look down now, hiding the amused look as you

watch her gathering her things up, pretending to be painfully shy. "Uh . . ."

She's standing up now, puts her arm around me. "Hey! I won't bite. I promise. Come with me. We'll go to a restaurant in Malibu. I can't stand to see anybody go hungry. Besides, I'm hungry too."

I lean against her, letting her hug me maternally, and we look each other in the eyes as if in that instant we know we are both going to be lovers.

I sigh but not for the reasons she probably thinks I do. I sigh because I've been to this well so many times before that the water no longer tastes wet, but what else is there?

We go to a fancy place in Malibu that looks like a Swiss château and smells like one. It's an expensive place and much better than I expected. I order double portions and eat like a pig. All through the meal I pass myself off as a nice-guy type out on the road because my girl left me (recent heartbreak being a good key for the opening of bedroom doors) and now am fallen on hard times. She eats like a bird, spending most of her appetite on hungry looks at my body. She doesn't even blink when she gets the bill, just digs out her credit card and charges the whole thing.

"How do you feel now?" she says, as the waitress hands back the credit card.

I almost belch in her face. "Better. Much better. I feel almost human again."

"Have you got a place to stay?" she says, almost managing not to sound too desperate.

Jesus! She's a little bit previous. Doesn't even give me a chance to be clever about it. This is almost too easy. I look her over. She's no beauty. But her car is expensively new and she doesn't dress like she's rich, which means she probably is. The more money you got, the worse you can afford to dress. Besides, I had seen her digging into her purse to get her credit card. She had credit cards for everything except maybe a trip to the moon.

"Uh, no. I thought I'd sleep on the beach. I didn't know where else to go." I sigh, looking the part of the homeless orphan. I'd be more eager to jump her if she were a little better looking and one hell of a lot younger, but she'd do until something better comes along.

She looks at her watch, suddenly shy. "How would you like to stay with me?" She looks up at me suddenly, as if she expected to catch me laughing at her or something. I understand how she feels. After all, she's got to be thinking I'm probably around eighteen and she knows I know she's at least thirty-five, if not a little older.

She could be ten years older and I wouldn't give a shit. I put my hand on her hand, jiggling her coffee cup with my arm. "I'd like that very much. You've been so nice to me. I don't know how I'm ever going to repay you."

"You'll think of something," she says with a smile and we both know what she's talking about.

I squeeze her hand and her smile widens and her false teeth slip a little and she closes her mouth quick to cover it up.

I just smile, pretending like I haven't seen it. I had to pick this fossil! Sometimes you lose when you win and this is going to be one of those times. I hope she leaves her teeth in when she makes love.

We stand up and I move next to her, leaning against her affectionately as we walk out. "Oh, damn," she says, looking at her watch again as we go out the restaurant door.

"What's wrong?"

She looks put upon. "Listen, I've got to get to work. I *have* to go. Can't get out of it." She stops walking, trying to think out the logistics of the situation. "I'd take you to my place right now but I'm not going to have time. I've got to be at the studio by two and I'm barely going to make it if I leave right now."

She looks upset.

"Hey, no problem. How about taking me back to the

beach? I'll meet you there when you get off work?" Of
course, maybe I'll meet somebody better before she
gets back. I hope so.

"Oh, that would be great 'cause I go right by the
beach where I met you," she says, looking relieved. "I
do set design and I've only got a little work to do but I
have to do it today."

Holding hands, we walk to the car. "I'll be back no
later than five. You'll be there waiting for me?" She
seems afraid I won't show up.

I put my arm around her waist, give her a reassuring
hug. "Meet you in the same place where we first met,
okay?"

She smiles, relieved.

In the car, before she drives me to Venice beach, I
kiss her once, not too frigging sincerely, afraid her false
teeth will fall out in my lap, and I paw at her flabby
breasts a little just to show her I know how. What a
drag!

Back at the beach, I strip off my clothes and lay back
down in the sun, wearing nothing but an old pair of
cutoff blue jeans with no pockets and so many holes I
am practically nude. I ate too much. I feel lazy, feel
like a bloated dog who's caught too many rabbits. I put
my shirt over my face, dig out a comfortable hole in
the sand with my shoulder blades and doze off, the
sound of sea gulls lulling me to sleep.

And it's one long dream about Tamara. But sometimes I see Deirdre in it too. But mostly it is Tamara.
She's lost and I'm trying to find her. I am lost too and
we pursue each other through the night. I almost catch
her in the dream and sometimes she almost catches
me. Sometimes it isn't Tamara with tears and love in
her eyes when I get close, it's Dierdre, an evil witch
with the sun burning in her hair who kills everything
good I try to touch.

In the dream I am running up a hill, a crazy dream
hill that glows with the warmth of summer, a hill that
gets higher and higher as I run. And Tamara stands at

the top, free and beautiful with the wind in her hair, beckoning to me. And I run and run, hear her crying out, hear her calling to me, and the only thing that matters is that I reach her.

The top of the hill is before me and I break through some barrier I can't see and Tamara's there with tears on her face and her arms out to me. I seem to be floating toward her.

Just as I touch her, just as her hands reach out for me, Tamara melts like wax. It's Deirdre now who stands before me, her hand reaching for my face. Her fingers become knives and drive into my eyes.

I wake up screaming.

My hands are pressed tightly against my face, covering the eye I lost to a knife long ago. A knife that still pursues me in my dreams.

I roll over on my side, feverish, sweating. Suffocating under the shirt that covers my face, I throw it off, as if it were a snake that might bite me.

It's dark, the edge of night. I must have slept for hours.

Fully awake, still haunted by the dream, I slowly sit up. The world I see before me, a sullen beach turned silvery by the coming dark, seems no better than the world of my dreams.

Somebody was supposed to meet me, I remember, at five o'clock. I look up at the sky. It's a lot later than five. More like eight thirty, maybe nine o'clock. Looks like the lady with false teeth stood me up. No loss. I got a big meal out of it. Better than nothing, but that still leaves me with where to spend the night.

I stand up, my body stiff and sore, and begin walking down to the boardwalk, after pulling my clothes on against the cold. There's some fires on the beach, people partying, drinking and drugging. I'll crash one of those parties if it gets too cold. Getting kind of late to hustle a place to stay now. Might have to sleep on the beach. Not a real thrilling prospect.

I need a little something to help me make it through

the night. Check my pockets, not enough money to buy a bottle of wine. But a bottle of wine is the best friend to have if you have to sleep on the beach. Without money, it's going to be a little tricky getting one but I'll get one. I leave the beach, head for a liquor store.

I ease into the store and float around the aisles until the clerk turns his head, then I grab a bottle of cheap wine, stuffing it down my pants in back and pulling my shirt down to cover it. I do it quick, only takes a few seconds. The clerk's head is still turned the other way.

I wait until he's waiting on somebody before I slide out the front door. The clerk doesn't even glance in my direction. It's almost too easy. Reminds me of the winter I lived off what I could shoplift. The slum dweller's version of living off the fat of the land.

It's darkest dark now, and I button my shirt all the way up, shivering in the cool sea breeze. Start toking on the warm wine. Tastes like horse piss but warms my insides against the cold.

Walking out on the pier, staring out at the dark waves crashing on the beach, I see a young couple walking toward me, arms around each other, obviously in love. I don't want to see them because I'll see Tamara and me in them and I don't want to see anything. I don't want to see anything or hear anything or feel anything. Wish I had some drugs, some real heavy drugs so I can get wasted, really totaled. Wish I was slipping into peaceful unconsciousness, temporary unthinking oblivion.

I climb off the pier and jump down into the sand, start walking under the pier. There's a body down by the water's edge, tossing and turning in the sand. I hear a voice, the sound of words not clearly spoken. Curious, I move down the beach, coming closer.

"Father! Father . . . I want . . . I want to . . ." It's a threat and the voice gets lost, mumbling nonsense. I've heard that voice before. It's Morrison, in the grip of some nightmare. He rolls in the sand, face gleaming with perspiration in the fading light, arms digging into the sand as if he swam into the night in his sleep.

I watch him with a peculiar sensation of disquiet. That is me there on the beach too, trapped in the same nightmare. We both sleep in all the rooms of hell. And we wake up screaming.

I hold out the wine bottle, tilt it over Morrison's face. Let a few drops splash on him. He comes awake instantly, looking like an animal driven into a corner, fighting for its life.

Morrison sits up slowly, not speaking, gathering his senses.

"It's you," he finally says.

I bend down, offering the wine bottle to him.

He takes it and belts back a healthy slug of wine. Politely, he doesn't gag at the taste, even though he's got every right to. It's really rancid stuff.

"It's been me ever since I can remember and I've been able to remember years and years too long," I tell him.

Morrison gets up, rubbing his eyes, stiff from sleeping on the beach. "Learning to forget is the only important thing," he says. "Christ! What a nightmare!"

Morrison staggers around, unsteady. "I need a bath, a shave and a real bed to sleep in. And something female with long legs and a talent for entwining."

"Is that order to go or will you have it here?"

"I'll take it to go. You got any ideas?" says Morrison.

I shrug. "Don't look at me. I am in exile myself."

"Chick throw you out?"

"I threw myself out."

"No difference," says Morrison with a scowl. "I smell like a sock taken off a hibernating bear. We've got to find us someplace to hole up for the night. Find us a cave where we can be blind cave fish, eyeless, safe and warm."

"There's a party," I start to suggest, thinking of an ugly girl with terminal acne I know in Hollywood. I know she's having a party 'cause that's all she does do, is have parties, seven nights a week.

"Fuck parties," says Morrison, holding his head as if it were ready to fall off. "I need to get out of the trenches."

I'm thinking, considering the possibilities. "Well, there's this girl. She's following the band I came into town with. Far as I know, the band's still in town. If I call them, they can tell me how to find her. That would solve everything."

"How would that solve everything?"

"She's got money coming out of her wahzoo. Her old man owns a chain of hotels. She gets free rooms for herself wherever she goes, and a free room for anybody who balls her. If you jumped her bones, she'd get us a free hotel room."

"A free hotel room? You mean like with beds and baths and room service with booze and food we can charge to her? Just for screwing her?" Morrison grins like an idiot, liking it. "Oh, wow! It's a gold mine! It's the frigging mother lode!"

Then he frowns, thinking about it. "Uh, just how ugly is she?"

I shake my head. "Ugly is not one of her problems. She's built like the girl *Playboy* magazine puts staples in the middle of. Also she's got one of those cute little-girl faces you see on magazine covers and a backbreaking routine in bed that any cathouse would be proud to rent out."

"Charge!" says Morrison, swinging an imaginary saber. "Onward to horizontal victory!"

I have to warn him a little, though. "Uh, she's a little bit weird, you know," I caution Morrison. I sigh. "Actually, she's a whole lot weird."

"Weird like whips and chains?" says Morrison, not really giving a damn.

"On her, that would be pretty close to normal. No. I mean she's really weird. Like mentally disconnected."

"For a few days' free ride in a hotel, I could overlook

cannibalism," says Morrison. "Let us not hesitate. Let us hurry hence. Lead on, Macduff, and all that razzma-tazz!"

"I don't know if she's into cannibalism yet but she'll probably get around to it. Like I said, she's strange. I mean *really strange!*"

Morrison and I start walking off the beach, sharing the wine.

"How is she strange? I mean, you really got to work at being strange in L.A. I mean, everybody's so brain-fried here anyway," says Morrison, belting back some wine. "Is screwing her going to be a hassle? Like how strange is strange?"

"Listen," I tell him, hoping I don't scare him off but feeling he at least ought to know, "she travels around with this St. Bernard. And she and the St. Bernard drop acid together and ball together. She gets it on with her St. Bernard. I'm not making that up. That's for real."

"A real dog lover," says Morrison, shrugging, think-ing about it. "You mean I have to take sloppy seconds from a dog, from a frigging *St. Bernard?*" The idea seems cosmic. Morrison's face lights up. "Outta sight!"

"Also she did about a million mikes of acid a year ago and she hasn't come down yet. Her mind is kind of like a disconnected phone number with static and no dial tone."

"I could screw a buzz saw," says Morrison. "Call those guys and let's find out where she is."

"Okay. I did my part. I warned you she was strange. I'll find her, that'll be my half of the deal, and you hump her brains out, that'll be your end."

"Far out," says Morrison. "I can ask her if she's ever had any dogs better in bed than me. I've never had to compete with a dog before."

I sigh, reaching into my pocket for a dime for the phone. Maybe Morrison never had to compete with a dog before, but I had.

Should I tell him I lost?

The phone only rings once before somebody picks it up.

"Mort's Mortuary," says a voice on the other end. "You stab them, we slab them."

"Spence. Is that you, Spence?" If it's Spence, he sounds loaded, as usual.

"I don't know," says the voice happily. "Let me look at my navel and call you next week when I find out."

"Hey, asshole, it's me." It would have to be him answering the phone. Spence is the biggest brain-damage case in the whole group. Ever since Russ split for another group, these guys have been self-destructing. No one sane around to hold them together.

"Hello me!" There's a pause on the other end. "Oh. Am I talking to me? How am me?"

"Spence, you asshole."

"Now I know who it is! It's Mickey Mouse. How's Minnie? Putting it to her regular, are you?"

"Spence! Shut up! Tell me where I can find Sheila!"

"Look under the nearest dog."

"Knock it off?" Just my luck to get Spence. You could say he takes drugs. You could say that. I've seen him so ripped, he's walked into a bar and tried to light a bottle of beer and drink a pack of cigarettes. "I'm serious. Let me talk to somebody else!"

"Who?"

"Anybody!" I shout into the phone. "Anybody! Let me talk to the nearest sane person!"

There's a pause on the line again. "Uh, sorry, Mickey. There's just a bunch of rock and roll musicians here. I don't think there's any sane persons here. I think we ran out of them last week."

There's the sound of a struggle on the other end and then a new voice comes on the line. "Anchovy pizza and no mushrooms!" says the voice, bellowing into the phone.

"Chris? Is that you, Chris?" The only semi-sane one in the bunch.

"No mushrooms," says the voice, belching loudly.

"Chris, can you tell me where I can find Sheila?"
What's wrong with these guys?

"How soon?" asks the voice, still yelling into the
phone.

"What do you mean how soon? How soon what?"
What the hell is he talking about?

"The pizzuh!" Chris yells. "How soon do you bring
the pizzuh!"

"Forget the frigging pizza! Where can I find Sheila?
Sheila?" I'm screaming into the phone now.

"Oh, it's you," says a third voice, after the sound of
another struggle. The voice sounds like a 45 record
played at 33, slow motion, words dragging against each
other. "Look, you better get over to our hotel right
away. I mean, yeah, uh huh, 'cause, uh, like we, uh, got
this gig, and uh, well, ain't nobody in any shape to,
like, uh, drive." The voice drifts off, as if the person
speaking has passed out, then comes back in again. "I
mean, uh, can you dig it, we got this, uh, gig, and, uh,
no driver. So, um, you better come over and . . . and . . .
hmmmm, drive us . . . okay?"

"I'm trying to find Sheila!" I try not to scream in the
phone and just barely succeed.

"Who? What? Uh, oh . . ." There's a long pause, and
just when I begin to think he's passed out, he comes
back with, "Oh, uh, who?"

"*Sheila!*"

"Oh yeah. She's here, she's like, you know, loading
the truck, man. On account of everybody's so wasted,
you know. And um, I think, um, she's gonna drive, uh,
'cause you're not here, right?" Whoever's at the other
end, and it sounds like Mick, seems to be trying to puzzle something out. "Oh yeah, and you ain't here, right?
Is that right? Right?"

I feel like tearing the frigging phone right out of the
phone booth. In the background I hear Chris yelling for
his "pizzuh."

"Oh, Christ! Listen! I'm coming right over, me and a
friend! Don't let that dog-loving maniac near that god-

damn truck! Sheila couldn't drive a merry-go-round horse without crashing! You hear me! Keep her away from that frigging truck until I get there!"

"Uh, yeah. Don't let her drive the, uh . . . keep her away from, uh . . . what was that you said?"

"*Don't let Sheila drive the fucking truck!*" Christ! She couldn't find the right side of the road if it came with her period.

"What about my pizzuh?" a voice screams in my ear.

I hang up, thoroughly cranked off.

"Did you find her?" says Morrison, finishing the last of the wine.

"Yeah. I know where she is." I frown. "Looks like we are gonna have to do some frantic hitchhiking to get there, though. I hope we get there in time. You can't join people in a graveyard."

"Wanna bet?" says Morrison. "That's the only place where they start to get real."

Morrison's energetic, beating me out to the highway. "Let's go! Let's get it on!" he says, talking to the cars as they whizz by.

Maybe if I told him how much competition a St. Bernard is, he wouldn't be so eager.

We get lucky. Practically the first van that goes by stops for us and on the inside is a stoned guy with ten pounds of beard on his face and a girl with a chest so flat it could be a landing strip. She's like maybe on a good day twelve years old but friendly. We know she's friendly 'cause she pops a joint in our mouths as soon as we get seated in the back and practically ignites us in her eagerness to get us lit up.

Good smoke. So smooth you don't know you're getting too much until you damn near choke. Nice folks. They go out of their way about six miles to drop us off exactly where we want to go. So lucky for us it's like magic.

"Outta sight," says Morrison, standing in the hotel parking lot, waving at the van as it pulls away from us.

I lead us into the hotel, hoping those idiots in the

band haven't split with Sheila driving. Sheila couldn't
back out of the hotel parking lot without driving into
the hotel swimming pool.

Spence is standing outside their hotel room, leaning
against the wall in the hallway, looking absolutely
wasted. He looks wasted because he is wasted. It's no
big surprise.

"It's good old me," he says, pointing at me.

I see Morrison staring at Spence, sizing him up.
Spence is something to see. About six foot five, coal
black hair like a lion mane flowing over his shoulders.
He's got a face carved out of granite and a chest a thor-
oughbred racehorse would be proud of. He used to be a
weight lifter and his body still looks like it.

He's dressed like Bela Lugosi, sort of a cross between
Elvis Presley's gold lamé country hick suits and what
the well-dressed Transylvanian count wears to a neck-
ing festival. Lace ruffles no less.

"I'm glad you guys haven't left yet."

Spence looks confused, scratches his head. "You
mean we're still here? Jesus! I thought we left!"

"Far out," says Morrison, not sure whether Spence is
kidding or not. He's probably not.

"Asshole," I say, passing Spence. I go into the room,
Morrison at my heels. Chris is on the bed, stretched
out, trying to blow smoke rings with an unlit cigarette.

Chris is wearing a ripped-up vest, tight white cordu-
roy pants and a glitter-covered top hat made out of
black velvet. Chris is about twenty-five pounds under-
weight, sort of a walking skeleton type with a face that
concentration camps usually get the credit for.

"Are you guys out of your frigging minds? You know
you're getting the look-over for an album shot and
you're sitting around here getting polluted right out of
your fish bowls!" I start in on him. "You guys can't
keep going into gigs totaled out and still expect to get a
record contract!"

I've told them all this stuff maybe a million times

but they have the attention spans of guppies.

"Welcome back, mother hen," says Chris, choking on an imaginary lungful of smoke. "Glad you came back to the fold. Man! Wheeew! I'm hungry as hell. I sent out for a pizzuh. A frigging anchovy pizzuh!"

It's like talking to a blank space on a death certificate.

"Where's the gig? How much is it? Is it a warm-up for Mitch Ryder? That was what Masters promised us. That was supposed to be next. Is that it? How long before you have to set up and go on?"

Chris shakes his head, staring at me with a blank look on his face. "Oh, wow. It's like twenty questions." He fumbles in his vest pocket, then takes a crumpled wad of paper out of his shirt pocket, tosses it in my general direction. "Uh, it's all written down. All you gotta do is get us there. Don't worry about us. We could play with rigor mortis. You get us there, we'll do our stuff."

I unfold the crumpled ball of paper, stare cross-eyed at the chicken tracks on the page. "Jesus! Did somebody write this under water?"

I can make it out, but just barely. And it doesn't look good. To make the gig on time, it's going to be a leave-right - now - and - drive - like - a - mad - bandit - straight - through-and-we'll-just-barely-make-it kind of thing.

Morrison's restless. "Like what's happening? Are you going off with these guys or what? And where's this Sheila you were talking about?"

I almost forgot Morrison. I turn and look at him, shrugging as if to say I'm trapped, I got no choice. "Look, these maniacs will kill themselves if I don't go with them. You wanna come along? We'll drag Sheila along. You can hump her until she breaks out in overlapping poodles. When we get to the other end, she'll get us a hotel room and we can live like kings for a couple of days. How's that sound?"

Morrison shrugs, ready for anything. "Why not?

Can't be any worse than going back and sleeping on the beach. Might be an interesting diversion. Do they have any dope?"

"Are you kidding? You think these guys got like this licking postage stamps? Food they can do without, sleep they can do without, sex they can do without, not that they've ever tried, but do without drugs? *Never!*"

"The music bone is connected to the dope bone," says Chris.

"Let's do it," says Morrison. "Might as well get our kicks while we can."

Chris gets off the bed, stepping into the wastebasket beside the bed. He stands there like an idiot, up to his knee in it.

Mick walks into the room, looking almost straight, except he walks a little too fast and runs face first right into a wall.

"Truck's loaded. Almost loaded anyway. We got everything out by the truck that should be out there. Except we're missing a couple people, I think," he says, sounding more or less coherent. He stares cross-eyed at the wall his face just hit. Walls are always surprising his face. Floors do it to him too.

Time for me to take charge. "Okay, we got to get rolling. Round everyone up, get them in the truck. If Sheila's out by the truck, load her up too. She's gonna go with us. I'll drive and I'll make sure you guys got everything loaded."

I stuff the paper with the info about the gig in my pants pocket. I don't know how we're going to make it there in time but I'll give it a shot anyway.

Chris, still in the wastebasket, looks like he's gonna cry. "Aren't we gonna wait for the pizzuh?"

It takes Morrison and me both to get him untangled from the wastebasket. We get everybody out of the room. We find a chick passed out in the bathroom, a groupie who's had too much fun all at once, and we

leave her there as a kind of tip for the chambermaid.
We don't really have any use for her.

We get out to the truck, carrying a guitar case and
some clothes that didn't already get picked up. "Did
anybody pay the hotel bill?" I remember to ask.

"I remembered not to," says Chris. "You better
write it down. I mean, the name of the hotel, so we remember not to stay here again."

"One of these days they're going to get wise to you
guys and you'll do your next gig behind bars. You guys
really ought to pay every once in a while." What a
bunch of fuckups!

"We paid a month ago," says Chris, trying to remember where and when. "Yeah. It was in Atlanta."

"We never were in Atlanta."

"Well," says Chris with brilliant logic, "if we had
been in Atlanta, we would have paid."

Morrison and I get Spence, Mick and Chris out to the
truck. There's a pile of equipment sitting beside the
truck, still not stowed away. Sheila's dog is sitting on a
guitar case, looking like a furry Buddha. Under the guitar case, which is under the St. Bernard, is another
passed-out groupie. Where are they all coming from?
This one must be a keeper because somebody went to
the bother of dragging her outside. I'll probably get in
the truck and find one packed in the glove compartment and one stored inside the snare drums.

Sheila jumps out of the back of the truck, skids on
her high heels and goes over backwards on her ass.
That pretty much describes her, inside and out. Morrison reaches down and helps her to her feet. "First im-
pressions are always the best," he says to her.

Sheila smiles at him, liking him already. She's not
hard to get acquainted with. Her average seduction
time must be around fifteen seconds. She's dressed
in—and it's hard to believe, but it is what it is—a frigging girl scout uniform. It's so tight on her, her vacci-
nation is showing through the fabric. It's about three

sizes too small and only misses covering her knees by about eight inches. Sheila is also wearing high-top black leather boots with silver stars sewn into the sides and a tricorner hat that Errol Flynn probably wore when he was swashing his buckle on the high seas of some Hollywood sound stage.

"Who's you?" she says, hanging all over Morrison. "Are you famous? Did I sleep with you already or what?"

Morrison blinks, she's really lovely, but without a cigarette in her hand, she really has no attitude. What a space case!

"I think it was or what," says Morrison, amused.

"Stick around," she tells him, touching his face with one crimson-nailed hand. "If you're not famous, you should be. That's my karma, you know. I sleep with famous people. And Sagittarians. But no football players. That's bad karma. They try to bite your nose off." That makes no sense but that's Sheila.

"She's good-looking," Morrison says to me, looking surprised. I hadn't lied. For an idiot, she's stuffed to the limit with good-looking.

Under his breath Morrison adds, "But somebody gave her mind an enema."

Sheila latches on to Morrison. "Have you met Snowflake?"

Morrison shrugs, finds himself dragged in front of a bored-looking St. Bernard. I busy myself with loading the rest of the goodies in the truck.

"Like say hello," Sheila says to Jim. "His name's Snowflake but you can call him Snowflake. He's a far-out cosmic real-like person only he's a St. Bernard at the moment, which is like his karma. He's not a vege-tarian, which is like his trip, you know, and he's bummed out, you know. I mean really bummed out, 'cause like Elvis Presley, you know, and like the Bea-tles, you know, and anyway, say hello. He's really very sensitive, you know."

Morrison just stands there with his mouth open.

The dog stares open-mouthed at Morrison. It's a Mexican standoff.

"Does he speak French?" asks Morrison, not about to rap with a dog, no matter how sensitive the pooch is. "French is the only literate language."

Sheila taps one bright painted nail against her teeth, thinking it over. "I don't know. Remind me and I'll ask him later."

I continue loading up the truck. It's gonna be super-crowded. The people who ride in back are going to have to be either very very friendly or so fried that they aren't going to mind being stacked on top of each other like Oreos in a cookie bag.

At least I don't have to worry about Morrison getting together with Sheila. I can sense room service in the immediate future. Sheila's attached to Morrison like a leach. Morrison keeps rolling his eyes heavenward. The longer she talks, the more brain damaged she sounds.

"What are you getting me into?" says Morrison with a sigh, as I help him and Sheila up into the back of the truck. Snowflake's already loaded up, taking up most of the room in back. Sheila wouldn't go anywhere without Snowflake. I don't envy those guys riding in back. Twelve hours up close with a bummed-out St. Bernard is not my idea of fun.

"What if Snowflake has to go peepee and doodoo like, you know, while we're traveling?" asks Sheila as I close the rear door on her face.

"Pray for constipation," I tell her.

Spence and I get into the cab. The cab is full of beer, must be four six-packs of it. Spence touches me on the elbow. "Hey, what about that?" he says, motioning out the front window.

I look out and see a guitar case, and the groupie who had been sleeping under it, crawling across the parking lot in front of the truck. "That's my guitar," says Spence. "It's trying to walk away."

Spence looks at me with a very serious expression on

his face. "You know I can't play my guitar if I don't have it with me?"

This guy is brilliant! I get out and get his guitar and the chick and stuff them in the cab with us.

"Now is that it? I mean is that everything? Is there anything else that's going to hold up the parade?"

"Uh, nothing," says Spence, "except maybe the hotel manager who's coming out of the office and is heading this way."

I look out the side window on Chris's side. Oh, Christ!

I start the truck and go roaring out of the parking lot.

The manager runs out into the street, shaking his fist at us. I can see his lips moving, as he memorizes our license plate number.

"Gee," says Spence, "that guy looks likes he's really pissed off."

"Assholes!" I say. "All he has to do is call the cops, report the license number and our asses are grapes."

"Don't sweat it," says Spence. "Soon as we get out of sight"—he reaches into the glove compartment and takes out two license plates, hands them to me—"all you got to do is stop, take the stolen plates off, throw them away and put the new set on. Take your pick. We got six different sets."

I shake my head. These guys would make good gangsters if they practiced a little more. Spence especially. He could be another Al Capone, except he lacks his compassion.

"I got a bad feeling about this," I say, zipping through the traffic, heading for the freeway. Spence leans back against the seat, not paying any attention to what I'm saying.

I feel something cold crawling up my spine. I have this uneasy feeling I can't quite shake or explain.

"I got a feeling we're headed for the big nasty."

CHAPTER 17

I know what I'm in for so I raid the glove compartment and take a couple of Benzedrines, the patron saints of truck drivers everywhere.

The tape player's going full volume. Spence, beside me in the cab of the truck, bangs the dashboard in time to the Grateful Dead. "Jerry Garcia is my main squeeze," he says, popping the top on the third can of his second six-pack. The inside of the truck cab smells like a brewery.

A groupie, underage, with crooked teeth, is passed out between Spence's legs, one arm wrapped loosely around the gear-shift lever. She'd been awake for a little while, talking disjointedly about downers and beer and weed and too much of everything. Her poor little brain had its mental tongue hanging out. Spence and I were glad when she slipped back into unconsciousness. It was when she was at her best.

I wonder where Spence finds these pigs anyway.

Spence is tapping his foot on the floor and her head bobs up and down on his knee in time to the music that blares from the speakers. Spence is drunk. Completely shit-faced. Nothing new. Far as I can tell, he's been drunk every night for the last two weeks.

"Pull over. I got to piss."

"Christ! I just pulled over," I growl, and it's true.

"I gotta piss."

"I ain't stopping. You wanna piss and I wanna make it in time for this gig. You guys ain't exactly rolling in money, you know. If we don't get to this gig, we're going to all end up working in a friggin' gas station again!" The stupid maniac! Spence downs a can of beer every ten minutes and has to piss every five.

"Stop the truck, you dumb bastard."

"Climb a pole!"

"Hell with you. I'll piss out the frigging window."

Next thing I know, Spence whips it out and is hosing down a fat woman in a blue convertible. In broad daylight no less. Piss splashes in a yellow stream all over the fat woman's windshield.

The woman panics, jams on her brakes, weaves across the road crazily and ends up with her car, ass backwards, in the ditch.

"*You frigging maniac!*" I scream at Spence. Spence zips up, unconcerned, totally aware of what's happened, but indifferent.

Chris has his head through the window in the divider and sees it all. The window slaps shut. Out of sight, out of mind.

I slam the accelerator to the floor and we speed away. The situation suggests distance and I want to get as much of it between us and the accident as I possibly can and fast.

Getting stopped by the cops is the last thing in the world we need right now. We are a traveling mass of illegalities.

"Eat my biscuits," says Spence, and then, as if for the first time, he notices the chick passed out between his legs. He grabs her hair and lifts up her head so he can take a look at her face. "Hey! Who's this?"

I don't say anything, concentrating on my driving, passing everything in sight. Ben Hur has nothing on me.

Spence says, "Is she yours?"

"What?"

"Is this thing yours?" Spence bangs her head against the dashboard to see if she's still among the living. She doesn't respond.

My eyes open wide. "I thought she was yours! I thought she was your chick. She was passed out under your guitar case. You saw me dump her in the cab with the rest of your stuff."

"She ain't mine," says Spence. "I thought she was yours."

"No way. I never get that desperate."

"Who does she belong to then?"

Spence bangs on the divider that separates the cab from the back of the truck. The little window flies open and a small cloud of marijuana smoke blows into the cab through the window. Chris sticks his face through the window. He has a pencil in his teeth, a totally destroyed look on his face. He holds up a crossword puzzle book. "Hey, you guys! What's a three-letter word that means 'suck my donkey'?"

Spence flips his hand over his shoulder, dumping the rest of his can of beer through the window. Chris splutters as the beer hits his face, then reaches through and hits Spence in the face with the crossword puzzle book. These guys are what you call real intellectuals.

Spence calls out, "*Truce!*"

Chris stops hitting him in the eye with the cross-word puzzle book.

Spence says, "Hey, piss-eyed wimp! Is this your piece of nooky out here?"

Chris sticks his beer-wet face farther through the window, looking down at the face that Spence drags into view by its hair.

"Nah! It ain't mine, man. She's got the terminal ug-lies and I swore off that kind of chick until the VD clinic gives me their seal of approval."

"Well, then, whose is it?" asks Spence, still holding her head up by her hair. She's lucky she's out cold 'cause it would hurt like hell otherwise. "She's giving my legs cramps. Find out whose she is. I'm tired of her already."

The faces at the divider window come and go. All ex-cept Morrison's and Sheila's. They are busy in the back, being overfriendly. Nobody claims her. Not too surprising.

"Pull over," says Spence, throwing an empty beer can out the window. He lets go of the chick's head and it smashes back against the dashboard. She's going to have some terrific bruises if she survives.

"I frigging-A do not believe it!" I say. "You just pissed five seconds ago!"

Spence is mad. "Pull over or I'll ram the frigging gear shift through your heart!"

A rest stop is coming up, so I turn signal, bitching all the time, and pull off the highway. At this frigging rate, we are definitely not going to make it.

I pull up in front of the john and park. Spence bangs open his door, swings one leg out and then shoves the little chickie out, head first.

As her head spangs into the concrete, it makes the sound a watermelon makes when you kick it. I flinch, glad it's not my head.

"You maniac!" says Chris, looking through the win-dow, seeing what Spence is doing. Chris's head disap-pears and we hear a scuffle in back as if somebody is walking over bodies and then we hear the back door of the truck slamming open.

Chris comes tearing around the side of the truck, looking really pissed off about something. Maybe it was his chick after all and he was just too embarrassed to admit it?

"What's his problem?" says Spence, glaring at Chris.

The dump on her head hasn't done real good things to the little lady. Her nose is bleeding and she's up-chucked in her sleep, coating herself in what looks like three boxes of Oreo cookies. What a pig!

"Spence, you frigging maniac!" says Chris, pointing an accusing finger at Spence. Chris looks furious.

Spence looks indignant, slouching on the seat in his top hat. "Well, shit," he says, "it ain't all that far from the cab to the—"

"You animal! You frigging, heedless animal!" says Chris, and he grabs the chick by her ass and hauls her up, more or less on his shoulder, careful not to get vomit on his shirt. "How many times do I have to tell you! They got laws in this frigging state! *Laws!*"

Spence jams his top hat further down on his head and just glares at Chris. "She isn't my chick! I never even touched the maggoty piece of jail bait! And dropping her on her head, man, I don't have to put up with—"

"*Laws!*" says Chris, and he starts hauling the chick away. She's still zonked, not even close to being in this world. "I mean, Jesus! Who can afford to get arrested!" says Chris, and he's standing over a green metal trash barrel with the girl. "I mean the penalty in this state for *littering* is no frigging joke!"

He up-ends her in the wastebasket and she sinks in. She's like a jellyfish and she slops down into the garbage can so far only her bare feet are sticking out of the barrel.

Spence leans out of the cab window, opening another beer. "Jesus!" he says and he puts his hand over his heart. "You've saved me from a life of crime!"

Chris dusts off his hands. "No need to thank me, son. Doing the deed was its own reward."

"Balls," I say. "Holy Christ!"

Spence turns and looks at me. "What's wrong with you? Ain't you got no sense of humor?"

"Not anymore. It just got arrested." I point at the rearview mirror on the side of the truck. Parked right behind our truck is a state highway patrol car and a fat lady in a dirty blue convertible with bent-up fenders. I've seen that dirty blue convertible before.

So has Spence. It looks suspiciously like the one he pissed on. It is.

I take the keys out of the ignition. "Looks like my truck driving days are over."

"Spence," says Chris, aware that we are tits in the wringer, "you see, I warned you about that littering!" His face is white in spite of the joke.

Spence hurriedly downs the beer he's just opened. "Anybody got a suicide kit?"

That's not a half-bad idea. Suicide sounds very tempting. We've got maybe five pounds of weed in the truck, assorted miscellaneous dangerous drugs including cocaine, acid and all kinds of speed, an underage chick in the garbage can, which is carrying a minor across state lines, which is some kind of superheavy federal crime number, and so on and so on. And leaving the scene of an accident, causing one, public urination (which may be assault with an undeadly weapon) and you are talking about enough flight time in the slammer to make us all old and gray.

If you count all the crimes, the list is probably endless.

Like me, innocently driving the truck even though I'm only fifteen and my driver's license is fake, fake, fake. The picture on it doesn't even look like me. It shouldn't. It isn't me but we have the same color hair. The resemblance stops pretty much right there.

"The shit," says Spence, "not only hit the fan, but some of it has gone into the wall socket too."

The state trooper gets out of his car slowly, like his car is giving birth to him. Some birth! The trooper is maybe ten foot tall and looks like the kind of guy that will either have only one eye in the center of his forehead, or raised eyebrow ridges, hairy knuckles, and when he walks, his hands will drag on the ground, gorilla style. A real intellectual with raw meat on his breath.

This is a high cab we're sitting in and I swear, without even bending over, he's leaning directly on the window frame of the truck cab.

"You fellows see a bunch of long-haired faggots that maybe pissed out of their truck window?"

He smiles and he's got maybe three or four thousand teeth, all rotten. "Hell! I'm sure you boys have seen these freako perverts."

The trooper puts one hand the size of a basketball on my shirt collar and kind of gathers me like a handful of potato chips. I sound very crispy as my bones crack. He yanks.

I go out the truck window. I am glad the window is rolled down. Real glad. It's less painful that way.

Before my feet barely touch the ground, he has my head up alongside the truck and he's pushing his hand against my face so hard I can feel the metal of the truck door bending out of shape around the back of my head.

"All you faggots out of the truck!" roars the cop.

Nobody disagrees. At least nobody conscious. Sheila and Snowflake are in cloud cuckoo land and they don't come out. Everybody else pours out fast, like ants out of a burning anthill.

The cop lets go of my face so my nose can bleed freely, which it does. Morrison comes and stands beside me. He looks like he's in a controlled rage.

"Get your faggoty butts over here and lean up against the side of this truck!" the cop yells in his best SS stormtrooper voice.

We rush to obey. All except Spence. He's a little too drunk to move quick. The cop helps him out by giving him a shove that puts his head into the side of the truck as hard as a baseball gets hit by a bat.

Spence slides down the truck, nearly knocked out cold.

The fat woman is sitting in her car. I can see her clearly. She's shaking her fist at us. Muttering curses under her breath. I can tell she feels safer inside the car than outside with all us hippy, long-hair freako perverts.

The cop goes through the motions of slapping us down for weapons. Some motions. His idea of a frisk is short vicious jabs with his nightstick to see if he can hear the sound of metal, knives or guns.

He puts everybody on the ground, holding their stomachs and sides, all except Spence, who's already down on his knees. Spence is lucky in a way. He's built like Tarzan's foster parents and can take quite a beating.

Me, I'm tough as a crate of eggs. The first chop of the nightstick puts me away. Morrison and I end up together on our knees, our faces against the side of the truck.

"Some fun," says Morrison under his breath.

Chris turns around, faces the cop. He digs his hands into his pockets, stares at the cop defiantly, pissed off. "Hey, man! Like this ain't cool, you know."

"A smart-ass," says the cop, delighted to meet some resistance.

"Yeah," says Chris. "How do you know? Did you see it doing tricks?"

The cop draws himself up to his full height. He looks very pleased with himself. "I'm gonna love kicking your fucking teeth in!"

Chris starts to say something else, something sarcastic, and the cop swings, lays him out with his billy club. Really lays him out. A vicious shot to the kidneys, and then, when Chris bends over double, another smash of the club against the back of Chris's head so hard he is driven head first between the cop's legs.

"Who's next? Who's gonna be next?" The cop's really excited. "C'mon, you faggots! Let's see somebody else shoot their fucking mouth off!" He slaps his billy club against the palm of his hand.

There's a noise inside the truck and I clearly hear Sheila saying "Don't be like that." She sounds frightened. I hear Snowflake growling. A bad sign. Sometimes Snowflake gets a little crazy, gets a little vicious from the drugs, and two hundred pounds of bummed-out St. Bernard can really be hard to take. Even Sheila isn't safe from him.

"Who's in there?" The cop slams the side of the truck with his billy club. Snowflake growls, upset.

The cop turns and stares at us, hate flashing in his eyes. He pulls out his gun, holds it in his right hand, switches the billy club to his left hand. "I'm going around the back," he tells us. "Anybody moves gets his fucking head shot off."

The back doors are standing wide open but it's dark in there and I guess he can't see who's in there.

I see his legs from under the truck where I'm still on my knees. He's standing square in front of the doorway.

"You better come out of there, you dumb son of a bitch!" snarls the cop. "Or I'll shoot the fuck out of you!"

Something's moving inside the truck.

I hear the cop banging something with his nightstick. There's a loud slap. It's a mistake.

I hear a frenzied growl and then something smashing inside the truck. I'm there beside Morrison, holding my aching sides, watching the cop's legs.

I hear the cop scream, then a gunshot, and suddenly the cop is flat on his ass with two hundred pounds of enraged St. Bernard dancing on his face. The gunshot's driven the dog mad and he's biting into the cop's chest like the cop is made out of dog food and Snowflake has been on a diet too long.

I hear the massive jaws snapping, biting, tearing. It's

like a lion at the zoo at feeding time.

Morrison and I get up, run around the back. The cop is bleeding from a big wound in his chest and he's out cold, his head slammed into the concrete, driven hard by two hundred pounds of dog. The cop looks seriously damaged. He looks more than that. He looks dead. There's lots of blood and the dog's jaws are still tearing at him.

Morrison kicks the dog in the side and Snowflake turns, enraged, forgetting about the cop, and starts for Morrison. That is Morrison's idea all along, but as soon as it works, he regrets it.

The dog leaps at him, begins chasing him, his muzzle red with blood. Morrison flies around the truck, running for all he's worth, the St. Bernard snapping at his heels.

The only thing saving Morrison is the corners as they race around the truck. The dog's so frigging big he can't make the sharp corners.

The rest of us are standing behind the truck, staring at the body of the cop, except for Chris, still lying face down.

"He looks dead," says Mick, looking genuinely scared.

Spence comes up and stands beside me. Morrison thunders past us, the dog yowling at his heels, leaping over the cop's body, tearing around the truck again. It's comical but nobody's laughing.

"What do we do?" says Spence, staring at the cop.

The woman in the blue convertible roars out of the parking lot at high speed, looking horrified, probably thinking we're gonna attack her next or something.

"Change the license plates and let's split," suggests Mick. "They *kill* people for doing in cops in this state! We got to get the fuck out of here!"

Nobody disagrees.

Mick starts changing the plates. Morrison leaps into the back of the truck, somehow gets the doors slammed before Snowflake can get at him. Spence and I are clumsily putting Chris, as gently as possible, into the cab of the truck. He's maybe got a concussion.

Mick finishes changing the front plate and goes to the back to change the rear plate.

We hear a snarl, a scream, and then Mick comes bolting full speed toward the front of the truck, Snowflake hot on his ass.

Mick dives into the cab, falling across Chris's body. Snowflake jumps for him, his jaws just missing his legs.

The dog leaps up against the door in a frenzy, teeth snapping against the door.

"The fucking dog is insane! He's turned killer!" says Mick, wild-eyed, freaked out of his mind.

There's a crash in back of the truck, Sheila screaming, Morrison yelling. Sounds like a fight going on. Maybe Sheila's trying to get out, trying to get to Snowflake, and Morrison's not letting her.

The cab is sardine-can tight. Mick, Spence, Chris out cold and me, all trapped inside by two hundred pounds of maniac gunshot-freaked-out St. Bernard.

Mick's still got a license plate in his hands. "I couldn't change them! That sucker turned on me! He's gone mad!"

"Get us out of here!" says Spence.

I can barely shift the gears. Spence is sitting where the gear shift has to go.

"If we leave that dog, Sheila will murder us in our beds!" I say.

"Drive! That dog is flip city! We can't bring him in the truck! He's gone killer. Just get us the fuck out of here!" says Spence. "If another cop comes, our asses are grapes."

The dog keeps leaping up the side of the truck cab, trying to get at us. The whole thing is a dream, an out-of-focus comedy that happens to someone else, and that nobody finds funny.

I get the truck rolling and the dog, foaming at the mouth, chases us up the ramp, following us back onto the freeway.

I watch the dog running behind us, watch cars slow down, trying not to hit him. The dog runs behind us maybe a mile before I lose sight of him.

Nobody says anything for a while. It's too unreal.

There's a crash in the back, sounds like somebody got his face popped hard. There's a thud, like a body falling down. Maybe nobody notices that but me.

We are so supercramped nobody can move. Chris is still gone, maybe seriously injured.

"Did that really happen?" says Mick, shaking his head. "Was that real? I think I'm tripping." Nobody answers him. The whole thing was like a film. Once it's gone by, it's gone, lingering like the memory of a very insubstantial dream.

"Maybe he'll get lucky," says Spence, meaning Snowflake. "Maybe when he calms down, somebody will adopt him."

"I bet the cop will," says Mick. "He looked like the kind of guy who would get along good with animals. He could relate to them on their own level."

"Morrison!" yells Spence. "Are you all right back there?"

Morrison's face appears at the window in the divider. "Everything's cool. Except I kinda had to deck the lady. She was hysterical, trying to jump out of the truck while we were moving. What's happening now?"

Spence shakes his head. "We are getting away from it and with it. Pull over in a little bit and change the rear plates. Rest of us will come back with you. Hope you didn't break her jaw?"

"She's all right. Didn't knock her out, just down. She's quiet now. Getting into some downers, enough to make a horse laid back."

"That was a close thing back there," says Morrison. "That frigging dog damn near got me."

"That dog is Lizzie Borden with teeth trouble," says

Mick. "It is Lucretia Borgia with a tail. Damn near got me too."

"And that cop was the Marquis de Sade of common sense," adds Spence. "He was the delivery man for the ready-to-wear electric chair."

I smile at Morrison, the miles spinning by adding to our safety. "We escaped."

Morrison shakes his head, staring at us, packed in like human sardines. "Nobody ever escapes," says Morrison. "Nobody."

I am probably the only one there who knows he's right.

CHAPTER 18

I shut off the truck engine. "There's still magic in the world. We made it. This is it. Let's unload."

It's dark in back of the warehouse that's now a rock and roll palace. The truck doors go open in back and in front and we all crawl out of the truck, very much the worse for wear. We look like a country that did not win in World War Two.

Chris is back among the living with a probable concussion but able to function. He refuses to see a doctor. Spence, dead drunk, is still sober enough to stand up. That's something anyway.

I am wired, speeded up and speeded out. We got there and that's all I know, all I can really understand.

It's a strange place we are in and no one's there to help us get our gear in. Already too weary, it's up to us, with Morrison and me doing most of the work, getting our rig inside and getting it set up.

Five bands tonight, that's what the posters outside say, and we are first on. Feels like we traveled a million light-years to get here. In some ways, maybe we have.

Sheila's gone deep-sea diving on downers, stomach-pump city, mourning the loss of Snowflake. We roll her over on her stomach so she doesn't choke to death on her own vomit, and just leave her in the truck. If she dies, she dies.

The place is packed, full of teeny screamers and rock and roll animals. The rock palace is an enormous empty cavern like the inside of an abandoned airplane hangar, rapidly filling with the young of our own kind.

We are them at their most desperate.

Spence peeks through the heavy black curtain hiding us as we set up onstage. "Lots of animals out there tonight," he says, his voice slurred. "It's gonna be a rock and roll weekend!"

Morrison, clumsy, helps me set up the equipment. Mick's staring at a wall. Chris, eating raisins and pain-killers, his face of mask of boredom despite pain, talks disinterestedly to a groupie chick with green eyeshadow and big tits.

She keeps volunteering to give everybody head but nobody's interested.

Randall comes in, the bass player. He didn't travel with us. He almost never does. He's never with us until it's time to play. He's, like now, usually at the gig ahead of us. He's got a couple of band groupies in tow.

Randall's maybe the only honest-to-God musician in the group. He can even read music. Remarkable. He is always crawling off somewhere to jam with other musicians, and always bringing back minichicks too.

He has a talent for scoring underage stick lickers that amazes everyone. He could find a groupie above the Arctic Circle just hanging round, jamming with polar bears.

He lets loose of the quickie bangers and goes right for his bass guitar, begins twiddling dials and tuning in, getting geared for his big moment, everything else forgotten.

Everybody is in their own oblivion, just barely existing, the waiting-to-go-on mood, a bad taste that is all too familiar.

The crowd outside is getting restless. The show's an hour late getting off the ground, partly because of us, partly because that is the way it always is.

The cat from management comes in, a fat guy with disk jockey eyes with as much depth as the hole in an album, and lays his number on us. We suffer his glad-you-could-make-it-here, now-go-out-there-and-kill-them routine in the silence it deserves.

He bitches a little 'cause we got here so late he didn't know if were gonna show or not, etc., etc., etc. We try to get our money up front but no go. After the show, gate paying us off, if we're lucky. Then it's hustle hustle, 'cause it's time to go on.

"We're set," I tell him, being the only one who can talk to this kind of guy without puking all over his shoes.

Spence staggers over and picks up his guitar. He's so drunk, everybody's a little bit surprised he can even lift it.

The crowd outside is stamping their feet, getting ready to riot, demanding some action.

The management guy goes outside to lay down his fire-marshal-says-clear-the-aisles routine, which is bullshit since everybody's sitting on the floor and there ain't no aisles anyway. There's the usual joke about no smoking cigarettes unless they are funny ones. These guys are always lame. Always. The whole place is already full of the sweetish crowd-pleasing scent of weed. As many joints as there are fingers, it looks like, out there in the crowd. Looks like a chain-smoker convention.

Morrison and I are standing together on the side of the stage. The P.A. is all fucked up. I hope it gets us through to the end because there's nobody in any shape to fix it.

Chris looks up at the ceiling, waiting for the curtain, looking like a bored rocking horse that died of inertia. Mick is rolling his head from side to side like a drunken marionette. They are all on the edge of imminent collapse. I don't know what keeps them from falling over.

Randall seems mechanical, as if his life was fine tuned and carefully engineered. He looks like a giant clock about to strike the hour with the precision of the weight of the ages.

Spence's head is down on his chest, as if it were too heavy to lift.

"These guys are going to play rock and roll?" says Morrison, having been with them long enough to doubt it severely.

The management dude finishes his speech, announces the band, to thunderous cheers.

Morrison looks at me. "Why do they even bother getting up there, man? I've never seen a more destroyed-looking bunch of defectives."

The guys on the ropes begin dragging the curtain open.

"Just watch," I tell Morrison, having been with these guys long enough to know what it's all about. "This is their only moment to be alive. Just watch."

The crowd gives off an immense primal roar, thousands seething in the dark. The lights flash, spotlights exploding like a nova, sending unreal shadows curling up the walls of the stage.

Spence steps forward and his hands slam the strings and suddenly he's not drunk anymore. He's an electric Samurai warrior and his guitar is a deadly weapon.

The group moves as if it had the same wild heart, as

if it were a wild horse that no one could tame.

Chris is a fever, a human dynamo flinging electric thunderbolts into the night, into hungry ears and minds. The crowd roars again, letting the first big burst of electrified sound roll over them like some tidal wave that nothing can stop.

Suddenly they are larger than life, towering above the crowd, all the guitars, the drums, the amps, transformed into high-voltage energy weapons. And the darkness flashes with the sound of aural death rays, kiss and kill rushes roaring through amps turned up to full gain.

Sex and death, the crash of skin against skin, all exploding outward to infect the vast ocean of the crowd mind, huddled religiously in front of the altars of massive speakers.

High-charged guitars slash and scream, big Sun amps pushing megavolts through the waves of stoned bodies on the floor.

Inside the ballroom there's a sensation of all-consuming force, of rivers wearing down mountains, of day destroying night, of the ever-powerful, unstoppable rush that is youth streaming through one vast shared bloodstream.

Long-haired stonies, trippies drugged into one massive sensation, sit directly in front of the speakers, tossing their hair around their heads in frenzied abandon, like electric horses tossing their manes.

Morrison stands beside me, absolutely transfixed. He has a look of total fascination on his face.

He says something under his breath, spoken not to me but to himself.

I can just barely hear it.

He says, "I am the Resurrection and the life."

And there is in his voice a sensation of wonder, as big as any that travels with childhood.

The music drives on into the night, building and building, to die without cause or ceremony forty-five minutes later. To die on schedule, to die right on time, so the next group can come on and do it all over again.

The equipment gets dragged off. Spence is drunk again. Chris is bored and Mick stares at nothing, thinking of nothing, the moment gone for all of them.

Randall, the only one who never lets go, holds his guitar as if it were a camera and he's trying to take a picture of himself.

Randall walks off the stage, not speaking to anyone, holding his bass guitar under one arm, preoccupied.

"I don't believe it," says Morrison, helping me move the stacks of amps. "I cannot believe the fucking incredible animal energy!"

Morrison calls out to Spence, "You were fucking-A great, man!"

Spence looks at him, indifferent. "Oh, yeah. It's over, man. It's already gone by."

"But while it lasted it was incredible! The—"

"But it doesn't last. It never does. Fuck it!" says Spence, walking off, a little unsteady on his feet.

"What's wrong with him?" asks Morrison.

"You got to realize they only live for that moment onstage, that spark that sets them up above the world. While they are up there on that stage, they're living, really living, but everything else, the traveling, the waiting to go on, tearing down, chicks, all that is just so much broken glass," I tell him, having seen it all before.

"I want to do that!" says Morrison, with a fierce light in his eyes. "I want to feel that energy driving through my body!"

"I wanted to be a Negro," I say, picking up a guitar case and putting the guitar back inside. "Even when you get it, you don't get it. You can't always get what you want."

"We'll see," says Morrison, coming over to help me with the gear. "Someday I'm going to ride right through the heart of the night and everybody's going to believe that rock and roll will save their mortal soul!"

Rock and roll will save your mortal soul?

CHAPTER 19

Hours go by and we struggle to get through each slow century, the truck long since loaded. Just waiting for the night to end and the money to come so we can go someplace else.

Sheila doesn't die because I call an ambulance after dragging her out behind the back door so the cops can't connect her with us. They pump her stomach and take her away.

Nobody is sorry. Nobody cares. This is rock and roll. You do only what you have to do and you don't have to care, so mostly you don't.

Everybody splits but me. Morrison goes off somewhere with some new girl who's promised him something sweet and a free ride back to L.A.

Me, my time, hour by hour, gets spent waiting for
the money. And the longer I wait, the harder it gets to
get it. Finally, while the last band is going off, I march
in past the guy hired to keep us out of the office and
stick a shiv in the fat face of the suck ghoul from management and ask politely for my money. I practically
have to knife the bastard to get him to cough up the
money, and he tries to short-change me six ways to
breakfast and back. I get every penny of it.

I gather everybody up, get them back in the truck.
We are ready to strike out for the nothing we have set
off from. Make haste.

I really want to leave, get away from these guys, but
anything I do is like anything else so it doesn't matter.
I'm in for the whole tour.

It's as good a way to get lost as any other.

And we get very lost.

Little strange eyes
Well, you know what you've been
Tell me what are you winning
We made you alone
Back there at the beginning
I have all I am and you
You are all I know
Little strange eyes
We made you alone
We made you a stranger
Trapped inside your home
Why are you grinning
Little strange eyes
Have you been sinning?
Please take it easy
Please take it slow
I have all I am and you
You are all I know
You looked so nice
I wanted your fire
And touched all of your ice
Little strange eyes
We knew who put out the light
We loved you all the time
Before the death, at the birth
We were together when
We buried it in the earth
Little strange eyes
Little strange eyes

(The police saw what we did)

Jim Morrison and Craig Strete

CHAPTER 20

We are five weeks into the tour, burning out with too many one-night stands too far apart. All the signs are wrong and the tastes are wrong and all the women we see make us feel unclean and wicked.

None of us sleeps. It just doesn't seem to happen. Spence, our lead guitarist, is drunk, has been drunk three weeks straight. Mick, our drummer, is stroking the skins with a toothache. For four days he has been doing up downers, heavy doses. Traveling like we are, it'll be a couple of weeks before we're in one place long enough to see a dentist. Long as Mick's got downers,

he's sure he can hold out, even though one side of his
face is swelling up pretty bad and the downers have already dropped him down two flights of stairs. Somehow he manages to play the skins but his timing is off
and the band is constantly slow.

Randall's traveling with us for once and is driving us
all crazy, yelling and screaming about how fucked up
everybody is, how we're ruining his chance to be a star,
the whole tired routine.

"I could be a star but I am surrounded by assholes!"
Randall screams, slamming out of the Memphis hotel
room we all share. We're sleeping six in a bed. Have
been doing it seven nights in a row 'cause money is
tight, like always, like always. Seven different beds in
seven different cities. Sometimes one of us scores on a
chick who has a bed and there's only five of us in the
same bed. I think we look for chicks just so we can find
someplace to sleep. But most of the chicks we meet are
band groupies, underage and usually still living with
their parents. What a drag!

The tour! The trip! And the V.D. clinic at regular in-
tervals. I should have jumped ship when Morrison did,
crawled back to bitch goddess L.A. to burn in the California summer.

Anything but this, this drug-crazed, sleepless slide
down the sleazy side of the night. This meaningless
shuffle, the endless check-in-and-check-out routine in
a thousand heartbreak hotels.

The hotel room comes equipped with livestock,
shiny-backed roaches who've escaped from some cattle drive somewhere. And you can't get tired of the
kind of places where you eat because the thrill is always there: Will this greasy dogshit hamburger kill
me? Is it ptomaine? The fear of poisoning is the only
legitimate thrill.

And there's girls to jump. Lots of that. Like the one
I'm looking at now. I don't have far to look. I seem to
be lying down on the bed and she seems to be lying
down under me. I swear she wasn't there when I start-

ed to get on the bed. Well, they must breed like rabbits. They are everywhere.

She is my age, maybe a little younger, but with all that speed in me, too many days' worth, she is the closest thing to rest I can get. Usually, though, it's not tender, it's not clinging softly afterwards. It's usually more like an efficient billiard ball game between experienced players. But this one is into having and holding.

Rock and roll chicks are usually made out of leather—as soon as they get wet, they get stiff and hard. But not this one. She's really almost nice. She even sounds a little less dumb than these kinds of girls usually are.

"You know why I sleep with the bands?" she tells me, lying next to me in the bed, her pitiful little-girl breasts brushing against my bare back.

I don't say anything, just enjoy the feel of her next to me. "It's 'cause I want to sleep with someone who's famous, or might become famous. I know that sounds crazy to you."

"Un-huh." So what if it is crazy? I've heard it all before, anyway. Does she think she's the only one? There's a hundred thousand faceless ones of her.

"I know it sounds crazy, but you see, you don't know what it means to me. 'Cause, see, you guys have got some kind of power, some kind of bigger-than-life something or other, maybe it's like glory or something, you know, like it's I don't really understand, you know, but I want to sleep with you because . . . because somehow I think whatever it is, that magic, maybe some of that power, maybe . . . just maybe . . . maybe some of it will rub off on me. Then I'll really be somebody. I want to get close to you, close to your power."

She puts her arms around me, hugging me tight, reminding me of an affectionate puppy. "It's important to me."

"You're already somebody now. You just don't realize it," I tell her, playing with her hair.

She frowns, very serious about it all. "No! I'm not. I'm nobody. All I have is my body. It's the only thing I've got to offer."

She makes me sad, maybe even a little angry, although I don't know why. "Why don't you go home to Mommy and Daddy and straighten yourself up?"

She jumps like I stabbed her in the back. Jesus! She's almost crying.

"Home? You think I'd be here if I had a home to go to? My father! I never seen him. He's in prison for something. And my mother, she's just a whore. I've been gone two months already and she probably don't even know I'm gone yet. She only knows I'm around when she's sober, and she almost never is."

It could be all lies. Almost everybody you meet is selling you some kind of wolf ticket, some parade that never happened where they claim they were the best float. But she sounds like the truth.

She rolls away from me, now just a lonely little girl that somebody didn't love enough. "This is my *home*," she says. "These are my friends and they take care of me. I belong here."

I get up from the bed abruptly. I must be losing control of my personal steering wheel 'cause I feel sorry for her. She's like a little sister or something. Maybe she's got an echo of Tamara. I can't deal with it.

Spence, undressing, jumps on the bed. "Sloppy seconds time!" he says, struggling with his boots.

I put on my shirt, not looking at her.

"I liked you," she says, looking up at me. "Didn't you like me? Why did you just jump up and leave?" There is an ache in her voice, a lasting sorrow.

I look down at her, trying to think of some answer. Spence is on top of her, acting like the animal he is. I see tears in her eyes and suddenly I can't answer, can't even stand to look at her anymore.

Rock and roll will save your mortal soul?

I have to go, have to get the hell out of there. I go

outside and smoke a dozen cigarettes, standing down there in the hotel lobby, watching the rain falling on the water-slick streets of Memphis, waiting for the look on her face to fade out of my mind. I let a few hours go by, aimlessly.

I had seen that look before, on Tamara's face, the night I left.

And I know something then, for the first time, between cigarettes. I am going to go back to Tamara. I am tired of trying to live like a dream whose meaning has been lost. I am going to be in love just like everybody else.

No more holding back, no more lies, no more promises I can't keep. I know that's what I'm going to do.

Fall in love just like everybody else

But I am not like everybody else. I am not.

The only thing I know is games and all my games contain the idea of death.

I am a vulture descending on life.

I am a camera in the coffin, interviewing worms.

Knowing and believing are two different things.

I am going back to Tamara anyway.

I stub out a last cigarette and head back to the room. It's getting as dark outside as it is inside and there's no place to go.

Back in the room, somebody gave the little girl some drugs, some unfriendly chemicals to keep her warm, and we get something we've all seen before, too many times before.

A screamer.

They run through your hotel room at four in the morning with a bad trip exploding inside their heads and the inevitable hysterical confession that they lied about being eighteen. That's what we got on our hands now, live and in person, a screamer making a hysterical appearance in our crummy hotel room in Memphis.

Down here in good old Memphis to play a gig that

didn't even exist, drug all the way down here by a bullshit promoter who couldn't promote a bowel move-
ment let alone a rock and roll concert.

So we are overnighting it in Memphis, six to a crummy hotel room, seven if you count the groupie screaming at us, all of fifteen years old with bad chemicals in
her bloodstream, and haven't we danced this dance before?

It's four in the morning and the little lady suddenly
doesn't know who she is anymore or who we are, and
like a hundred times before, it's those screams of out-
rage, those screams of rape from the once willing, and
we all get that uneasy vision of some cold prison cell,
doing twenty trips around the sun for statutory rape.

We sit in a kind of shock, listen to her screaming at
us. Nobody does much about her, we just let her
scream. Nobody even knows her name or remembers
where she came from. Maybe we won her playing
cards. Who cares? No one. They all look the same after
a while, all the little ones with the same tired faces and
the tight little bodies that drugs and drinking and living loose are slowly killing.

There's this guy traveling with the band. I think
maybe he joined us in Detroit. Not invited, just some
brain-damage case who has lots of money and some big
talk about being a hot-shot record promoter. He's
gonna make us stars, he says, and it's a lie we never get
tired of hearing no matter how badly it is told.

None of us believe a word he says but he is useful
when it comes time to pay for gas and for the usual garbage you get to eat in crummy restaurants along the
way. So nobody tosses him out. Besides we'd be afraid
to.

This guy's Mexican or Puerto Rican. His English
isn't too good but his money is fine. He's got an ugly
knife scar on his left cheek that goes from one eye to
the corner of his mouth. Just some crazy bastard from
Detroit, which is where hell moved to get to a bad
neighborhood.

He follows our truck in a new Cadillac with a big dent in the hood. Nobody says it to his face, but we all know the car is hot. Christ! He switches license plates more often than we do.

It's Saturday night in Memphis.

The little groupie is screaming. If this is a movie, the projectionist is on drugs.

Spence is out getting drunk or staying that way.

Me, I am wrecked with speed.

Mick, down on his knees in one corner, is passed out from downers, head flopped over on a chair, neck bent at a painful angle. Dumb bastard's been falling down all day. I am tired of picking him up. His neck's gonna kill him tomorrow when he wakes up, but I'll be damned if I'm going to move the son of a bitch. Let him suffer.

I keep hoping somebody will get up, that somebody will go over to her and make her shut the hell up. Nobody does anything. I am on the bed, with my head buried in a pillow, trying to shut out the noise, expecting cops to come.

My ears hurt. Chris is long gone, must be hours since he left, gone out to cop some penicillin 'cause a red-headed groupie from Alabama gave him a special gift that burns like crazy. He's also maybe looking to lay his hands on the four-eyed pimp that got us down here for a gig that disappeared before we got into town. Randall's out head hunting for the promoter too, threatening to kill him, and maybe he will if he finds him. We had been told we were gonna do a warm-up for a big-name band. Turns out the band isn't even in America. Just another scam artist wet dream.

I look at the screamer, trying to remember what she was like when she was soft, when she was sad and lonely. "This hotel's got cockroaches. Rude, nasty, screaming cockroaches."

Chris pops back into the room "Hey!" he says, holding his ears as he comes all the way into the room. "Enough is enough! Turn down that music or I'll put your head through a goddamn door!"

I keep hoping she'll use up all the air in the room and collapse. Nobody knows what she's screaming about.

Chris slaps her and she dives for him, fastening on to his leg. The drugs have burned her little brain away.

"Make love to me! Please make love to me."

Chris turns and looks at me, the chick fastened to his leg like a leech. "What's wrong with her? Did somebody stop her from getting sloppy seconds?"

"She's just scared. She only feels wanted when somebody makes love to her." I can figure out that much anyway. She's really freaking out.

Chris tries to push her away but she's holding on tight so he rams his knee into her head and she thunks to the floor like a dropped bag of lawn fertilizer.

Now she really goes berserk. Nobody will touch her, nobody wants her, and her brain is flipping over like an automatic record changer.

Our Spanish-speaking friend with the hot Cadillac and the knife scar comes in with a couple of sacks of greasy hamburgers. He probably stole them.

The little chick sees the goon from Detroit and loses it completely.

She starts yelling rape, and I mean really yelling. All the screaming before is nothing compared to this. Sounds like she grew an extra set of lungs.

"Rape! Rape! Rape!"

That's funny 'cause she's been sleeping with everything that wears pants or looks like it might wear pants. How could she ever possibly be raped? The only time she ever said no was when she didn't understand the question.

Four in the morning, underage and yelling rape loud enough to bring every cop in the world down on us. Who needs it?

Mr. Knife Scar Detroit gets nervous as hell. Me, I'm too wired. I'm professionally nervous, speed pumping through me like electric eels swimming in my bloodstream. Those screams go through me, make me feel like I am swallowing a mouthful of razor blades.

I move back, getting ready for flight.

He goes over to her. "Shut up! Shut up!" He slaps her. I get a look at his face. Suddenly I am scared. This guy is crazy. Homicidally crazy.

He starts beating on her, hard solid blows to the face. But the little chick is past stopping, she's off the deep end, screaming her guts out. Even more incredibly, she strikes back.

She gets her fingernails into his face, goes right for the eyes and rips into him, drawing blood. She's in a drug-crazed state, stronger, berserk, all that adrenaline pumping into her overloaded bloodstream.

I try to get between them but he one-hands me out of the conflict, smashing me against the wall, flung halfway across the room with one blow.

I couldn't stop him with a machine gun.

I turn my head, not wanting to watch. She's just my age, still a kid really, and my stomach turns. I don't know why we do what we do when we do ourselves in.

I want to scream at them, to tell them to stop, but I know it's no use. All those brainless bodies, like silent movies that don't know yet they will someday have to talk.

I turn away, maybe I'm going to run out, just split. When I look back, the man from Detroit has a knife in his hand. Oh, Jesus! He puts the knife through her back like threading a human needle. It's so fast she doesn't really know what hits her.

Rock and roll is gonna save your soul?

She staggers away, scream cut off in her throat, bumps into the bathroom door and falls on through. There is a hard slap as she hits the tile floor.

Next thing I know I'm on my knees beside her and blood is coming out of her mouth and she's flopping on the bathroom floor like a fish out of water. Fifteen years old and a hole in her back in Memphis, Tennessee.

In the other room the man with the knife wipes his blade on the bedspread and says something complicated in Spanish to no one in particular.

Chris is out there running around the room like a head with its chicken cut off. He splits.

The man with the knife comes to the door and looks down at the body in my arms. I've seen a thousand just like him, crawling out of the caves of the cities, quick hands and no light in their eyes. Demented hangers-on, grabbing onto the violent raw edge of life, onto rock and roll, moving like sharks at raw meat.

The son of a bitch wasted her with the same motion you use to put a penny in a parking meter.

Spence comes in with some chick who looks like syphilis with legs. They are both dead drunk, falling-down drunk. Spence pushes past the man from Detroit, forces his way into the john, ready to explode, he's got to piss so bad. Jesus!

Spence is so wasted he just does his "Man, is this for real!" number. He keeps repeating that over and over.

Then the bastard starts kicking her. I still got my arms around her, trying to hold her head up, so loaded with speed I feel like only three seconds have gone by. I am out of my mind. She's dying in my arms. I don't know what I'm doing.

"You stupid bastard!" He just kicked my arm.

"This ain't real, man!" He's kicking her like you kick a car tire to see if it's flat. He is out of his mind. "This ain't real. I ain't gonna piss on no dead bodies, man!"

Spence grabs her and tries to heave her out of the bathroom.

She looks like a broken doll that's fallen in red paint. She's dead. Spence drags her out of my arms, throws her into the next room. This is all her life came to.

This is a bad movie. None of this really registers in my brain yet. I've got blood all over me and my stomach is turning over. I start for the door and this other chick, the one that came in with Spence, explodes like a lightning bolt. She screams and goes for Spence, swinging a whiskey bottle at his head and screaming bloody murder.

Spence is standing over the dead girl, his cock hanging out of his pants for the piss he's yet to take. The girl hits him solidly in the face. He doesn't know what's going on.

The man with the knife is over in the corner, not moving, and the other chick is trying to tear up Spence's face 'cause she's screaming it's her sister, and Spence goes down under her attack. He doesn't understand her because he only understands taking a piss. Everything else, he can't handle.

The chick is beating Spence into a pulp, and he's too wrecked to defend himself. She goes for his eyes like a kamikaze pilot jumping to a screaming death.

It's all part of the tour. The trip. Rock and roll will save your mortal soul.

The man with the knife. I don't want to look at him. Don't want to know if he's going to use that knife again. I think he is and I don't want to know it. I don't want to see it.

I yank my duffel bag out from under the bed and run into the bathroom, slamming the door behind me. There's blood all over everything, all over me, and I lose it. I puke all over myself like a fucking four-year-old.

I take a huge step over the pool of blood, eyes averted from the hideous. I strip down, scald myself clean under the hot water of the shower. All the water in the world cannot wash the blood off.

Change clothes, wrap up my other ones to throw away. Still wet, I run out of there, run through the room and the screams with my eyes closed, but they never really close. I see it all more terribly in my mind. It burns up there inside me, inside my head.

The rooms of hell, you can't get out of them, they follow you everywhere, every door leads you back inside.

Outside the hotel I am a diseased creature, fleeing from a dollar hotel, running scared, never looking back.

I can't live like this. I can't make it anymore.

I think maybe the little one with the big hole in her back, I think maybe she is my little sister. I think she dies with Tamara's eyes looking at me, with hope and love denied in her eyes. Her only crime was that somebody didn't love her enough.

That was Tamara in my arms, all alone in the world and looking for a love she couldn't find.

I have all the band's money in my pocket, accidentally. I never go back. I just hitchhike out of there.

Three days to get back to Tamara and the look in her eyes. Three days and a dead girl in my arms as soon as my eyes close in sleep.

CHAPTER 21

It is a dream from which I do not wake. Forever. It lasts forever. Hotel room blood and the endless highway and the door, the door that opens and finds Tamara waiting, waiting for me inside.

It is as if there is nothing in the world until I get back to Tamara. Please be there when I get back. I can't make it anymore. Inside your rooms, in your soul kitchen, are all the things that wait, that walk and talk and breathe. All the things that matter that for so long I pretended did not and could not exist for me. Please be there.

I can't make it anymore.

I call in Memphis. In Little Rock. In Oklahoma City. In Amarillo, in a hundred towns whose names I don't know. The phone rings and rings. Nobody home.

This frantic journey to the end of the night. What was it for? Looking for a home in every face I see.

In Phoenix the same dime clicks in the slot, the same despair, the same urgency and frantic hope, all clinging desperately to that need to know she's still there.

My whole body is an instrument of hearing, tuned to some sign that she still is there. Is it the thousandth ring already?

There's a buzz on the line and the phone stops ringing. It's one in the morning and summer's gone. A sleepy voice says "Hello."

And there's a million words I want to say and they catch in my throat and I can't say any of them.

"Hello! Who is this?" The voice sounds like a warm little cat, rubbing its back against the floor.

"Tamara." It's the only word I find. I have too much to say and she's too far away.

And she knows. I don't know how but she knows. She knows everything from that one word. Maybe it is all in that one word somehow.

"I love you," she says.

"I'm coming home! I love you! I'm coming home to stay." The words rush out like expelled breath. Just hearing her, being able to say what I feel, the nightmare eases. I've found her again.

"I'll be waiting for you. Where are you? How soon will you be home?"

"I'm in Phoenix. I'm hitchhiking. Don't go anywhere. I'm coming home. I love you. We're gonna get married. We'll have the baby. Everything! Don't leave. Just a few hours, baby, and then I'll be there."

"I knew you'd be back," she says. "I knew." She sounds so happy.

"Be there when I get there."

"Hurry home, love. I miss you."

The phone goes back into the cradle. I go back to the highway. Put my thumb out. It's an easy ride from here on in.

An easy ride.

CHAPTER 22

It starts going wrong. Not her, me.

After three weeks I am climbing the walls. I don't know what's wrong. Not exactly. Maybe it has something to do with being too young, with trying to live past my years. Anyway, I am restless. Restless and crazy.

Tamara is doing domestic things, cleaning, cooking, singing happily to herself, alive like no caged bird is alive.

I've got all this money in my pocket, the money that I was holding for the band. I didn't steal it, just

couldn't go back to the hotel with it. No sense return-
ing it now. Wouldn't know where to reach them even
if I could. Unless they did something magical they are
all probably in jail somewhere anyway.

This money is burning my pockets. Tamara wants to
buy things, toasters and cookbooks and baby clothes
and whatever else. Half of the money ends up with her
and I don't mind, but with what's left, I feel I got to do
something. I don't know what.

Have a party, I guess. Haven't been going out at
night. Been a good little bastard. Even been out looking
for a job. Doing all kinds of mental numbers in my
head, trying to adjust to the idea of being a father and
husband, all this at the ripe old age of sixteen. Settling
down is unsettling.

Despite trying to keep it down, I still want something. I don't know what. Just something. Kicks, ex-
citement. I don't know what.

So a party.

I do it. I spread the word on the beach and with some
bands I know, with the hangers-on and druggies and
the party people I know in L.A. Telling them it's something loose, a party party.

It's a weird notion for Saturday night L.A. I think I
am celebrating being in love, celebrating Tamara being
four months pregnant. I tell myself that anyway. Tell
Tamara that too. Celebrating settling down.

Good way to celebrate not raising hell anymore is to
raise hell, right?

Party starts Saturday night at midnight and goes.
Really goes.

Snort, pop and inject. The mad and the maddening
arrive in droves. I become the kind of host, drugged up
to my freaking eyes, who cuts the hearts out of small
children to amuse his guests. Everything comes full
circle.

Cops come twice because of the noise. The last time
they come, somebody tries to stomp them. It's that
kind of party.

Innocent Tamara, in an apron, lost in a world of strangers, wanders from room to room, trying to impose something nice on nothing that is. Playing hostess while they laugh at her.

I try to stay with her but people keep dragging me off, talking dope, talking drugs, talking L.A. hard hip, and she's always left out. I keep wandering back to see her, feeling responsible, hugging her, keeping her calm when she gets scared. The wild animals are scaring her. I tell her not to worry when somebody breaks something. And they do.

And then there is a fight and some people overdosing and others getting naked and getting it on and it's only two in the morning and the accelerator is stuck wide open and we're gonna tear the roof off of Saturday night.

I keep ducking into the kitchen, avoiding the ladies, the ones I've slept with, the ones I haven't. Can't remember the names of most of them. I especially have to duck a space case with terminal horniness from Beverly Hills who's been grabbing at me ever since the world began. I avoid them because I am pushing it to myself and to everyone that I am spoken for. God knows I am trying to be. Trying.

I am feeling pretty good, maybe too good. Tamara is in the kitchen, hiding, scared because there was this fight and somebody grabbed her and tore her shirt a little, and she won't come out. She won't come out and I don't feel like going in. Don't know why. I am getting difficult.

And like a bad penny, a voice I know hits me and I turn around and it's Morrison. Can't seem to get away from him.

My mouth drops open to say something appropriately nasty and Morrison pops a pill in it.

I gag, have to swallow to keep from choking.

"Glad you could make the party! A swallow in time saves nine!" says Morrison, bowing.

"What do you mean, glad I could make the party? This is my party! I am your host, asshole!"

Morrison laughs, drugged up, drinking wine from a gallon jug.

"Well, then, I want you to have a gift," says Morrison.

He reaches behind him and hauls out somebody his body has blocked from view.

It's a girl.

And I look at her and remember all the promises I made and meant to keep. And something starts to break inside me. Maybe it is a promise.

Because she looks like the girl who makes you forget promises.

"I'm a gift?" She laughs. "Before you can give me away, you have to have me first. My name's Dawn."

I nod at her, trying not to be interested, turn away. I like looking at her too much.

I see Tamara coming into the room and I walk away from them, walk toward her.

Tamara looks like she wants to cry. She doesn't belong in this world. I'm a bastard to have put her in it.

Somebody knocks over a lamp and it breaks.

"Can't we send them home? I'm scared." She clings to me.

"Just stay in the kitchen." I hug her, trying to comfort her. "I won't do this to you again. After this party, this is it. No more parties. This is the last time, I swear. I just need this last run."

I kiss her.

"These people are animals," says Tamara with a shudder. At our feet two guys and a black girl make love on top of a pile of their clothes, put underneath them so they won't cut their backs on broken glass.

The apartment is being destroyed.

"We have met the enemy and he is us. Don't let it get to you. I was like this too. Before I grew up, that is," I tell her, trying to reassure her. She puts her head against my shoulder.

"I love you," she says. "I'm glad you're not like that anymore."

"I love you too," I say and I feel sad. How do I know

I'm not like that anymore?

She takes her head off my shoulder and my neck is wet from her tears. "I'll be in the kitchen. I feel safer in there. I hid all the kitchen knives. Some of these people are crazy."

"All of them are crazy. All of them!"

A nude girl sprawls on our couch while three guys paint her body. One guy paints a bull's-eye around her pubic hair. Maybe he's planning a lecture with visual aids.

"Remember all the things you promised me," she says, letting go of me. "Remember that I love you."

She goes back into the kitchen and I stand there, watching her go, feeling strange. Very strange.

The party is not going out of control, it is already gone. I feel something stirring in me that wants to get loose, that wants to match the violence of this party. Some kind of frenzy I know I should avoid at all costs.

The inside of my mouth feels strange. Then I remember that pill Morrison popped into my mouth. I smile, feeling something electric beginning to move beneath the skin. I'm going to get ripped out of my skull.

It fills me with a special kind of delight. Perhaps it's 'cause I might fuck up and now I've got an electric excuse.

Morrison comes up beside me, alone, having ditched the girl somewhere or vice versa. It's probably more vice versa. She looks like one grown independent and hard to master.

"I came out of a long line of souvenirs," he says. "My parents were two holes in the night out of which I tumbled genetically."

"And I," I say, "am a prayer kneeling in the snow. I am the blank spaces on a death certificate."

Some violent clown in black leather tries to take the back off of some guy's head with a bottle of beer. The bottle breaks as the top of the guy's head opens up, blood oozing onto the floor beside the guy's head. Why hit somebody who's already down?

Morrison watches the exchange, curiously affected. "The wooden soldiers are gnawing on the furniture. The counselors to the king are shooting horse in the john. The squires are doing weird things to horses. The planet is out of its orbit and all's right with the world."

"Don't show compassion. If you show compassion, they'll take you outside and take away your kingdom." I bow to him.

"Well, I can't help it," says Morrison, helping it. "I am an old movie on the late show. I am an old spectacle looking for a place to happen, heart in hand, sitting there, like a mouse, ready to crawl up the right pair of pants."

"You are either a philosopher or in love. Whichever is more infectious." I finish my bow, tipping an imaginary hat. "You try to be a good boy but you ain't nothing but a Nazi."

"Hail to the Fatherland! And rain and partly cloudy for the Motherland, highs in the ten thousands, tornado watches in the western portion of our mental health!" says Morrison, waving his arms.

Any minute I expect him to break out in song.

"If you wrote like you talked, everybody would read you."

"I'd still have to give—" The sentence gets interrupted by a black chick who stumbles between us, drunk as a volunteer fire department at a convention.

"Jive-ass motherfucking white boys," she says or something like that.

"You got your tits on backwards," says Morrison. "Either that or your falsies—" He doesn't get to finish that sentence either.

She passes out cold like a period at the end of a sentence.

She slides down Morrison's legs, coming to rest on his feet.

"Give me your tired, your weak, your huddled masses, yearning to pay income tax," says Morrison, staring down at her. "She's no fun. She fell right over."

"It must have been something you said, you insensitive asshole! You jive-ass white boys never get it right.''

Morrison laughs, moves his feet, pulling them out from under her.

"What was that pill? What was that monstrosity you tossed into my digestive system?" I ask. "What kind of strange, as yet unknown to science wonder drug have I taken?"

"A ceremonial hallucinogen from ancient Babylon. When you get off, your mind expands in an overlapping series of hanging gardens. Forbidden pleasure palaces!"

"Shit! I knew it! I swallowed a low-rent district!"

I hand Morrison a bottle of wine I steal from somebody passed out on the floor. Practically have to break the guy's fingers to get the bottle loose. Either rigor mortis or drinker's lockpaw. Lots of passed-out people having too much fun.

"What did you think of Dawn?"

"She's pretty." I shrug. I had tried not to look at her too close. She did things to my body and my body is being told it's a no-no.

Morrison jumps, backs away. "C'mon, man! Pretty? She's just about the best-looking piece of poontang you ever laid eyes on! I been chasing her all night and I can't get to her."

Morrison looks depressed.

"*You* can't get her?" Now I'm really surprised. "What's wrong with her?"

"Nothing," says Morrison, reaching out to take a joint from a roadie. Lots of band people here tonight. "She's just about the most independent girl I ever met. She drives me crazy. I want her so bad I can taste her."

"She looks like she would taste pretty good." I have to admit that much. She's beginning to interest me more and more, in spite of myself, in spite of promises.

"I wish I was in love," says Morrison.

I hear what he says and it registers. I knew this about him all along. He's a human being in secret.

I see Dawn across the room and I stare at her, really

give her a looking over. Everything male that can still function is panting, keeping hot eyes on her. She just stands there, listening to the music blaring full volume from the stereo, ignoring the stares.

I don't know how to describe her, not even to myself. It's a face you see on magazine covers. Her eyes are so big they look like they could steal your soul. Dark eyes and raven black hair and a golden-tan body.

She wears a short white dress that makes her look like a medieval princess. You imagine her walking through a field of flowers on a sunlit day in some other century.

"You know who she is? I mean, really?" says Morrison, also staring at her. "She's the girl of summer. *The Girl!* If you get to her, winter will never come."

"You don't sound like a lord," I challenge him. "You sound more like—"

"Put me among the creatures tonight," says Morrison, handing me the joint, his voice strange from holding in the dope smoke. "We all have to fall off our high horses sometimes. We have our public horse and our private horse. I'm telling you about my private horse. It's a horse of a different Technicolor."

Dawn sees us looking at her and she walks toward us.

Morrison is almost jumping out of his skin. "She moves like a wild deer," he whispers to me.

And he's right. She has the most beautiful body I've ever seen, all the graces in the world in the way she walks. A body bronzed gold by an endless summer.

"Having fun?" says Dawn, smiling at us.

"Till the day I die," says Morrison.

I don't say anything. I don't trust myself to speak. My body is telling me it wants her. My mind says no, but it's got such a small voice.

"What do you think of the people here?" she asks, looking back over her shoulder at the human wreckage.

"Pigs," says Morrison. "Happy, greedy little pigs

with all four feet in the trough."

"Is that why they act like this?" she says. She doesn't look like she believes him.

Morrison shrugs, trying to find the right lie.

"First you break a window and then you become one. Nothing else exists. Nothing else can touch you," I finally say.

She turns and really looks at me. "I like that," she says, thinking about it. "Did you steal it from somewhere, or make it up?"

"Made it up, I think. I don't remember."

"You're interesting," she says, and she smiles and it's like getting kissed for the first time, sly and wonderful.

"Hey! Don't bogart that joint!" says Morrison, taking it out of my hands. I didn't even know it was in my hand.

"You want a hit?" Morrison offers the joint to Dawn. She shakes her head no. Morrison shrugs, takes a huge toke. It's obvious to me this one has him running in circles.

Me too. I am going round and round and I don't even want to be running, period. At least I've told myself that.

Some people are clearing away broken furniture, moving passed-out bodies and sweeping aside broken glass. Clearing a place so they can dance. What a bizarre thing to get into! Who are these people? Escapees from a 1950s sock hop?

Christ! Some of these people still have their clothes on. It's maybe not un-American but it sure is un-L.A.

Somebody keeps changing records on the stereo. I've got lots of albums, free promos from my musician friends, and some of the band people are standing around playing their latest records and arguing with each other. People from six or seven bands here.

Somewhat confused by drugs, the arguments are either about claiming they are better than each other or listening to their own record and trying to remember the name of the group that recorded it. Most of them can barely remember their own names.

"This is some party," says Morrison. Somebody puts his fist through the wall, demonstrating karate. He breaks his hand and I laugh. It's that kind of party.

"Enthusiasm it has," says Dawn. "It reminds me of the San Francisco Earthquake. Or maybe the Chicago Fire."

"And I am Mrs. O'Leary's cow. Anybody got a lantern for me to kick over?" I ask.

"This is Sodom. When you leave, don't look back," says Morrison. "You don't want to turn into a . . . into a . . ." He can't think of anything.

"Can I quote you on that?" says Dawn.

"I can't even quote me on that," says Morrison.

Dawn comes up beside me, touches my arm. My whole body shudders at the touch of her. I smell her hair, like something sweet that stars could get stuck in. "You want to dance?"

"Me?"

Morrison frowns. I look at him, thinking I should say no. But I don't.

We drift away, her hand holding my arm, leading me across the room to where the other dancers are. Her touch sends warm rushes up and down my spine.

We plug into the music, just dancing. And she puts me away. Me who got taught dancing by black musicians who had worked for James Brown. She takes my breath away.

She could dance. She could do it all. Better than me. With more grace. Hers is a body free to move in all directions.

I try all my moves and she's with me and passes me and at some point, with the beat of the music driving us into the heat of the night, I begin pursuing her, Tamara forgotten.

I know when I look into her dark eyes that I want her as much as I want anything. She *is* the girl of summer.

Morrison disappears into the cold, uncaring heart of

the party. And I forget him too. I forget everything but Dawn. I don't even see the party anymore. There are only two people in my world at that moment, me and her.

Somebody forgets to put another record on and there's some space that goes by without music and I find myself sitting down in a corner, with Dawn leaning against my knees, talking about all the things in the world we can pretend are worth talking about.

My hands keep getting tangled up, keep reaching to touch her. My lips ache to get to hers. My whole body wants her. And now, so does my mind.

And I can feel it down deep, burning in her too. Her body wants my body and all promises are only promises, bound to get broken.

The music starts again, intruding on us. Rolling across the room like a summer thunderstorm, screaming guitars and high-voltage injections of desire and electric fire. It pumps through our bodies, and our blood races, driving on into the death of sex, the complete make-believe fire of aural climax.

"Do you like make-believe love?" asks Dawn. "Do you like making love when you aren't in love yet but you might be? When it's only to find out if you are going to find out if you're going to fall in love?"

"I like make-believe love. I like make-believe fire," I say. "I like make-believe everything. I don't understand anything else."

"I think I want you," she says.

And I go swimming out toward her. I pull her against me and try the taste of her lips. Tamara forgotten, promises forgotten. Dead girls who look like my little sister, who have Tamara's face. Forgotten. Love and hope and looks of betrayal. All forgotten.

The body says take her. The sweet touch, taste of her. Take her and hold on to summer.

We get up, arms around each other, looking for someplace to go. Our bodies know why.

The battle to get to the bedroom is a million miles

across a deserted beach piled high with the bodies of beachcombers who were cast adrift by the uncaring heart of Saturday Night.

Each delay just raises the temperature. Takes us into the tropics. Into the torrid zones.

I push into the bedroom, my arms around her, kick the door shut behind us, and we are alone with the thing we are building between us. This conspiracy of youth and summer. This is the most erotic dream, the most beautiful girl. This is the one.

She takes my breath away.

The old world goes away. The one with the promises in it.

The new world is skin on skin, dark eyes that tell you to come do the dance, you won't know anything until you get inside. Then, too, there is an electric edge to me, a loosening of inhibition from the drugs. The sheets are hot, tropical white zones. Our bodies are mine fields that explode against each other.

Arms around backs, bodies tightly held, lips burning, wrapping ourselves in a cooling cocoon of perspiration.

The voyage of discovery that finds everything in the world tasting better than it ever possibly could. And all into it, a million miles deep, all promises gone, there's no sense of ending, ever. This is the endless summer.

This is the endless summer.

I hear a door slam and someone screams. I look up, turning my head, startled, the dream jarred.

Tamara stands in the doorway. A look of hurt and loss and shock on her face. The ultimate cruelty. To take a girl in our own bed.

The moment lasts forever. There's a chemical fire inside me and the world isn't real anymore. My body hates the sensation of stopping, the withering of the erotic dream. I want to shout "Get out of here!" I don't want Tamara to exist. I don't want to see her.

I don't want to see myself either.

Morrison comes through the open door at her back.

To rescue me from what I cannot be rescued from.

He takes a couple of steps into the room, too drugged to really see much, for the way it is to register clearly in his mind. When it does, he smiles. Mysteriously.

And he turns and leaves. Moving quick with the strangest look on his face, turned into a total stranger in front of my astonished eyes. I watch him go. It's too hard to look at Tamara.

Dawn moves beneath me, struggling, the moment almost gone, the dance threatening to end. I won't roll over on my side, won't let her get free. My body, transformed by drugs into one big sensation, doesn't want the dance to end. Doesn't want the magic to go away.

Tamara looks like a child is dying inside her. You can't describe the look of betrayal on her face. No words are big enough.

My body owns me. I can't see her face in my mind. The words come. And sound as cruel as they are. "Get out of here! Leave me alone!"

I let the acid in me make Tamara unreal, a phantom I can pretend away. And I make believe against her as I make believe against all of life.

One little moment of guilt. One little moment of remorse.

"I . . ." There's nothing to say or too much, and it doesn't get said. First you break a window and then you become one. Nothing else exists. Nothing else can touch you. I live my own lies like I mean them.

Tamara turns and runs out of the room. Slamming the door behind her. I get my wish of long ago. Just once she sees me for what I really am.

I see that look on her face. And try to hide from it. Bury my head against soft skin.

Dawn moves under me, a sensual shudder, like a summer witch, stirring the cold ashes to keep the cauldron fire lit. Her body moves against mine, teasing, imploring, keeping the fire burning.

And I get pulled back inside, as if I never left. Two erotic animals out of control, trapped in the sensation.

Her fingernails dig into my back, as she climbs another climax. Her lips tear at my throat and the heat rises off of her. She drags me deep inside her. She cannot be denied.

She is every girl I will have in the summer of my life. It's that crazy thing about wanting every beautiful girl you see and thinking for a little while, just for a moment, you can really have them.

We drive on into the night as if there is no morning.

But the untrue heart of Saturday Night cannot last forever.

The party goes on without us. Doesn't notice us when we go back to it.

If there's remorse, it comes now, as soon as the body lets go. If there's guilt, it comes now, as the drugs that smothered inhibitions fade.

I look for Tamara. Suddenly terribly afraid for her.

I can't find her anywhere.

Morrison's got a hot-looking blonde up against the wall in the kitchen, running his hand over her breasts, kissing her on the neck passionately.

He sees me come in and lets go of her body. "Hey, man!" He makes a V-for-victory sign with one hand, nodding at me.

I have the sensation I have never seen him before in my life, not in this light.

He lets go of the girl altogether, disengaging, comes over to me. The girl, drugged into partial oblivion, stares blankly at his departing back. If the wall wasn't behind her, she'd fall down.

"Where's Dawn?"

She had been hanging on to me when we rejoined the party but I had pushed her away then, seized up by a look on a face I couldn't find anywhere.

"Where's Dawn?" asks Morrison, thinking I haven't heard his question.

I shrug, not interested. "Have you seen Tamara?"

"Who?" He doesn't know her. Doesn't know anything about her.

"I got to find her!" I feel empty inside, as if I have torn a part of me out of myself.

"What did you do with Dawn? Where is she now? You lucky asshole! You're one of us, ya know! A frigging lord!" Morrison stands in front of me, ripped out of his mind. "I'll get her yet. I'll enslave her in my mesh."

I look around the room, eyes darting everywhere, seeking her face in the crowd. Maybe she's gone. Maybe she's fled. It's possible, but there's no place for her to go. Somewhere deep inside I know I was the last place she had left to go to.

"That's it!" says Morrison. "Enslavement! I will trap the world in my vision. I shall take the young women of summer, the strange girls from the island!"

Morrison's all wound up, an electric crusader, standing in his own temple, blind to his own religion.

I can't get away from him. His voice freezes me in place. Words tumble out of him.

"That's the only power in the world!" His voice rises like a gathering storm. He sounds like a shaman who knows all the words in the world. "To enslave others. To trap others in our hopes and dreams and desires! My make-believe can do anything!"

"I don't know what you're talking about."

"Don't lie to me," says Morrison, suddenly angry, pushing on my shoulder. "I am the prince of liars and in my presence all the lies should be mine! You know what I'm talking about!"

The crowd shows me no face I want to see. I start for the next room, to make another hopeless circuit of the place, and Morrison follows, moving quick, ending up leading me as if I were his own personal Roman legion.

"My strange device. The power of disguise," says Morrison. "I cannot be seen because my exits and entrances are all lies."

"I'm tired of lies," I say, suddenly angry, at me, at him, at the world.

"You mean you're just ready for some new ones,"

says Morrison, looking like a prophet.

I don't say anything. Because I am afraid he's right.

The party is still going full force. The place is a wreck. Furniture smashed, broken glass, naked bodies, conscious and unconscious. Discarded clothes and spilled drinks and cigarette burns. Zonked bodies everywhere and the stereo blaring above it all, a scratched record repeating itself hideously, over and over, and nobody in any shape to even notice, or noticing without the energy to deal with it. There's a thin little chick passed out in Tamara's favorite chair, a hypodermic needle sticking out of her skinny arm, blood dripping from a cut on her face. Maybe she's thirteen years old.

A roadie I know comes up to me, taps me on the shoulder. "You looking for your lady?" says Russ.

I turn, startled. "Yeah! Where is she?" I sound frantic.

"Locked herself in the bathroom," he says. "People been trying to get in but she won't open up. Thought you should know." He moves off.

Morrison's blonde peels herself off the wall and grabs him from behind, whispers something in his ear.

Morrison nods, puts his arm around her. "I'm splitting." He hugs the girl against his body. "We're gonna go get it on and get it off!"

We are strangers who met in the heat of a streaming summer.

Morrison touches me on the shoulder. Our eyes meet. There is something final about this, as if this is the last time we will ever meet, ever run together.

"Go tell them wicked lies," says Morrison and then he's gone.

I run. Smashing my way through, knocking people down in my panic to get to Tamara. I know something terrible has happened.

Two guys are trying to break down the door. Making half-hearted attempts.

"Tamara!" I yell through the door. There is no sound

on the other side. I know what I'll find in there and I am scared. *"Tamara!"* I scream at her.

The silence comes out at me. The two guys at the door are freaked out, just trying to get in to piss or something, and suddenly I'm doing some kind of number they don't understand.

I throw myself at the door, hurting my shoulder. The door is thick, hard to break down.

"Help me! Help me get it open!" I scream, and the urgency, the panic in my voice, gets me some volunteers.

Four of us hit the door. Hinges start tearing loose. We hit it again, hard, and this time we knock it off its pins. The door crashes open, hanging by one hinge.

The door hides her from my sight. I grab the door and drag it aside, flinging it away from me. The light is on in the bathroom and she is in there.

Oh, Jesus!

Four months pregnant, love and hope betrayed.

I walk inside, my insides frozen.

"Tamara."

There's blood everywhere.

I put my arms around her, pull her to me. I lift her head up. The arms, wrists slit and bloody, dangle loosely against me. The razor blade lies beside her. Her eyes stare up at me. She has that look on her face.

That look.

I hold her against me, hold her tight.

I see it as it happened. See her bolting the door. The look in her eyes as she takes the razor and runs it across both wrists. And then, bending over the toilet, so the blood doesn't get on the floor, kneeling there. Waiting to die, feeling her life draining away.

And the loss of blood makes her weak. She gets dizzy and leans over and all the lies and promises I made are rattling around in her mind.

My body betrayed her. It betrayed me. It couldn't let go of the idea that you can be young forever.

I brought her to this, as surely as if I had held the razor blade in my own hands.

I see it all.

And that look on her face.

The head falls, the knees give out. The heart slowing, so weak now, she faints, falls forward. Maybe by now that other little heartbeat inside her falling silent, dead.

Tamara. I have not given you a pretty way to die.

She falls.

Her head goes into the toilet.

And she drowns.

CHAPTER 23

I turn the stereo on. Put some old blues records on to suit my mood.

It's my birthday and I want to do something different. I don't want it to be like the way I usually spend Christmas holidays, the way I usually spend my birthdays. For a change, instead of sitting in a hotel room full of strangers a thousand miles from a home I don't have, instead of staying alone in an empty apartment with bare walls, I want this birthday to be special, unlike all the others.

Not gonna get drunk all by myself or in a bar with

strangers or with some girl I pick up in a bar and whose name, tomorrow, I won't remember.

No cake. No party. No friends to catch me by surprise. That would be the same as always but this birthday will still be different.

I go in and turn the record player up, let the blues echo through this empty apartment. Take the phone off the hook. I'm not expecting any calls on my birthday. Not that I ever do. Cancel my subscription to the Resurrection.

Sit in the kitchen staring at the birthday present I gave myself.

The music pounds in my head. I've heard that song all my life. Always the same song. That song that says "I've been singing the blues ever since the world began."

Her cat comes into the kitchen, a gray bedraggled-looking tomcat with fleas and sad yellow eyes. He had been a stranger once who had appeared one night at her door, cold and hungry. She fed him and got him warm and loved him and . . . he had stayed.

She really loved that cat.

The cat comes all the way into the room, walking all around the kitchen, putting his nose into every corner, still looking for her. I've tried to get the cat to eat but he won't touch his food. In the middle of the night I had heard him crying out for her.

He just prowls restlessly through the apartment now, as if she were behind some door he had yet to go through, where somehow, magically, she waits for him.

And she is behind a door. The one that never opens after you go through it once. The one on her coffin.

I didn't go to her funeral because I wanted to sit here and celebrate my birthday. I didn't go to the funeral because I had no tears, because in the hard life I'd lived, I had never learned how to cry and I would want to at her funeral.

It is on the table. My birthday present.

I open the bottle and tilt it. I count my present out into my hand.

Twenty birthday presents.

It is going to be different this time. Not like my other birthdays.

I open my mouth and drink some beer so my birthday presents don't stick in my throat. They feel good going down. I swallow them all.

I feel comfortable here in the kitchen because it is a room that belongs to her.

The cat rubs up against my ankle, lonely. I bend down and pick him up. I hold him in my lap. But touching him is like touching her and I have to let him go. Gently, I put him back on the floor.

He stares at me, with sorrowful eyes from under the kitchen table, wanting to be held and not understanding why I can't do it.

The truth is, I don't want to touch anyone, living or dead. Not anymore. I am too tired. I am having a busy morning on my birthday and I am too tired. Very busy.

I spent the whole morning trying to write a suicide note that would say it all.

Couldn't.

Forgive me, Tamara. This suicide for my birthday is the best apology I know. There is no apology in the world that can apologize enough because ultimately what I have to say to you is . . . I am sorry I killed you. I am sorry I wasted your life and love on someone who did not know he needed either of them until it was too late.

Today I lose your face in my birthday celebration, but never that look, that awful look of betrayal and loss I saw in your eyes.

There is something I should have done but forgot to do. Forgot to lock the front door. Too late now. Not that the world outside has any reason to want to come in. The light is gone in this cave, in this soul kitchen, and no one will ever live here again.

Not that it matters about the front door. Nobody can stop me from celebrating my birthday now.

I can feel my birthday presents opening up inside me.

Happy Birthday!!

It all happens so slowly. My head gets heavy, as I knew it would, and I try to lean over on the kitchen table. I slip and fall out of the chair. It is like diving into a tunnel, a tunnel made of black winds and approaching night.

"You take my breath away." I said that to her the first day I met her. It seems a good time to remember that now.

Funny how the ceiling looks as I lay on my back on the kitchen floor. I stare at the bright light hanging from the ceiling, watching the blackness eating away all the brightness. Funny-looking ceiling, all wavy and shimmery.

The cat touches my face with his paw, missing her too, his loneliness matching mine.

I want him to go away. Don't want to be touched. I want to punish myself by being alone, by being totally alone. Too weak to push him away.

He lays down beside me. Puts his head against mine. We share the same broken heart.

And then I am glad he is there.

And I cry for both of us.

Here's More from Warner
on Your Favorite Stars

NO ONE HERE GETS OUT ALIVE

by Jerry Hopkins and Danny Sugerman   *(137-377, $3.50)*

Here is Jim Morrison in all his complexity—singer, philosopher, poet, delinquent—the brilliant, charismatic, and obsessed disciple of darkness who rejected authority in any form, the explorer who probed "the bounds of reality to see what would happen. . . ." Seven years in the writing, this definitive biography is the work of two men whose empathy and experience with Jim Morrison uniquely prepared them to recount this modern tragedy.

SHOUT: THE BEATLES IN THEIR GENERATION

by Philip Norman   *(130-337, $3.95)*

At last! The complete story never before told! Behind the myths . . . behind the masks . . . behind the secluded walls. . . . For the first time here's the definitive biography of the incredible rise of four boys in scuffed boots to beings more pampered and adored—and in many ways deprived—than any in the history of popular entertainment.

To order, use the coupon below. If you prefer to use your own stationery, please include complete title as well as book number and price. Allow 4 weeks for delivery.

WARNER BOOKS
P.O. Box 690
New York, N.Y. 10019

Please send me the books I have checked. I enclose a check or money order (not cash), plus 50¢ per order and 50¢ per copy to cover postage and handling.*

____. Please send me your free mail-order catalog. (If ordering only the catalog, include a large self-addressed, stamped envelope.)

Name _____

Address _____

City _____

State _____ Zip_____

*N.Y. State and California residents add applicable sales tax.